Dive Tour

Volume One
Raptis Trilogy

Tracee Raptis

VOLUME ONE: RAPTIS TRILOGY

****

Dive Tour

**Volume One
Raptis Trilogy**

Tracee Raptis

Metaterra® Publications

****

Metaterra® Publications
DIVE TOUR
VOLUME ONE: RAPTIS TRILOGY
Tracee Raptis
Copyright © 2017, 2016, Tracee Raptis and Angela Browne-Miller.
Copyright © 2017, 2016, Metaterra® Publications.
www.Metaterra.com
Library of Congress Cataloging-in-Publication Data.
Raptis, Tracee
DIVE TOUR
VOLUME 1: RAPTIS TRILOGY
/ Tracee Raptis, Author / Angela Browne-Miller, Afterword /
1. Thriller. 2. Mystery. 3. Crime. 4. Drug Smuggling. 5. Treasure Hunting.
6. Scuba Diving. 7. Romance. 8. Psychological. 9. Heroines. 10. Adventure.
Title:
DIVE TOUR
VOLUME ONE: RAPTIS TRILOGY
ISBN-13: 978-1-937951-36-8 (paperback)
See Amazon.com for Paperback and Kindle Ebook formats of this book.

ISBN information for the other volumes in this Raptis Trilogy
(also on Amazon as paperback and Ebook):
TREASURE HUNT • VOLUME TWO: RAPTIS TRILOGY
ISBN-13: 978-1-937951-37-5
REDEMPTION • VOLUME THREE: RAPTIS TRILOGY
ISBN-13: 978-1-937951-38-2

Published in the United States of America for U.S. and worldwide distribution.
Metaterra® Publications, www.Metaterra.com
Book interior design by Metaterra® Publications & Angela Browne-Miller.
Afterword and Editing by Angela Browne-Miller.
Book Cover Concept and Design by Alicia Beulow with Tracee Raptis & Angela
Browne-Miller. Interior art – Basic Scuba Diver Gear Diagram by Tracee Raptis.
Book Cover Illustration by Alicia Beulow.
AUTHOR, PUBLISHER, RIGHTS, & PRESS CONTACT: DoctorAngela@mac.com
Ordering information and bulk ordering information available through:
Amazon Paperback and Amazon Kindle. Also contact Info@Metaterra.com.
****

DIVE TOUR

****

To my parents,
Russell and Korryn.

VOLUME ONE: RAPTIS TRILOGY

****

Table of Contents

VOLUME ONE: RAPTIS TRILOGY

****

Prologue

It was thirty-five feet underwater at six thirty in the morning. A weak light offered by the peeking sun had yet to penetrate the water's surface. A slight breeze blew, rippling the water and jiggling the reflected sky. Three men swimming below used small handheld flashlights to guide them back from their underwater destination. They had been in the water less than twenty minutes and were already heading back, each kick of their rubber fins propelling them forward.

At first Enrique thought the clumsy weight he felt on his back was one of his diving buddies floating into him. He had stopped to admire a sizeable parrotfish they'd pointed out, which was lurking deep in a crevice. Now exhaling the air in his lungs, Enrique began to back out of the crevice, gently pushing himself upward and outward, using his gloved hands against the coral walls surrounding him.

However, the weight on Enrique's back increased and seemed to nudge him forward. Enrique pushed harder, and was met again by unknown resistance. Head down in the crevice, he couldn't see what it was. Sea urchins in their spiny purple-black globes stabbed into his forearms as he was shoved further and deeper inward. Enrique struggled still harder. Then he realized he could not back out. He was trapped.

Enrique's struggle ended abruptly. His eyes grew wide with terror when his next inhalation was restricted. He could hardly pull a breath from his regulator's mouthpiece. Indulging his fear for only a moment, he held his last breath of air and pushed out harder. Again he was met with resistance. Once again he was propelled forward as the stinging jabs of the sea urchins caused him to exhale some of his precious last air.

John and Jerry held him firmly in place as he struggled to extricate himself. John had turned off Enrique's air valve.

Enrique's momentary pause, followed by a wild struggle, told the others he had drawn his last breath.

John's eyes darted now, ricocheting between Jerry and the desperately struggling diver. Momentarily distracted, John's grip accidentally loosened. With a violent surge, Enrique catapulted himself backward, shaking free of his companions and gaining the open water as he saw the glow of daybreak at the surface.

With lungs full of carbon dioxide, his first exhale made his throat spasm, then restrict his inhale. Enrique sucked at the mouthpiece in desperation as he thrashed upward against John and Jerry's hands.

Kicking, turning, gyrating against the renewed grip of his captors, his oxygen was at last fully depleted. Now blackness enveloped Enrique.

Losing sight of the surface, shooting stars streaked his vision as his struggling subsided into unorchestrated jerks and eerie spasms. Jerry's hand met no resistance as he reached over and pulled the regulator out of Enrique's clenched teeth.

Enrique floated lifeless between his two companions.

DIVE TOUR

****

PART ONE

TRUTH

VOLUME ONE: RAPTIS TRILOGY

****

1

She opened her eyes just a little. Off in the background, a low light was softly diffusing into subtle streams. Everything from far off right up to the sharply illuminated foreground was blurry. Somehow that blurriness was tied to the strange streaming light in the background, which in turn connected to the sudden sharp throb in the back of Terri's head. These muddled sensations were all too familiar.

Still half asleep, Terri carefully shut her eyes again, moving her lids as little as she could for fear the ache in her head would grow. It did.

"Oh not today, shit, ugh," Terri groaned. The same old signs of a full blown hangover were there. She felt the bed swaying, and her head swirled as if she were in the bowels of a boat in rough, choppy seas. But she wasn't. She was feeling sicker by the moment.

Abruptly, Terri bolted upright and opened her eyes as if seeing the horizon would help her avoid her rising seasickness. Things were still rocking. And the warmth of the morning air, stiff with humidity, added to the illusion of being on this rocking boat.

Then the bed moved again. An arm reached out and wrapped around her waist. "Good morning … uuugggghhh!!!" The hand attached to this arm fell back, as this arm was unable to muster the strength to hold this hand up. The loud groan that accompanied this attempt at intimacy out matched Terri's. Clearly they were on the same rocking boat.

Terri's head swirled out of control as the inevitable rushed to the back of her throat. Struggling to unwind herself from the top sheet, she stumbled out of bed and ran the three steps to the toilet. She could barely get the door half shut before she found herself in the throes of dry retching. This condition felt far too familiar. Last night's drinking rushed back to her. *When will the lesson, never drink on an empty stomach, let alone never drink so much in the first place, ever sink in?*

Slowly, Terri regained enough composure to stand up and find her toothbrush. Her head throbbed in pain with every move as she squirted toothpaste on the end of the brush and ran it back and forth across her teeth. She turned the water on and off in strategic movements, trying to not waste a drop, her gag reflex responding to each stroke in the back of her mouth.

She splashed some water on her face and then her body. Washing away the sweat made her feel a little better. The brief coolness on her skin was a relief from the stifling humid air in the bathroom, where only a small window above the tiny shower stall provided any fresh air.

Now she peeked through the doorway at her bedmate. As she made her move back to bed, she saw that his eyes were shut and his hand covered them to seal off any additional light. Walking quietly, she pulled the loose top sheet up from the bed and quickly covered herself. Her head spun with vertigo as she sat down slowly, trying not to rock the bed.

The room was starkly decorated, one bed with sheets that clearly didn't match, one wall with a map covered in notes and in colored pins that correlated to colored marks on the map. An old low dresser stood below this map. On this dresser was a small rotating fan working quite hard to push the heavy tropical air around.

"Well ... Darren...." she started to say. *What have I done here?*

The even now gorgeous young man uncovered his eyes and looked over, giving the best smile he could muster.

"This is a tad embarrassing," she said. *What have I done, oh no!*

His eager smile shifted to slight confusion, as if he were being rejected.

"I mean, after all, I am your boss," Terri reminded each of them as she looked down at herself and shut her eyes. Her head was still trying to adjust to the rocking movement. In nothing but a sheet, and fresh out of the bathroom from relieving herself, she realized she was the major source of the embarrassment. She wanted to open her eyes and see that all this was just a bad dream, but the pounding in her head told her otherwise.

"I guess things moved a bit fast last night," the young man in her bed offered.

"Zero to fifth gear in a few hours is beyond fast. It's the stuff major pileups are made of ... and I'm afraid I might have caused one. A pile up." Terri looked away, ashamed to look Darren in the eyes.

He attempted to sit up. "Oh wow." The expression on his face made it clear he was not that much better off than Terri. "Well, it takes more than one car to be in a pile up. ... What kind of cars were the two of us driving last night, anyway?"

Darren's half attempt at humor got to Terri the way he intended it to. She couldn't help but crack a partial smile, even though she couldn't remember the night they just spent together. *Too bad I missed it, I bet it was great,* she said to herself. Standing up again, she surveyed the room looking for her clothes. She didn't see them in the corner where she usually threw them at the end of the day. She passed through the yellow tiled bathroom into the front room where she spotted her clothes on the arm of the couch. "All righty now," she said to herself as she picked them up.

After securely tucking the sheet around her body like a toga, she scrambled into her clothes underneath. A big stain covered the front of her shirt: she had spilled beer all over herself last night. "What a boner move. What were you thinking? You weren't thinking," Terri scolded herself relentlessly, under her breath so as not to be heard.

Perspiration beaded on her upper lip as a new wave of nausea rose. She sat down on the couch and put her head between her legs. She shut her eyes and let herself drift, wondering how she was going to work all day like this....

Terri was awakened out of her trance by the sound of the toilet flushing. Terri took a long deep breath and looked up to find Darren standing in front of her. He looked in pretty rough shape but somewhat more stable than she felt.

He offered her his hand. "Come on, show me how you make coffee here. I looked last night and no luck. Thought it would make more sense this morning."

"Hmm, coffee. Well let's see ... I don't have a coffee maker."

"No coffee?"

Terri thought she heard a hint of desperation in his voice. She smiled for a moment, briefly forgetting the throbbing pain in the back of her head. "I said I don't have a coffee maker, but what I can offer you is a small substitute."

She stood up with the help of Darren's strong pull. His six-foot-four stature towered over Terri's tall but seemingly dwarfed five-foot-eight inches. They walked over to the kitchen area. There, Terri reached up into her open cupboard and pulled out a small metal contraption that resembled a large hourglass figure.

Darren's eyebrows raised in surprise, as he had never seen anything like it before.

Terri's face lit up, delighted to be showing him something new. He leaned past her, brushing his bare chest against her as he picked a banana off the bunch on the counter. Pulling the peel back, he offered Terri the first bite.

At first she refused. The sight of it just didn't look good.

8

"You should have a bite. Potassium is very important, you know."

Terri relented and opened her mouth. Darren gently pressed a piece of banana on her tongue. She closed her eyes. She knew she needed something in her stomach. Slowly, carefully, she chewed on the small bite, wondering if it would stay down. Then she turned her attention to the sink and unscrewed the hourglass. She rinsed out one end of it and filled it with water. She packed the middle portion of this hourglass with coffee, carefully pressing it down, filling the small metal filter object to the brim with grounds.

Darren observed all this from an uncomfortably close distance. For Terri at least, it was uncomfortable. She could feel his breath as he exhaled onto the back of her neck, admittedly sending vague ripples of excitement through her aching body. For just a moment, Terri found herself thinking, *Well, gee, I'm actually only a few years older than he is. So this is alright. ... What am I saying, I'm his boss. And Mitch, then there is Mitch. But Mitch doesn't own me. Oh geez, I need to stop this.*

With the top part of the hourglass screwed back on, the contraption was sitting on the stove top. Striking a match, Terri then held the flame next to the burner and slowly turned the gas on. The stove lit with a flash as a wave of gas hit the flame. Darren touched her for a moment, then stepped back a bit, unsure whether she was liking this.

Terri backed up quickly, half intentionally bumping into Darren, as if to claim the personal space around her (or to touch him again, she wasn't sure). Now her head was spinning for reasons other than the complete overindulgence the night before. What was she going to tell the guys? How was she going to talk her way through this one?

"This is what we call Cuban coffee around here. Well, at my house, that is. Don't ask me why, someone gave this to me and that's how I've been making my coffee ever since." Terri found herself babbling nervously now, waiting for the water to boil.

As if on cue, the sound of bubbly froth began to seep out of the pipe on top and into the cup. Terri and Darren listened to the bubbling until it stopped and the top part was full. Terri set out two small cups and took the sugar out of the refrigerator. "Hope you like it sweet, cause it's going to be strong!" She poured them each a full glass and then doctored hers with a large spoonful of sugar. She gave it three stirs and then sipped. She motioned for Darren to do the same.

"Espresso," he said after his first sip.

"What–o?"

"Espresso, this is espresso."

"OK, whatever you call it. Expresso. I'll call it Cuban coffee. You like it?" She looked up at him for his approval as she sipped away.

"Hmm, yes. Sure. I like it…."

Terri wasn't sure whether that was a compliment or what. Remembering his impressive resume and family, Terri knew he was one of the privileged few whose daddy's fortune was always close by to afford any opportunity. Darren's current "whimsy," as his father called it, was choosing to take a year off from college and do something completely different—in this case, become a diving instructor and teach for a while. So here he was. In less than twelve hours on this tiny island, he had already managed to make quite an impression, as well as to make Terri. *Oh God, what have I done*, Terri asked herself again.

The acid in the coffee went straight to Terri's stomach and immediately messed with her bowels. Her stomach began to object to the harsh, sugary brew. "Excuse me," she muttered as she dashed away to the bathroom one more time.

Darren stood there and decided it was best not to finish his Cuban coffee. Tiny beads of sweat were already forming on his brow. These were definitely the symptoms of a hangover and of some very very strong coffee. Fortunately, his symptoms were not as disastrous as Terri's. Darren went over to the sink and rinsed out the tiny mismatched coffee cups. He thought about his bags now, all of which were still in the car, his rental car which he now remembered was parked out front. Terri had had a few too many drinks last night and everyone had decided she was unable to drive herself home. Clearly, Darren mused, this woman was a heavy drinker, probably in keeping up with the men around there. *Oh well, work hard play hard,* Darren told himself about this world he had just yesterday come to be part of.

Sliding open the glass door, he stepped onto the covered patio and looked out at the view. With a heavy sigh, he managed the biggest grin he could, and took it all in. He was no stranger to the tropics and had been on many vacations to exotic destinations. The heat of the morning didn't surprise him. A dozen or so frigate birds with their enormous wingspans circled high above, as if they were attempting to gain altitude for a better view. Having grown up in the hot humid southern USA, Darren's body had acclimated quickly to the heavy hot tropical air he was now faced with. He calmly shut his eyes and took several very slow and deep breaths.

"Whoa."

Darren looked to the moan to see Terri holding her head and shuffling out to toward him. Terri really didn't want to be seen this way, but there was nothing she could do about it. She felt humiliated once again. She was not going to keep track of her embarrassing moments and was hoping no one else would either.

"Hmm, nice day," she said as she put her hand up toward the sky to shield herself from the direct sun, a little like a vampire afraid to melt. Terri was sure a sight with her lush but tangled long blond hair which she didn't want to brush until well after the aspirin had settled in. But she was unable to keep aspirin down at this moment. She eyed birds flying by. "Oh boy, look at those frigates up there…."

VOLUME ONE: RAPTIS TRILOGY

****

"Yep, nice, aren't they? And don't they have over a four foot wingspan?"

"Hmm, I suppose so, sure. Remind me to put that in the tour." Terri looked up at the sky again and then down. Looking out over the parking area she realized her car was missing. "Damn it." Terri pounded her fist on the edge of the balcony. "My car, it's not here." She looked at Darren for answers.

"I drove you home last night, remember?"

Terri vaguely remembered. "Oh boy, this isn't good. I mean we can't...." She started walking in a circle as she was talking to herself out loud, not expecting answers but laying out the facts. "So, I have to go in to work without you, go in by the beach. It will take me longer, so I should go now." Her pacing shifted to the gait of a caged animal. "Oh boy, my head, this sucks. I need to see what the water's going to be like before dive classes start today. Those frigates tell me something might be up, maybe a swell. I don't see any clouds in the sky, but there is a breeze. Hmm. Seems like it could be stiff."

Darren stood there, puzzled, but he let Terri go on. He marveled at this beautiful strange creature he had just spent the night with. *Wow, she's so awesome, no women like this back home. I hope I'm not just a drinking mistake to her*, Darren thought to himself. *I hope this is the start of something great.*

She went into the kitchen and announced: "It's time to go."

Darren looked down at himself and took a quick inventory. Not the impression he would want to give on his first day at work here. He ran a hand over his beard, which felt as rough as he did. Right now a toothbrush would probably help.

"Me first." Once Terri made up her mind, no matter how much it hurt, she got to it. She wanted to get down to the beach, check out the conditions, and then retrieve her car so they could arrive at work separately. Maybe that way she could save some honor. They had one hour.

As Darren realized this himself, the door to the bath shut behind Terri. The water turned on and there was a loud shout. "Whoo hoo! This water is cold!" The water stopped. After a minute or so, the water came back on and was accompanied by another shout. And again, the water turned back off. Another couple of minutes and Terri popped her head out. "OK, your turn."

"My turn to what? What did you do in there?"

"Shower! But keep it short. Your dad may be able to buy you all the water you want, but just try and get it delivered here someday."

"Why?"

"Cause that's when they'll deliver it to you—someday!" She laughed out loud. "At this end of the island, we don't count on the most modern services being reliable."

Though he'd driven last night and was now going to drive Terri to her own car, Darren found himself feeling he might just be left behind if he didn't get moving. "Wait, before I shower I need my bag, some clean clothes, my toothbrush." He scrambled out to his car and picked out a few things as he had not yet unpacked after arriving on the island yesterday.

****

Terri was dressed and in the front room by the time he made it back. She thought it best to brush her hair later. *Why bother right now?* "OK, ready when you are."

Darren retreated into the tiny bathroom and shut the door. Within a couple of minutes, he was ready. They jumped into Darren's car, each fantasizing about last night's wild encounter. Terri couldn't remember it at all….

<u>2</u>

The beach they were headed to was a fifteen minute ride. It was only eight short miles, but the bumpy, winding, twisted road made people take it real slowly. Terri planned to get out at this beach and then walk to her own car.

The morning had a stillness to it now: the calm before the storm. Terri wished it would just blow by after work. She could see big dark nimbus clouds forming in the background as if they were huge sails hoisted, getting ready to blow in with the wind. The frigate birds were still working their way upward in ever winding circles. The morning darkened momentarily as the breeze drove under a line of large trees, their branches closing overhead, climbing vines tying them into a looming web.

In response, Darren's rental car lights automatically came on. The pair exchanged a brief glance, but Terri quickly refocused her eyes on the road. Her stomach was already borderline woozy, and she didn't want to lose her focus for fear of losing her cookies.

The darkness passed, and Terri motioned for a right hand turn. Now the sun was coming up behind the peak, and the colors of the sky changed rapidly as the new light began casting shadows.

"Hey, there's our dive shop's truck. What's it doing here?" Terri perked up, stretching her neck to get a better view. "Pull over here, please."

"OK. Is there a place around here I can take a leak?"

"Sure, over by that little building. Back in a minute. I'm going to see who's here."

VOLUME ONE: RAPTIS TRILOGY

****

As soon as Darren shifted into park, Terri sprang out and walked down to the water's edge. She had left her house in a mental fog this morning, and had forgotten to protect her ankles with a spritz of bug repellent. As she bent down to slap at the no-see-ums biting her ankles, she spotted two divers surfacing on the bay. She looked back at the truck as she tried to think who they could be. She was not aware that any early morning dive had been scheduled.

Stumped, she looked out to sea again, and now she saw three heads. One of them turned around and looked right at her. She raised her arm up over her head, then touched the top of her head with her hand. This was the beach signal used to ask a diver if everything was OK. There was a small pause—and then one arm went up in the air and began to wave. It was the diver's signal for distress.

Terri responded immediately by kicking off her sandals and running in. The coldness of the water briefly stunned her, but adrenaline took over as she swam out to the divers. They seemed to be floating, waiting for her.

****

As she swam up she saw it was John, the new manager Melvin had hired to take the job that should have been hers. He was with a gentleman she knew but couldn't place. The third party was floating face down.

"We found him, dead."

"What?" For a moment, given how calm the two divers seemed, Terri thought this was a weird joke. She looked at the third party, who she didn't recognize, who was face down, whose buoyancy compensator was not even partially inflated. Out of instinct, she grabbed at the man and turned him over. She gasped as his widened eyes looked back at her. His mask was filled with a combination of salt water, snot, and blood. She ripped the filthy mask off his face. There was no mouthpiece in his mouth. He released a large belch of dead air.

Terri turned around and swam away as she felt her stomach about to erupt one more time. She purged the contents of her stomach onto the surface of the water. After rinsing her mouth with salt water she quickly swam back toward the men like nothing had happened.

They were still floating in the same position.

She grabbed the dead man's buoyancy compensator hose and pressed down on the button to inflate the bladder. Nothing happened.

"His tank must be out of air," she informed them. She again pressed down on the button and blew into the black mouthpiece. The other two floated next to her, watching.

"Pull him in!" she shouted, taking control. The irritation in her voice was obvious. These two men had just been idling, doing nothing as she took action. She continued to press the inflator button and exhale into the mouthpiece until the dead body became buoyant. The two men began towing the dead man slowly toward the shore. Terri swam alongside them, continuing to inflate the vest to keep the body floating.

They quickly pulled up to the shoreline. Darren rushed out and immediately helped remove the man's equipment. Darren seemed so tall, so strong and alive compared to the small unmoving body. The dark skin of the dead man was now pale and bloated with salt water, and his black hair was covering half his face.

Terri found herself reaching down and wiping the hair out of the dead man's bloated face. The zipper on the front of his wetsuit was pulled half way down. Terri couldn't help but notice his gold Saint Christopher.

"Who is he?" Terri was down on her knees feeling for a pulse, although he was clearly dead.

VOLUME ONE: RAPTIS TRILOGY

****

John's companion spoke up for the first time. Terri noticed that he had already removed his diving equipment and had clearly made himself comfortable—as if he hadn't a care in the world. "The young man works with me. His name is Enrique." The strange diver held his own moment of silence with an almost practiced look of condolence, then put his hand out to Terri. "My name is Jerry, although most people just call me Captain or Captain Jerry—I'm Captain of the *Captive Sea*, that big tour ship. We've actually met. Been diving together before."

"Oh yes, yes, I knew I recognized you from somewhere.... What happened out here?"

John was standing in the background, watching.

****

Darren had already jogged over to the concession stand and was trying to connect with the police department. Darren was a responsible, take charge guy, Terri had noticed. She noted that he was self sufficient enough to already know exactly where he was—or at least the name of the beach. Darren returned as Captain Jerry was explaining the underwater scenario to Terri:

"I'm not sure where he swam off to behind our backs. We were taking pictures of seahorses on the outer grass patches." Captain Jerry, or Jerry, or Captain, it wasn't clear what he preferred to be called or if it mattered, pointed straight out to sea. "I can't imagine what happened. We were busy looking through our camera lenses. Enrique was such an advanced diver, I would never have thought he would get into trouble in such mild conditions. By the time John and I found him, he was like this."

They all looked down at the bloated figure. A distant siren broke the unnatural silence. No one spoke as the siren alarms drew closer.

Darren carried the deceased's equipment over to the dive truck. He began to dismantle it next to John, who was breaking down his own equipment. Out of habit, Darren turned the knob on the tank until it stopped, thinking he was turning the air off. But the hoses quickly tightened with pressure, so Darren reached for the regulator to purge any remaining air.

John abruptly reached over and all but grabbed the tank from Darren.

"Here, let me take care of that," John said, putting the tank next to his. "You go take care of Terri."

Darren, being the new guy, quickly relented and didn't question his new manager.

****

As the police car turned onto the road and approached the long parking lot, Terri noticed John was fidgeting by the truck, looking over at Jerry. She pretended not to notice as Jerry looked back and gave him a nod. Terri's instinct told her maybe she was watching some kind of code between these two. Reminded her of a first base coach. *What in the world could these two be up to?* Terri wondered. She stood back and observed them as the policeman sauntered over from his car.

"Terri, mon, what hap'n here?"

"Clift. Good to see you." She walked over, giving him a hand shake as she stood by him. "I don't know, ask those two, John and Captain Jerry. We got here a little too late."

Clift looked over at Darren and gave him the once over with a smile. "Yea mon, I see why you late." He started to chuckle.

Terri stopped him. "Clift. The dead man?"

"Oh yea, mon."

Out of the corner of her eye, Terri could see Captain Jerry rolling his eyes. He held his hand poised next to his head as if to hide his grinning face.

Terri looked at her watch; the dive shop was opening in fifteen minutes. Her head began to pound as she realized there would be no time to retrieve her car. She would have to drive in with Darren. She brought her attention back to the group and listened to Jerry's story one more time. This time she was watching John's body language and noticed that he was fidgeting from one foot to the other, and that he didn't look anyone in the eye. She broke in.

"Darren and I are going to leave you guys and head to the shop." She looked at her watch as she added, "We're opening in about ten minutes now."

John looked at the Captain, Jerry, with a look that seemed to say, *What do we do now?*

"Go ahead, Terri, we have this under control," the Captain told her in an authoritative voice, as if he was dismissing her.

She waved goodbye to Clift.

"I'll tell Melvin what's up," Terri offered as she headed out.

"That won't be necessary, Terri, we'll give him a call," the Captain spoke up again now.

Then John added, "Yeah, we'll call him, don't bother."

Terri was a little surprised, since John had been silent for a while. She had begun to wonder if John, this so called dive shop manager, had lost his voice or something.

"Hmm, whatever you need to do," Terri answered. There was something about this guy, Jerry, she didn't like. She felt somewhat uncomfortable leaving the situation. It wasn't any of her business, but something just wasn't right.

****

Darren opened the car door for her.

"Thank you," she said. "Did you think that whole scene was a bit strange?"

"Honestly never saw a dead person before—not by drowning."

"Not a pretty sight, I know. But I'm talking about John and that Captain, Jerry, or whatever he calls himself. John hardly said a word, did you notice? And Captain Jerry there was pretty silent too. It's like they didn't really care that the guy was dead. And I didn't see either of them trying to revive him out there." A visual of the dead man staring at her through the mask, and the thought of having to give him mouth to mouth, made her queasy again.

The ambulance with its siren blaring raced toward them and then passed them.

"Can't put my finger on it, but something's not right. Twenty-five, maybe thirty feet of water, three people—how can one get lost and run out of air? So dry, *real* dry. I tried to inflate his buoyancy compressor and the tank was bone dry. And those sea urchin spines all over his forearms. They said they were out there taking pictures, out in the outer grass patches. Did you catch that? Well, hey, there aren't any sea urchins out in the grass patches." Terri stopped and rubbed her chin as what she'd just realized began to sink in.

Darren wasn't sure how to respond. He had met John, the dive school manager, briefly last night. After his plane had landed, Darren had rented a car and driven over to the shop, surprising everyone just before closing. And when he extended an invitation to take everyone out for drinks, Darren had found an instant camaraderie. "Gee, I don't know Terri. I didn't walk up until late in the whole thing, and I don't know these people. I honestly don't remember sea urchins on the guy's arms."

"Seriously Darren? Shit, they were all over—and bad, as if he'd crawled through them or something."

Darren was hesitant to give an opinion, not knowing who all the players were. Also, he was still new to driving on the left

VOLUME ONE: RAPTIS TRILOGY

****

side of the road. He held both his hands on the wheel and tried to focus on the road. He wondered if Terri remembered he didn't exactly know where he was going.

But Terri was deep in thought. "When John arrives at the shop, I want those tanks they were using put aside so I can check them out later. Can you help me remember that?"

"Sure, no problem. There was air in that tank. I turned the knob, thinking I was turning the valve off and the hoses tightened with air. Hey, am I going the right way here?"

Terri wasn't paying much attention to Darren's driving. "Hmm … strange. Jerry said this guy ran out of air. … Oh, we're almost there. Look, its late so I want you to drop me off a block away, and I'll walk up on my own. I don't want the guys seeing us drive up together." A moment's pause: "So you're saying that his tank wasn't empty?" Terri rubbed her forehead. She was fighting off another awful headache and the urge to just go home. But she couldn't. Not now.

"It didn't appear to be empty. But I didn't get a chance to check the gauge, now that I think about it, because John grabbed everything from me. I mean he wanted it, took it, and I let him. But Terri," Darren's meaning shifted as he grew more serious, "don't worry about us going in together."

"I do worry, Darren. You don't know the guys you met last night. They won't let me live this one down."

"Terri—I mean nothing happened," Darren said reassuringly with perhaps a touch of regret.

Terri found herself momentarily surprised and perhaps just a little let down. Then a wave of relief swept over her. "Oh my God, wow, good to know, as I couldn't remember, I woke up without my clothes on and all. I'm so mortified." Terri was quite nervous. She liked Darren a lot, he was hot and fun and smart and magnetic and had manners, almost irresistible, *but all that is not relevant*, she told herself. *Hands off. For now.*

"Look, it's not that I didn't want anything to happen, because I did. You are so beautiful and fascinating. I'm blown away by you. Who would have ever guessed I would be with the woman of my dreams on my first night here? But you were passed out. That would have been totally bad form. I'm not that kind of guy."

"Hey, thanks. … You know, Darren, there aren't many guys like you."

"Maybe we can try again sometime?"

Yes, let's do that, for sure, Terri wanted to say, but she stopped herself. "Sounds good. But, well, let's see how things go. You just got here, and I am your boss, one of them anyway, OK?"

"Yes." *Well then, it's a date, isn't it,* Darren thought to himself.

"Now, can you just drop me off a block away from the dive shop. And, don't kiss and tell, please keep all this to yourself. Because the guys'll for sure insist something else happened, not nothing. Drop me off, right up there." She pointed forward and closed her eyes for a moment as if to grab just a second to pull herself together. And to stop herself from thinking about a next time with Darren….

VOLUME ONE: RAPTIS TRILOGY

****

DIVE TOUR

****

<u>3</u>

The door to the dive shop opened and Terri walked through. Everyone was busy getting ready for the day and she was uncharacteristically late.

"Ooohh, you're alive!" Henry called out across the floor to Terri as she walked in.

Darren came out of the back, working hard, already shuffling tanks in, one in each hand. He had his trademark smile on. Terri wondered for a moment if she could trust this new guy. She wanted to, but the jury might still be out. Maybe he was just a bit too perky this morning for her to trust him completely.

Terri walked over to the schedule board. One hundred twenty tourists today. One hundred twenty people leaving the comforts of their tour ship, choosing what to do on the island. She would be happy they chose to spend either a morning or an afternoon with her people. *Not a bad day, we can handle this,* she told herself as she massaged her temples. She felt a hand on her shoulder and turned around. It was Melvin, her boss.

"Heard you had quite a morning."

"Big excitement. We should talk about this. Boy, that Jerry guy, Captain he calls himself, is quick. It was this Jerry that called about this, right?"

As she said it, Melvin was already guiding her gently by her elbow off the sales floor toward his office.

When they were in Melvin's office she told him, "I asked Darren to set the tanks aside when John gets here."

"What do you mean?"

"Those guys said that man ran out of air. But Darren started to take the equipment apart and saw that there was air in that guy's tank. And I saw that there were sea urchin pricks all over his forearms." Terri spit out that last part without knowing exactly what she meant.

"Now wait a minute Terri, that's quite an accusation. Accidents do happen. Both John and Jerry are experienced divers. I myself have been diving with Jerry."

"I don't know exactly why this sticks in my mind, but it just all seemed weird."

"You just keep this to yourself. I'll talk to them and find out what happened."

Terri was still rubbing her temples as she listened.

"I don't like this guy Jerry, Melvin. Something stinks."

"Go take some aspirin. Terri. Looks like you're barely hanging on." Melvin had a furrow in his brow suggesting agitation. Captain Jerry was bringing his dive shop and school a great deal of business. "Another late one last night? Think you might want to watch that a bit?"

"I'm OK, I'm OK. You know I'm OK and that I'm not the one to watch." Terri immediately wished she hadn't added this hint about John right then. But she had dodged the accusation about her own over-drinking. "I've really got to get to work; we've got a hundred twenty coming today, you know."

Melvin put his hand on Terri's shoulder. She thought she briefly felt some tension ease away. "We'll talk about this later, OK?"

Terri looked back at him, looking him right in the eye, and nodded. She trusted Melvin. He was a scuba diving entrepreneur.

******

Years earlier, Melvin and his wife had honeymooned on a cruise in the area. He had fallen in love with one of the most natural facets of the island's beauty: tourism. Then he had convinced his new wife to leave the comfort of the States and move to the islands to forge this new business. And they had done this. They filled a niche for the more adventurous tourists on the many cruise ships that came in and out of the harbor and around the island.

Then, after seven years and two kids, his wife had left him for the comforts of her family and hometown, not to mention for an unlimited source of hot running water, air conditioning, and up-to-the-minute news.

Melvin never married again. Not that he ever had a problem finding a date. With his charming looks and Texan hospitality, he had already been through several short relationships. And no one could match his passion for what he loved to do: dive.

Terri had met Melvin in Acapulco. It had been a long way for Terri to travel for an interview, but Melvin was unwinding after a week at a diving convention. And Terri had wanted to move; anywhere she could find work would do. She actually had wanted to end up in an exotic foreign place, scuba diving the days away. So Melvin and Terri immediately hit it off. The two of them had a wonderful time in Acapulco and Terri landed her first job diving in a foreign country. She still remembered her excitement. As soon as her plane landed back in California, she had arranged to leave school, sell all her worldly goods, and buy a one way ticket to the Caribbean.

She had only looked back once, when she was already boarding the plane to take her away. She could see her mom and dad standing there. Her dad was waving goodbye with one hand and holding her mom up with the other. Her mom was beginning to sob and mouthed the words, "I love you." Terri waved back and smiled to assure them she was OK, while she was choking back tears herself. She turned away, and looking forward, boarded the plane.

****

Terri's reverie was interrupted when the bells on the front door of the shop started jingling. A busload of people had arrived and were bursting through the doorway, eager to start their morning adventure. The dive shop was a scuba retail store, training facility, and tour business. People always felt the urge to shop the minute they walked in the door. They couldn't help it; Melvin had set it up that way. Colorful t-shirts with the dive shop's logo or other Caribbean graphics supplemented the entire range of things people coming in would want. They covered the wall everyone saw the moment they walked in.

"Mom! Mom! Can I get a t-shirt?"

"Ohhh! Underwater postcards!"

"Wow! Look! Underwater cameras! Excuse me—can we rent one of these?"

"Good morning everyone! We've been waiting for you!" Terri weaved her way through the crowd and stepped onto a bench so she could be seen as well as heard. "We're going to head straight back into the classroom and get you folks started on some diving knowledge. All your questions will be answered, and more. We don't want to hang around here too long, we want to get to the beach!"

"Yeah!" The crowd roared back. All eyes were on Terri now; she was their new leader.

"My name is Terri! It is my job to make sure this tour is better than an e-ticket ride at Disneyland." Terri got a few chuckles with this, but made a mental note to come up with a better line. *People just don't remember those Disneyland e-tickets and the thrill attached to them.* "For those of you that don't know what that means, trust me—you're in for a good time!" Terri let them see her contagious grin, and when she waived her hand to send them into the back room, off they went.

Danny was inside his classroom, inviting them to sit down for a video.

Terri spied the ten-year-old staying back. He still wanted a t-shirt and was determined to pick one out. "Don't worry kid, I'll personally work on your mom about getting you a shirt."

"Thanks!" He looked up, totally putting his trust in her.

"Now go sit next to whoever you're with, because the movie's starting."

"But I'm not with anyone! I'm by myself!" He proudly pulled out his wallet, opening it up to show off to Terri the amount of cash enclosed. "I'm going to buy that shirt!"

"No foolin'. Well, let's buy it later. The video's starting and you can't miss it." Terri ushered the boy into the back room and sat him down. *Who let this young kid come here? Alone? Shit.* Terri made sure the kid's attention was on the TV before she left the room.

Melvin and Kathy were on the sales floor. The instructors were busy loading the air tanks onto the bus. Terri wanted them to explain the boy. Terri kept her voice down as she walked up to Melvin and Kathy. "What the hell's goin' on here? I got a ten year old who says he's here all by himself!"

"Wait until we find out who he belongs to. Gotta' be someone important." Kathy had an almost giddy excitement in her eyes.

"We may never know the father's name, but he's a pretty big guy I hear. And the kid, well, he's not alone; he has a bodyguard with him at all times," Melvin added. "Special guest from the *Captive Sea*. That Captain sends us some big customers. This kid's one of his main guy's kids. So let's be great with him."

"And, the kid doesn't know he has a bodyguard, so no telling," Kathy quickly added in a hushed tone and then walked off.

"And let's just say the 'extra' we receive for this unusual arrangement will be split among everyone. Everyone is going to keep an eye on him, pass it on," Melvin told Terri. "Let's do a great job, it'll keep the *Captive Sea* sending us great business. Let everyone know this."

"Does Kathy know about this deal? She should know, she should tell everyone about this, not me. I mean, she's in charge, not me, right?"

"Good point. I'm going to tell her right now, Terri." Melvin called out to Kathy, "Come with me for a moment, Kathy." Melvin led Kathy away to his office, leaving Terri standing there.

But Terri was not alone for long. Another bus load of tourists had just pulled up in front of the shop. The door began to jingle.

4

"Good morning everyone!" Terri exclaimed as she again went into her act. She began the song and dance: "Line up for your masks here, line up for your fins here, you can rent an underwater camera for only fifteen dollars over here!" Terri gestured wildly to Donna behind the counter, ready to take their money. Young Donna was always eager to help and did her job well.

A hardy roar of laughter from the crowd flowed out of Danny's classroom in the back. This cued Terri so she could be ready when the video was over: five minutes. Then all these people just arriving and all those in the back would trade places, with the first group going out to the beach. And five more busloads of people were still coming in today.

****

Eventually, it was five o'clock and the last bus drove away from the shop. Terri looked around. She had not seen John or Kathy the whole day. She found them both in Melvin's office. Melvin looked up as she walked in.

"Can you pick up the money at the *Captive Sea* tonight?"

"Sure, Melvin, like I always used to...." Terri didn't want to look at John, but she wanted to know about the tanks. She just came right out and asked, "Hey John, what did you do with that, you know, that empty tank. From this morning?"

"Put 'em back. Everything's put away now. Hey, let's go have a beer. Melvin just bought everyone beer and pizza."

"You put everything all away? You didn't think that someone might want to look the equipment over?"

VOLUME ONE: RAPTIS TRILOGY

****

"Terri." The way Melvin said it was louder than Melvin ever talked. Terri knew to stop her line of questioning right there. "Get cleaned up, put something in your stomach, and hit the road," Melvin told her.

She walked out without saying a word. She went into the back with the rest of the crew and picked up a piece of pizza and a beer. Then she sat on the outer perimeter.

John entered without Kathy, picked up a beer and sat on the opposite side of the group.

John blurted out without being asked, "Showing Darren 'the ropes'—or should I say—*your* ropes, Terri?"

"Shut up, John." Terri shot a look over to Darren that accused him of spilling the beans.

John kept it coming at her. "These guys say it usually takes a week of fresh meat landing before you sniff it out, *him* out. It is always a 'him,' right?" John let out a howl and tipped his beer toward his fellow workers as if to egg them on into joining the banter. A few small smiles may have cracked at that, but they all knew better than to laugh out loud. Terri was edgy like a loaded gun and no one wanted to be in her sights.

"Oh, is that what they say?" Terri's face reddened with anger. Her eyes sharpened and locked on to John's. John had crossed a line, *her* line, in front of the guys, *her* guys. She wasn't going to be humiliated without jabbing back. But her wit was still a bit dulled with this morning's headache. The day's events had only compounded her stress.

Terri stood up, tipped her head back, and slugged down the rest of her beer. All the while, she managed to keep one eye on John. *Silence will kill this guy. Let him guess what I'm thinking.* As she lowered her beer, she had both eyes locked on John's.

The room was terribly silent, the tension making everyone uncomfortable. They all knew Terri had wanted the job John and his wife, Kathy, now held. Kathy was part of the deal. But John *was* the deal, for some reason Terri could not understand. *Could this be something that big customer, Captain Jerry, asked Melvin to do, hire John? Melvin always seems to feel he has to cater to this big tour ship, this big source of business,* Terri told herself.

Suddenly, Kathy walked into the room and interrupted Terri's stare, which shifted to the woman's wide eyes, filled with the naivety of a young doe. Kathy was always fresh as a flower, even in the middle of a storm.

John's eyes also shifted to the safe harbor of his wife. "How are you doin', honey?"

Kathy walked over to John, put her arms out, and rested her hands on his shoulders. She started to rub. But John jumped in response, as if Kathy were a total stranger. His head went down, unable to look his wife in the eye.

Everyone quickly looked the other way, pretending not to notice the man's quirky behavior. Kathy's initial response was confusion, then embarrassment. Why wasn't her husband reaching out for her?

Terri chose that moment to leave. As she walked by the two of them, the words she had been trying to put together, the right jab, came out of her mouth just loud enough for them to hear. "What a great guy." Terri kept walking until she was out of the room and on the sales floor.

******

Everything was put away, neat and tidy, all ready for the same pace tomorrow. The indoor outdoor carpet smelled slightly damp. To the right of her was Melvin's closed office door. She stopped next to it, poised, ready to knock.

Leave Melvin alone—what am I going to say? That I "have a feeling"? A chuckle actually erupted from her mouth, a complete contradiction of the way she felt inside. She knew Melvin was not interested in her feeling, whatever it was, especially not today. Anyway, most likely Melvin was on the phone, discussing the need to keep this morning's events out of the four page local newspaper. No pictures had been taken. And the few employees of the dive shop who knew about what happened knew not to talk. Rumors on this island spread faster than southern California wildfires, scorching and burning everyone and thing in their paths.

But Terri was having a very hard time keeping her mouth shut. She felt a burning desire to talk, to express her disgust for John and this Captain Jerry, and this venom was bubbling to the surface. Furthermore, Terri's emotional state was poor, and she was on the verge of letting it all out. She had to get out of there fast. So she turned to leave.

But there was one minor detail that opened the gate. She suddenly remembered she didn't have her car. Darren had pretty much driven her to work that morning, letting her walk the last hundred yards or so to arrive alone. Now she was trapped. She felt like crying.

Closing her eyes, Terri chanted to herself as she tried to drive back the tears. *Not another meltdown, not today.*

The front door jingled. Someone was walking in. It was Mitch. Mitch was Terri's closest friend, or something like that.

She walked over to say hello, but on the inside she wanted to run to him. "Oh Mitch, I need a hug, what a day! Can you take me to my car?" Her frustration had immediately decompressed to a more manageable level.

"Sure, Terri. A little bird told me you might need help. Melvin does watch and pay attention, you know."

"Oh, you've talked with Melvin. Then you know I have to go and pick up the money at the *Captive Sea*. Are you joining me?"

"Sure, go change your top. We'll have a drink on the ship."

"Maybe Jackie up at the ship will join us." Terri turned and darted to the back room. Soon she emerged with a different top on. "There, this is better."

"Terri." She heard her name called from across the sales floor. She turned around to see Darren walking toward them. "Hey, what's up? You need a ride to your car? Can I buy you some real dinner?"

"Oh, Darren, yes—wait, I mean no. I mean—Darren this is my good friend, Mitch." Terri was obviously flustered.

Darren stuck his hand out to Mitch.

"Nice to meet you," Darren and Mitch said in awkward unison, each giving a firm handshake.

"Nice island you've got here." *Nice woman you have here*, **we** *have here*, is what Darren wanted to say and was thinking. Darren's grin was contagious and he always seemed to be wearing one. He towered over Mitch with about five inches to spare.

"Mitch is going to take care of me, thank you for asking."

"Everything is under control," Mitch added in a somewhat authoritative tone. Darren may have been taller, but Mitch had years on this young man, *looks like almost fifteen of them*. Mitch told himself this, hoping no one heard him thinking.

Darren assessed the situation and, in his young innocent stag sort of way, grabbed Terri's hand. She blushed as he gave it a quick kiss, half teasing, half wishing.

"It can only get better after today, right? Lot's better." Darren was looking at Terri for confirmation.

"Absolutely!" Mitch had his hand on Terri's shoulder and maneuvered her out of the shop.

Darren wistfully watched them leave.

******

Mitch was parked right in front. He walked Terri around to the passenger side and opened the car door for her. A BMW sports car with air conditioning and leather seats, this car was more comfortable than anything Terri had ever owned. And it was a rarity on this relatively basic island. But Mitch took his driving seriously. If he was going to drive up and down a mountain every day, then he was going to enjoy it. In this case, however, the cruise ship docks where the *Captive Sea* would be berthed were only a mile away.

"Where's your car?" Mitch asked.

"At the Conch Shell."

"Ahhh, the Conch Shell conch'ed you again. … And Mr. Perfect?" Mitch tried to figure out what young Darren had to do with all this. *Could he be after Terri?*

"Funny." Terri let out a slight huff to accentuate her sarcasm. "His name is Darren. He's our new instructor." She closed her eyes and sunk her head back into the headrest. *Ahhhh....* But just as she found her comfort spot, they pulled into the parking lot at the base of the mammoth ship. Steel drums sounded out to welcome the buses and taxis filled with people coming back to their floating home. This was Captain Jerry's kingdom.

"You've had quite a day," Mitch said.

"You wouldn't believe it, Mitch. I really think something's up. Can't put my finger on it. But something is not right." Terri was punching her right fist into her left hand as she made her point. It was as if she wanted to slug someone, which she did: herself. "How come this guy died in less than thirty feet of water, and they're saying he ran out of air? Darren says he knew that tank had air. He didn't know how much but—"

"Terri." Mitch cut her off. "We both know accidents happen, all right?"

36

DIVE TOUR

****

"Yes, I know, but—"

"But what? Let it go right now. You're not even giving the guy the benefit of the doubt. I think you're a little upset at seeing a dead man again. We know what that's like." He looked over, trying to catch her eyes.

"I have no doubt, Mitch."

"What, so you think the captain of this ship, and John, took this guy out into the ocean and killed him? Think of what you're saying before you speak, Terri. That's called murder."

"Well, uh," Mitch had totally unnerved the usually unflappable Terri. His voice was so stern now. She had not heard that tone come out of him before. "But, Mitch. I'm just saying.... Hell, I don't know what I'm saying. It's just that—"

Mitch had turned the engine off and was still looking at her, waiting for her to spit the words out.

"Shit, Mitch!" Terri was exasperated.

"Come on." He opened his door and got out.

Terri followed. They walked up to the gangplank in silence. Terri was feeling somewhat like an ass and not really sure why. While steel drums banged out their calypso beat, the pair walked inside, showed the officer in charge their IDs, and gave their reason for being there. It was all pomp and circumstance, as Terri had been on this ship umpteen times, many of them with Mitch in tow. She knew that right now over in the bar they were serving free hors'dourves, and she had her heart set on one or two.

Walking through the maze of hallways, they passed passengers who recognized Terri from earlier in the day at the dive shop. She kept her smile, nodded, and exchanged hellos as they made their way to see the petty officer. Her name was Jackie.

VOLUME ONE: RAPTIS TRILOGY

****

DIVE TOUR

****

<u>5</u>

They walked into Jackie's office and saw she was alone. Jackie was always fastidiously dressed in her neatly creased uniform. Her petite frame had perfect, unblemished white skin. It was a stark contrast to her jet black hair which flowed loosely around her shoulders. Over-sized black glasses topped off her tiny frame. Although Jackie had only six years on Terri, the two gals seemed centuries apart. The thought alone of wearing a uniform and makeup made Terri cringe.

Jackie sorted and counted the scuba gear and diving school tickets at breakneck speed. She quickly calculated the monetary value and counted out the money in front of Terri. It came in a combination of traveler's checks and cash. With that quick exchange, business was complete. Terri put the checks and cash in the envelope in her bag.

"How's life on the ship these days, Jackie?"

"Oh just fine, Terri. You know, every week another loop! How's everything on your end? I met your new gal, Kathy, last week."

"What time do you get off? We're going up to the bar for a drink. Would you like to join us?"

"I'm expecting two more operators, they should be here shortly. I could—"

"Hello, folks." Terri recognized the voice before she turned around. It was that Captain Jerry she had talked to on the beach that morning. This time he was in uniform. He stood tall, and smiled as she looked right at him. "Hello, Terri. Two times in one day. Imagine."

"Yes sir. We're doing a little ticket exchange," Terri answered, surprised to see him there. An unexpected sensation raced up her back into her neck. There was something about this guy; she just didn't trust him. He, like Jackie, looked neatly pressed in his uniform, but he still wore that smug, arrogant look on his face.

"Of course." He turned and directed his full attention across the desk. "Jackie, can you meet me in the upper conference room as soon as you have business wrapped up? We have an unannounced meeting scheduled. I'd like you to be there."

"Yes sir, of course. Two more clients and I'll be able to get away."

"Perfect." He smiled widely at Jackie and then turned to Terri. "Terri." He nodded to her in a military style, letting her know she was dismissed. All the while he had completely ignored Mitch.

"Say, Captain?" Terri added quite spontaneously. Once she had gotten his direct attention, she wasn't quite sure what she wanted to say. "I'd sure like to see your pictures of the sea horses, the ones you took out in the grasses this morning."

"Unfortunately, we didn't get any."

"But that's what you said, right? You were out in those shallow grass patches?"

He shot her an annoyed look.

"Yes, we were out that way." He nodded to her once again to let her know the interrogation was over. Turning around, he disappeared as quickly as he'd come.

"Well, I guess that answers that. Evidently I am needed." Jackie jumped right in, not sure how to interpret what she just saw.

"Maybe next time you can join us," Mitch pitched in, as if he needed to assure his own existence by the sound of his voice.

There was a brief silence as both ladies turned and looked at Mitch.

"Yes, that would be nice. We'll catch up then."

Terri looked right at Jackie. "What do you think that meeting's about? Anything happen today?"

Jackie, in turn, looked at Terri and gave a light sigh. "Terri, you know as well as I do. Loose lips sink ships and honey, I live on one!" She followed it up with a maternal because-I-said-so look.

"Yeah, yeah, well I had a big day." Terri was fishing for a response.

"So I heard."

OK, so she has heard something, she's just not saying what. Maybe that Jerry is listening somehow. Terri stepped sideways, poked her head out of the room, and looked down the hallway. All she saw was her good friend Hook coming up to the door. No Captain in sight.

"OK then, how about next week. It's a date?" Terri wanted confirmation.

"I'll try my best."

"Well mon, good to see you here." It was Hook, a long-time bus driver coming in to do his share of business with Jackie. "And you look so beautiful, my dear."

"Oh, thank you Hook. You're so sweet."

"Ya, but you still won't go out wit me. What will it take, girl?"

"Hook, you give that line to all the girls." Terri gave him a friendly pat on the back, knowing it was Jackie's time to leave for that meeting. "I'll see you next week!"

Terri and Mitch walked away through the long narrow halls. They eventually found their way to the bar, which was already filling with passengers ready to unwind.

"What convenient timing for the Captain to steal Jackie away from us."

"What do you mean?"

"He knew I wanted to talk to her."

"About what? What are you talking about?"

She leaned over and answered in hushed tones. "You know, this morning."

"Oh please, are you serious? You're just not going to let this go, are you? So what, now you think Jackie is in on it?"

"No Mitch, I don't think Jackie is in on it. Gosh, stop making me look so silly. I'm telling you, I'm going to get to the bottom of this. Maybe Jackie knows something—like, who was the guy that died, anyway? Enrique? He worked on this ship. What did he do?"

Mitch didn't respond. He didn't know what to say. Maybe if he just sat there, she would stop talking. But she didn't.

"And you know that if this would have happened in the States, the police would have been all over the death scene, held an investigation, the whole nine yards. And here, a simple report, a pat on the back, and everything's washed and put away, and that's it! I don't get it!"

"Terri, I think you need some sleep. Finish your drink. I'm taking you to your car. You need to go home." Mitch had reached his limit.

"You just don't see it, do you Mitch?"

"I see a tired, frustrated young lady who needs to go home now." He had emphasized the "now" and thus quickly finished his drink and stood up to go.

Terri complied. They walked out to Mitch's car. The drive to Terri's car was silent. Mitch was trying to unwind from his own complicated day, and Terri was in a mood because her best friend just wouldn't listen.

When they got to Terri's car, Mitch said gently, "You'll feel better tomorrow. We'll talk then, OK?"

That was Terri's signal to get out of his car, he wanted to go home.

"OK Mitch, thanks for the ride. Sorry I'm a wet blanket today."

"Go home, get some rest. It'll all look different tomorrow."

"Yeah, right. Tomorrow." She walked over to her car, feeling defeated and lonely. And what the hell, it was barely seven o'clock! She dropped the money off, then diverted from her path and went to a bar instead, half hoping she'd run into Darren and half hoping she wouldn't.

****

<u>6</u>

Kathy stood waiting for John in front of the dive shop. She was perplexed and frustrated. *Where did he just come from, and then where did he just go, the bathroom? And now what in the world is he doing in there?* It had been a very long day and she wanted to go home.

Everyone else had left, everyone but Melvin, who was waiting for Terri who was to return soon with the money.

John seemed to have six different reasons to delay his and Kathy's departure. Right now he was in the bathroom for the second time in fifteen minutes. The fourteen minutes in between were spent waiting for him to check one more thing, just one more thing, and now back to the bathroom. Kathy felt that John was quickly drifting away into his own little world. It left her feeling stranded, all alone.

John came out of the bathroom.

"Are you OK?" She looked at John, his skin was pale. He looked twenty years older for some reason she couldn't put her finger on.

"I'm fine, I'm ready."

"Are you sure?"

"Yep, yep, let's go." He walked out to their car at a fast pace while leaning forward, almost bent over. He opened the passenger side, got in, and shut the door. Kathy let out a brief sigh of disappointment. This was just one more sign John was changing; he always opened up the car door for her. She looked at him as he sat in the passenger seat, swiping away at his nose.

John laid his head back against the headrest to let the cocaine he'd just ingested sink down into his nasal cavities. The trickle of mucus mixed with cocaine began to numb the back of his throat as the drip continued. He started to sniff through his nose to keep it from running, not to chance anything by blowing the contents out into a Kleenex.

Kathy looked away. She stared out the window trying to find anything else to look at. She was sick of watching John wipe and sniff his nose.

Down in his lap, John was clenching his fists and releasing them over and over without even being aware of it. His palms were reddened from the pressure of his finger nails pressing in. In a weak attempt to be nonchalant, he gave Kathy a quick glance. *Is she watching me?*

The car started. John snapped to when the engine noise caught him off guard. He felt extremely anxious, so he focused on his breathing. The air seemed unusually heavy this evening. Kathy pulled the car out and merged into traffic.

****

Driving home, the windows were down. Neither spoke as they inched their way through single lane downtown traffic, always odd to see on this island. John sat with his hands folded on his lap, fidgeting as if he were forcing those hands to stay still. As the car moved forward in the stop-and-go traffic, John tilted his head out the window a little so the slight breeze would bring some relief from the humidity.

After leaving the sounds of the busy town, the silence between them grew more and more awkward. Soon it became a challenge. For Kathy, it was trying to figure out what to say to connect with John. John's challenge was to avoid eye contact, as he didn't want to connect or talk at all.

Kathy was craving details. *What happened out there? Where are you, John?* Frustrated, her hands clenched the steering wheel tighter. She was trying to keep her emotions from bubbling up to the surface. This was not the perfect ending to the perfect first week on this perfect new job here in this perfect new place that they had planned when they were back on the island of Aruba. In fact, nothing had been right since their arrival on this new island for this new job a little over a week ago.

Kathy had not felt accepted at the dive shop, though they'd both been hired, as a team. John fared a little better with the staff, but barely. It seemed the crew didn't trust either of them very much. And Terri was downright rude to John. And now this, a diving accident with John smack in the middle! Melvin had told them there would be a time of adjustment, as they were replacing Dave, who had been the shop's dearly loved manager for years. It seemed that Terri had it in her head that Dave's job should have become hers. And now Kathy and John were treated as though they were responsible for some kind of hostile takeover.

Kathy couldn't take the silence any more. "John? Maybe if you talked about what happened, it might help relieve some of your anxiety." She could see his fingers clenched tightly around each other. She was about to burst out of her seat because he looked so uptight.

"Can you believe it?"

"I know sweetheart, I am so sorry." Kathy reached out to touch her husband's leg. John jumped. He uncurled his fingers and began to drum them on his knee. Kathy pulled away, as if the energy field around him repelled her. "You've had an awful day."

"I know, can you believe that bitch?"

"What? Who are you talking about?"

"Terri, of course."

Kathy put both hands on the wheel. She focused forward, noting a landmark not far from their new home. She had stopped talking. John's behavior was confusing, not at all what she'd expected. It wasn't as if anyone blamed John for the accident, but Kathy thought his responses were peculiar, kind of defensive or something. He didn't seem to be upset about the dead man, not exactly. He was more wrapped up in whatever was going on in his head. And the death of that man—well, John just didn't want to talk about it. As if it didn't happen.

An unexpected shudder whistled through Kathy as she wondered how someone could change so rapidly. She glanced over at him; he was daydreaming as he gazed out the window. He was transforming into an oaf right before her eyes. Now he was a big overgrown child, so self-absorbed that no one else mattered.

****

Making a quick right, Kathy maneuvered up the steep and narrow drive which led to their home. It was a rental. It had sounded so perfect over the phone. With two bedrooms, a full bath, and one whole acre of land behind them, there was plenty of room. There was a separate cistern to collect water for the main house. This important plus meant they had an extra water supply to depend on, and since conservation was mandatory, all water used in the household was supposed to be collected rainwater.

Kathy parked in the covered driveway. John immediately bolted out of the door as if he had been being held hostage. Kathy didn't even care. His strange scent had been overtaking the interior of the car. She shot a brief puff of air out through her nostrils to rid them of John's smell. *Even his smell is grossing me out.* She took a deep breath as she stepped out of the car.

Soon it would be dark. When it was dark, it was really dark out there; no neighbors nearby, or lamps on the road to guide drivers at night. And now, this coming dark only increased her feeling of aloneness. John had just run into the house, leaving her standing outside. Tears started to well up in her eyes.

Relax. She didn't want to go in at this moment. Her emotions were so two-sided, behaving like Gemini twins, one side trying to feel compassion for John and the other swimming in despair. She loved this man, but right now he was both Dr. Jekyll and Mr. Hyde. Today, she was admitting to herself she was seeing someone very different, someone she wasn't sure she even liked, one she did not want to see or even admit existed.

Finally relenting to the inevitable, she went inside. Looking around, she spotted John sitting out on the porch. His briefcase was just dropped there on the kitchen floor. She scanned the counters. Something there was different. Kathy reached for a small bottle of Vodka sitting there. *Where did this come from?* She looked down at John's briefcase for answers.

Suddenly footsteps and then clinking broke into her chain of thought. John was standing next to her dropping ice cubes in an empty glass.

"Can I mix you a drink?" He talked as if this were a nightly ritual, a mixed drinks routine.

"What are you drinking? Vodka?" She stared at John in disbelief. In the year and a half she'd known him, she had never seen him drink anything. He always said alcohol wasn't good for him. So now it was?

"To take the edge off." He swirled the ice cubes around in his glass again. This sound set Kathy further on edge. "You want one?" He turned and looked right at her, catching her off guard. "What, you have a problem with that?"

Kathy was stunned; now it wasn't just the drinking, but his tone. He was scaring her.

"Well, no, John. I don't think so. I've just, you know, never seen you drink before. You said it wasn't good for you. What did that mean?" She wasn't sure what to say here, as she was afraid of setting him off. "Where did you get it?"

"Where in the hell do you think I got it? I bought it, after work." He began to mix himself another one.

"I couldn't figure out where you went. You left the dive shop and then came back." Kathy stood there stunned and puzzled. Why shouldn't she believe him? Why would he lie about that? None of this was making sense.

"I had to get some more fresh air."

"I'm sorry." Kathy didn't know what else to say. She went to sit down, sinking into an uncomfortably hard wooden dining chair. She so wanted to understand, but didn't.

"I'm going to sit outside. It's too muggy in here for me." John turned and walked away. Her ideas, her opinions, they didn't mean anything to him.

Kathy sat there for a long while feeling stunned, like there was a stranger in her house.

DIVE TOUR

****

7

It was dark out. The sun had set three hours ago. City lights glowed in the background. Momentary glimpses of headlights on the mountain flickered now and then without rhythm. All but one of the cruise ships had left the harbor, sailing on to their next exotic destinations.

No one noticed what was unfolding out at Coconut Point. The forty-five foot yacht that had been lolling in the bay all day had raised anchor and set sail to its next destination. No music, no chatter, no fanfare. Nothing to draw attention to itself. There were only two men on board, two brothers. They had been told to dive at Coconut at nine o'clock, but they had chosen to take their time.

The two brothers had been suspicious about a trap or something. Diving at a specific time seemed odd to them. They would go when it felt right, and they would do their job: retrieve the tanks and be in Miami with them on time.

It was simple and clear. Appear to be two underwater photographers out for a night dive at nine o'clock, and instead retrieve two tanks stashed in an old culvert forty feet underwater off Coconut Point. They were then to motor in the dark to nearby San Dominguez, and from there, it was a simple private flight to Miami with the tanks. In Miami, they would deliver the tanks to an as yet undisclosed address.

******

By ten o'clock, both men were on the back deck donning light wetsuits for the short dive. They certainly looked like two avid underwater photographers. They had large cameras and strobe lights. Slowly, they descended into the water off the back of the boat. The moon was at a sliver and the ambient light was low. They turned on the flashlights strapped to their wrists.

The pair descended to the sandy bottom, down about sixty feet. Before them, the soft glow of the flashlights lit a five-foot diameter. Drawn up off the sand beneath, a layer of silt danced in the glow of the light. Most fish were still, asleep within the comforts of protective coral on both sides. The two divers checked their compasses and began to swim on a course to the culvert. With their destination in sight, they were to take extra precautions: only one would swim up to this culvert, without a light. The chances of anyone watching the point this late at night were slim. Still, they were careful not to draw attention to where exactly they were going.

With clear visibility, their eyes adjusted to the darkness. From the bottom of a long sandy slope, the cylinder loomed in the dark up ahead. A massive artificial inlet, approximately four-and-a-half feet in diameter, was guarded by four large blades at its mouth. Goosebumps ran up the diver's back as he saw where he was headed. It was just as described.

He handed his flashlight to his partner and swam up to the entrance. There was a neglected cage-like wall of fine gauge steel wire across the front, which appeared to have been unmaintained for years. He looked inside and let his eyes adjust to the darkness. There in the back, yes, there the tanks were.

The thought of swimming through, moving between those mammoth blades, made his breathing accelerate. He shut his eyes and said a short prayer, trying to slow his breathing down. His diving buddy was below him off in the distance with both flashlights on. With a quick crossing of his heart, he pulled back on the face of the screen. Satisfied the screen was going to stay back, he removed his tank from his back and pushed it through the narrow opening between the blades.

His body glided through the opening as he pushed his air source ahead of him. He was surprised at the lack of sediment inside. Forward, about ten feet away, sat the two tanks, just as

DIVE TOUR

****

promised. With his tank removed, he found himself able to turn around in the cylinder so he could swim out. He slid three tanks ahead of him to the entrance.

He slowly pushed the two lone tanks out the bottom, watching each one glide down the sandy slope. He saw his partner swim over to collect them. Then, before he could leave, he had to shove his own tank out between the blades. And he did. Just then, he heard an unfamiliar noise, something like a mechanical buzz, then a click. He paused briefly, trying to identify the source of the sound.

The intake fan became alive in reverse. With one quick slice, horror and shock were permanently engraved on the man's face. The current had sucked his mouthpiece out of his mouth, leaving it wide open as if he were screaming. The fan lasted all of five seconds. The wide blades minced and spewed out his lower torso. It all rained down on his diving buddy below. Small pieces drifted in the current.

His partner had swum halfway up the slope to retrieve the tanks. He now found himself pushed back down with the current. The upper torso of his partner swirled in the current as if it were dancing while trying to find a place to land, his eyes and mouth remaining wide open. The partner was hit with a wave of nausea. He was paralyzed with fear. He watched as small fish were zooming overhead, snapping on raining body parts. Panic overcame him and he bolted for the surface.

He got to the boat, threw his equipment up onto the platform on back, and quickly scrambled up as if someone were chasing him. He had to slow his breathing, catch his breath. He didn't want to look down.

******

Sitting there on the boat a half hour and two drinks later, the man nervously looked at his watch. His time was growing short to reach San Dominguez. He was numb and shaking. He didn't want to see the horror of his partner's body, but he knew he had to. To leave anything behind would mean sure death for him as well. He then realized he had left the two tanks down there. Now another fear set in. They would kill him if he forgot those. He started to put his equipment back on.

Looking over the edge he could see the glow of a flashlight left behind. A frenzy of small fish swam around the light. Waiting for an opportunity to dine, larger fish alerted by the movement were circling this swarm of smaller fish. At the edge of the reef a small shark had taken interest in the scent and movement.

Descending down to the bottom, his first priority was to retrieve the tanks. This was, after all, the whole point of this trip-turned-disaster. The tanks were heavy and weighed him down while he tried to carry both. Reluctantly, he left one tank behind and took two trips to do this, placing both tanks on the platform's edge. He then had to remove his own equipment, climb up, and carefully stash the two tanks.

Bordering on complete exhaustion, he again checked his watch and knew he had to keep going. On board he found a large mesh bag, probably meant for laundry, and some rope. He took this back down with him.

He had to begin the task of retrieving the remains. His partner was drifting about one foot off the bottom, his arms still extended. He wanted to shove the body in face first so he wouldn't have to look at his eyes again. The arms stiffened, refused to cooperate. The dead man's hands were too long to fit all the way in, it was if the man was reaching trying to climb out of the bag. Stuffing what other remains he could locate into the bag, his own breath became labored. Reaching for his pressure gauge he wasn't surprised to see that he was breathing so hard he was using the last of his air. He only had minutes left.

Fish were darting back and forth as he cleared out their feast. Suddenly he felt another rush of fear, or was it instinct? He swung his flashlight around. He felt as if he was stealing a wild dog's bone. He didn't want to meet any wild dogs in the guise of sharks down there.

Moving faster, with an additional rush of adrenaline, he quickly had his partner's equipment fastened together. He tied the mesh bag to the equipment, inflated the buoyancy compensator with air and slowly rose to the surface. With much effort, he made it back to the boat.

He talked to himself as he pulled everything aboard, his skin now whiter than the sliver of moon. He was shaking down to his soul. He was sorry now that they had dallied at the harbor earlier. They were supposed to have been there before nine o'clock and they weren't in the water until almost ten.

Time to go. Now the engines came alive and the anchor cranked up. Pushing the throttles full force, he sped away as if a demon was chasing him. He had to reach his destination in the dark, alone. It was going to be three hours—if these weather conditions held up. If not, longer.

Once in San Dominguez, he would have to dispose of his partner's remains while it was still dark. He briefly thought about dumping them somewhere between here and there. The sharks would take care of him.

But what was he going to say? He had to disclose what happened.

****

That same evening, far away in the hills outside of Caracas, a phone rang. A gentleman named De Gerlick had finished eating dinner with the phone beside him, waiting for a confirmation.

"Hello?... Gracias," was all he said. He set the phone back down in its cradle, then attempted a smile. As De Gerlick was not accustomed to smiling, the right side of his mouth simply reached slightly upward, then quickly retracted: the left side remained motionless from a deep knife wound to the face. An unpleasant task had been taken care of just as planned. And De Gerlick's own son (fully equipped with his own bodyguard employed by big daddy De Gerlick himself) was having fun, too. The coded message he received from the *Captive Sea* was: "Having a great time. And your boy is, too."

He reached for the phone again and called for a car to meet him out front. Reaching into the top drawer, he pulled out a bottle of Sea Breeze cleanser for an antiseptic splash to revive him. He splashed some on his hands, and then rubbed it on his face. He stood tall, holding on to his cane, and made his way to the front of the large home that was secured like a large compound. Lit for effect, large tropical foliage graced every corner. There were large pavers throughout the home; the inside an extension of the outside. The scent of the Sea Breeze lingered in the garden behind him.

The driver opened the back door for him. De Gerlick passed a piece of paper to him without a word. The driver studied it, then handed it right back. De Gerlick demanded this sort of memory from anyone who worked with or around him. Almost to the point of paranoia, the man was afraid of leaving any paper trail. The car drove through the heavy opened gate and wound down the hill to the center of town.

****

The neighborhood they arrived in was far different from the one they'd just left. High rises loomed above, and strewn down below in between the high rises were less fortunate homes— old cars and cardboard boxes. Cautious eyes watched as the long, sleek sedan pulled up. There was no reason for a stranger to wander into this part of town. There were no streetlights to illuminate the surrounding area. Feral dogs sniffing at the trash on the streets showed no fear of the man as his driver opened the back door.

De Gerlick stepped out of the car and instinctively checked the inner pocket of his light silk jacket. Assured by the outline of his revolver, he walked into the nearby highrise and ascended four flights of stairs. His cane matched every step, taking the weight of his useless leg. It made an unusual sound as it hit each concrete stair and then echoed up the stairway. When he

DIVE TOUR

****

approached the door he was looking for, he knocked with the steel tip of his cane.

The door slowly inched open, an eye peering out to see who the visitor was. The scent of Sea Breeze preceded the steel tip of his cane. The cane quickly lodged the door open, immediately revealing his identity. Someone tried to slam the door shut, but was unsuccessful against De Gerlick's favorite tool. On his second attempt, the intruder pushed the door open to no resistance; everyone had stepped back. A young woman was escorting young children out of the room, not daring to look back over her shoulder. She lifted up the youngest and shut a door behind them.

"Buenas noches," De Gerlick greeted them in Spanish as he looked around the room. His eyes met with Fernando's. A young man in his thirties, Fernando, had been working for De Gerlick over ten years, and Enrique was his brother. Their older parents sat in chairs and three other young adults, two females and a man, stood cowering next to them as if to protect them. No one returned De Gerlick's greeting; they were terrified. Earlier in the day they had heard the news their son Enrique had died, drowned in a diving accident.

"I'm sorry to hear of your loss." De Gerlick reached into his jacket. Everyone gasped a deep breath and leaned back, expecting a gun. This amused De Gerlick and so the right corner of his mouth reached upward. Now twice in one day he'd attempted a smile. Instead of a gun, he pulled out a large stack of money and placed it on the table next to Enrique's father. "Maybe this will help."

"You expect money to replace my son?" The mother started to raise her voice.

"Mother!" Fernando shouted out, "Do not disrespect this man!"

"This man is the devil, Fernando! He killed your brother, you know he did!"

VOLUME ONE: RAPTIS TRILOGY

****

"Mother, please!"

"It would be wise to listen to your son. We wouldn't want two accidents so close together," De Gerlick said as he slowly walked backward toward the door, careful to never put his back to any one of them. He continued to back up until out the door, and then shut it.

****

Much later that night he woke to an unexpected phone call. He answered and sat up, listening.

"Yes, I see," he responded slowly, thinking. Then his voice slowly rose with anger as he went on, "No plans will change, he will not be replaced, it is up to you now, do you understand?" De Gerlick hung up the phone, almost slamming it into the cradle. This was getting too messy. The orders were to get those tanks before ten o'clock at night. *How many more imbeciles are on the payroll*? he wondered. *This is bound to draw some sort of attention.*

De Gerlick sat back down. He pulled a fresh cigar out of the humidor sitting on his desk and grasped the tiny guillotine tool to clip off the end. As he rolled the guillotine in his palm, he glanced at his right hand where the first digit was missing, lost to one of these same little devices. Pride rushed over him as the memory recalled honor and devotion in his refusal to talk, even when they cut off this digit. He'd been only twelve years old at the time.

Holding up the flame from the lighter, watching it flick and dance, he lit the end of the cigar and began to puff. This was a habit he'd picked up early, at fourteen, when he had already been a leader among the feral young men and women, kids with no home. He had organized, they had listened.

DIVE TOUR

****

8

At the dive shop the following day, Terri was the first to arrive. Taking a deep breath, she was glad to be alone. But this was not for long. Soon everyone shuffled in behind her and started preparing for the day like synchronized swimmers, not saying a word. Most of the group was still trying to wake up. They moved in unison, all with the same goal, each knowing his or her part in completing the tasks.

The rhythm was contagious. Darren joined in as if he were already seasoned. Terri walked over to the clipboard and examined it: three tourist ships today, the exact number of people taking diving lessons and or diving would be in shortly. All three ships would let them know. This was going to be another busy day. Melvin would arrive soon to write down the names of the tourists who wanted to dive. Terri left one eye on the door, not for Melvin but for John, wondering where he was.

Melvin came in with the number of divers they'd expect to come from each ship. Kathy would be there in about five minutes, arriving with the first bus load. As Terri and Melvin discussed the day to come, John walked up to them, wiping at his face with the back of his hand. His nose was running.

"Sorry...." John ran the back of his hand up his nose and sniffed. "Sorry I'm late."

"I wasn't sure if you were going to make it in today, John. Do you need another day to gather yourself?"

"Yeah, you look bad. What's wrong with your nose?" Terri couldn't help putting in her two cents.

"No. I'm sorry for the distraction."

Hmmph, distraction? That's a nice word for "dead man on the beach." Terri started to squirm; she wanted to say something out loud so badly. Melvin shot her a glance. She felt the chip on her shoulder weighing her down, making it hard for her to behave.

"I'll be fine," John added, sniffing his wet nose.

Terri was in disbelief that Melvin couldn't see through this. Looking at the clipboard she saw her next move. She would get out of there and let Melvin's boy wonder screw up all on his own.

"There's an advanced diving tour this morning, I see. I'd like to take this one out." Terri announced and looked up to field any questions. With that, she handed the clipboard to John and walked away.

Soon, the familiar jingle of bells announced the door was opening. There was sudden commotion as twenty-five people walked in, all dressed in their bathing suits. The smell of suntan lotion filled the room. Terri pushed her way through the back door. And for the ten thousandth time, she started her spiel: "Good morning, everyone! We've been expecting you!"

After giving instructions and sending them on their way into the next room, she singled out her people. They were easy to spot. There were four of them, a family. They each carried a mesh bag, each one filled with select pieces of diving equipment they owned and had packed with them. She introduced herself and showed them the truck. They'd be driving out to the beach ahead of everyone else.

Terri saw Kathy busy directing people. But Kathy was supposed to take off to get more people; directing people was John's job. Where was John now? He was nowhere to be seen to take over for Kathy.

Let it go Terri, let him sink. Too bad he's going to take his wife down with him. Terri looked back over at Kathy. *He's probably off packing his nose. Doesn't she see that?* With that thought, Terri motioned the Anderson family to hop into the truck. It was time to go diving.

****

The children were excited to be riding in the back of the small pickup. They sat on the bench seat with their dad, the equipment stowed beneath them. Mom rode in the comfort of the cab with Terri. Terri would have preferred the fifteen-minute drive alone for some solace, but couldn't refuse Mrs. Anderson when she asked so nicely. Terri asked a few questions and then let Mrs. Anderson do the talking.

The shoreline was picture perfect. As soon as the truck stopped, the young boys jumped out and ran down to the water's edge. Terri began removing the equipment from the back.

"Let's walk down to the boys at the water and I'll discuss the dive plan," Terri told the others. A few large nimbus clouds floated off in the distance. The water was turquoise blue; calm conditions. "Come on over here, kids!" Terri said as she gathered the family. The boys quickly obeyed and ran up to her.

"OK, this is the deal. We're going to enter the water here." She pointed as she talked. "We'll drop straight down, and move out. Do you see where the water turns from bright green to dark blue?"

"Yes," the boys said in unison.

"That's where the reef is. We'll drop down to forty-five feet and continue to the right. We'll keep following the reef until the first person reaches twelve hundred pounds. At that point, we turn around and follow the current on back. Any questions?" Terri looked at everyone and they seemed to feel she was being clear. "OK. Let's go up to the truck and put our equipment on now."

****

They gathered again back at the shore up to their waists in water, equipment on. They were all busy spitting into their masks and rubbing their spit around, then following this with vigorous swishes of their masks in the ocean water—a ritual most divers perform to keep the insides of their masks from fogging up. Terri ran through a few things with them such as counting underwater and other hand signals. Minutes later, they were dropping down to the sandy bottom.

The silence was always relaxing for Terri, even when keeping a watchful eye on others. The sound of the bubbles rushing up past her ears became a calming rhythm in the background.

This was a nice family. They were obviously experienced divers. Terri pointed out different creatures along the way, looking for something extraordinary to show them. They moved at a quick pace, making it a good way down the reef.

Terri stopped and motioned for everyone to check the pressure in their tanks. She was surprised to find everyone still had plenty of air. Before they started swimming again, Terri realized she had lost the young boys' attention. They were up the reef a little further examining a piece of coral. Small fish were swarming, frantically picking away at something on the coral. The boys' eyes were wide as they turned to point out their find. First the father swam up to look and then the mom was right behind.

Terri felt someone coming up behind her. This must have been her fifth sense, an instinctual feeling, because no one else had come out there with them, and everyone was in front of her.

Slowly, Terri turned her head to look down the reef. It seemed oddly darker out there for some reason. A strange chill raced up her spine. A friendly school of large grey angel fish gracefully swam by, turning their bodies ever so slightly as if to wave a greeting. Just as Terri was about to get quite concerned about what could be out there, she felt a tug at her arm. It was the dad, trying to get her attention. With one look into his eyes

DIVE TOUR

****

Terri forgot about the creepy feeling she was having and she followed the dad up to the boys' find.

Soon Terri was focusing on the object in the coral in disbelief. She moved closer to look at it from a different angle. It couldn't be. It looked like the remains of three toes, somehow held together by a few fleshy tendons that the fish were picking apart. Terri tried to look away, casting her eyes downward, and then saw what appeared to be a finger lodged in the lower half of the coral.

Backing away from the coral, still in disbelief, Terri looked again over her shoulder. Mrs. Anderson was a short distance away, waving for her to come over. Something in the back of her mind told Terri whatever Mrs. Anderson had found wasn't good. *What an exciting tour for the Andersons*, Terri thought to herself! Terri slowly made her way over to Mrs. Anderson. Then Mrs. Anderson held up her hand as if to stop Terri from coming any closer. She pointed with the other hand.

At first Terri couldn't focus on what she was seeing, she just couldn't. And then she saw it. In shock, Terri slowly moved closer. A large grouper was doing its best to hide beneath a large coral head. The grouper had what appeared to be a mangled foot protruding from its mouth. With his eyes bigger than his stomach, the grouper had apparently bitten off more than he could chew. *Where did these body parts come from*?

Terri flinched as she felt a tap on her shoulder. Turning around, she saw one of the sons with his pressure gauge in one hand and signaling his pressure with the other. She had to stop her mental whirring about the mangled foot and momentarily admire this young man's diving skills. He had listened to her. It was time to go back. Using hand signals, Terri told the group to stay there, she was going up and would be right back down. She intended to take a compass reading on this area below. That was until she realized she didn't have her compass with her. Looking over she saw the good doctor himself, Mr. Anderson, had one. She swam over to him and motioned for him to come up with her.

****

The two of them reached the surface and looked back down. Terri immediately gave the OK signal to anyone who may have been watching from a rocky point. She was surprised to see exactly how far down the reef they all had gone that morning. They were almost all the way to the point, which housed a natural underwater aquarium, Underwater World. Of course, it wasn't open for another hour and no one was there.

"Can you take a couple of compass readings for me? I don't have mine. How about one off of the tip there, and one from that point." Terri indicated with her hands as Mr. Anderson lifted his compass and read off the numbers. Together they chanted those numbers so as to remember them. "Let's bring those toes, or whatever they are, back. Something tells me we're not going to catch that grouper."

Mr. Anderson agreed. Together they descended back down to the rest of the family. Terri removed a glove from one of her hands. With her gloved hand, she removed the toes and pushed them into the empty glove's fingers.

She led the group back to the shoreline where the morning's adventure had begun. Now, the real challenge: *How do you keep a couple of young boys like these from talking about what they found underwater today?*

Terri would come back with other tools to collect the foot from the grouper. Maybe during the lunch hour she could come out there with her spear gun. That fish was sure to still be sitting there, as groupers digested so slowly. She felt it was her duty to retrieve the foot. It must belong to someone!

Terry and the Andersons swam back to the shoreline, which was like coasting downhill in the morning's current. They were swimming in just as busloads of people were unloading onto the beach. The shoreline was filled with groups of six, each a group of beginner scuba divers accompanied by an instructor. Teams of snorkelers took off into the turquoise water with abandon, shouting to each other through the barrel of their mouthpieces. When Terri and her group were spotted below, a few snorkelers followed them in with excitement. Every now and then one of them, taking a deep breath, would to swim down to say hello.

******

Swimming up to the shoreline underwater, Terri did her best to relax and take in the last moments of serenity. With only hand gestures and bubbles, her group popped their heads above water.

"Wow!" the kids shouted in unison. "Can I see those?"

"Well now, let's not get too excited," Terri told the boys. "Let's just wait, I think it might be some kind of hoax." Terri couldn't believe this had just come out of her mouth.

"A hoax?"

"Yeah, you know, maybe one of my buddies playing a trick on us. Let's pretend we didn't find them so they won't laugh at us."

"But can we just see them again?"

"No, I think you've seen enough now." Mom pitched in before Terri dug herself much deeper.

"Come on, let's go take these tanks off. We'll walk to the red truck up there."

They got to the truck to unload their equipment. Of all people, John was there. "Well now, how was that?" John started to help them remove their tanks.

"Wow!" the boys shouted, then sat down a short distance away, unsure what else to say.

"Where's Kathy?" Terri was not in the mood to talk to John, and wanted to change the subject. He nodded his head in his wife's direction. Their coolness with each other was evident to the Andersons.

VOLUME ONE: RAPTIS TRILOGY

****

"So, I think that was one of my top ten most interesting dives, what do you all think?" Terri began directing the conversation to the group. "Thank you so much for joining us!" Handing one of her business cards to the dad, she took him and his wife aside so John wouldn't hear what she had to say.

"I don't know what to say about the end of the dive out there this morning. I think I'm still having a hard time believing what I saw. I'm going to take our find to the authorities, and maybe go back and see if I can find that grouper again."

"What do you think they'll do with those?" Mr. Anderson wondered.

"Who knows. This island isn't exactly what you would call advanced in police work. If you leave me your name and number up at the shop, I'll tell you if I ever hear anything. Do you think the kids will be OK? I mean, body parts and all?"

"I'll talk to them. And let's write those compass readings down."

Terri looked over at the truck. John was still there and didn't seem to be in a hurry to leave the truck area. He seemed to being busy doing this and doing that. The more Terri saw of John's behavior, the more agitated she felt. Her focus was being split in too many directions. This caused her to rub her temples as she attempted to pay attention to the compass readings she had just asked Mr. Anderson for.

What in the world is John doing, folding all that up? He should be down there giving Kathy a hand with people. Terri resisted the urge to tell John to get to work, as well to give him a good kick. She wanted to see him fail. Again she looked over and saw Kathy, hard at work without any assistance from her husband.

****

At the end of the beach, a concession stand was opening up for the day. Gloves in hand, Terri snuck over and asked for a large

DIVE TOUR

****

soda with ice, hold the soda. Slipping around the corner, she opened her ice chest to add to its ice and, for the first time, peeked into the heavy glove. She clasped it shut immediately, ready to heave. She'd forgotten: thirty five feet deep, you only see in greens and blues, there aren't any reds unless you use artificial light. In broad daylight the redness of the meat, the detail of the tendons—down to the black toe hairs sticking out of the white skin—all became too real.

Terri folded and buried the glove deep in the ice. She urgently put the plastic lid back on the ice chest as if to hold in a bad spirit. Who had lost his foot? Certainly the hospital would know, someone was bound to complain of missing it. *Unless the rest of him was still down there.* Another one of those foreboding chills ran up Terri's back. *I felt something down there, I know I did.* Right then and there, Terri decided to keep the toes to herself until she saw Melvin, but first she'd go back down and explore that area again.

******

During the second part of the day, Terri explained to Kathy she was going on a quick dive. For an excuse, Terri said Mrs. Anderson thought she'd lost her watch on the dive and Terri would give it one quick look while everyone was wrapping up.

"I didn't hear anything about that, who's going with you?"

"Oh, I'll just be a minute retracing our dive; we didn't go far. What are the chances, huh?" Terri walked away while talking, before Kathy could ask another question. She was breaking a cardinal rule in diving alone, but Terri just kept going with a sense of purpose, hoping no one would notice. She'd kept the toes quiet this long. And she would continue to as long as she thought this best.

Terri swam out to the edge of the reef and down. She looked back over her shoulder several times. She didn't want a stray snorkeler to follow her out there. It wasn't long before she was at the coral where they had discovered the toes. The grouper had vanished.

Terri scanned the area, looking out into the deep, trying to figure out where these body pieces might have come from. She found herself swimming further and further out around the reef. At some point, she noticed that there was an abrupt change of scenery. Just as she had remembered, a sandy, sloping bottom. *Nothing down there to see, just sandy bottom.* She hovered in neutral buoyancy, looking around. She'd never had any reason to venture out that way before. She didn't know what was beyond this place. The underwater aquarium was way up at the top of the reef.

Ohhh, maybe an unfortunate accident at the aquarium. That had to be it. Satisfied with this answer to her question, she quickly swam back, knowing someone was certainly missing these toes and would like to at least know of the last foot sighting. She was acquainted with most of the people who worked at the aquarium and hoped the person was OK.

DIVE TOUR

****

<u>9</u>

"Now that's strange, you'd think 'man severs foot' would be front page news for this rag." Terri spoke aloud to herself as she was reading through the local daily newspaper the next morning. She was half hoping that someone would hear her ramblings and fill her in with the juicy gossip and details. But no one seemed to hear her.

She was eating the breakfast special at the deli around the corner from the dive shop. It was a small slice of classic New York, attitude and all, right in the middle of the island. Fumbling through the six quick pages of this little local paper, she was sure the story would be printed somewhere. *Hmmph, how can someone lose his foot and not complain? Fingers maybe—but foot too? Not even at the hospital—no one was even missing a foot at the hospital?*

The door to the deli opened. Melvin and Mitch walked in.

"Mind if we join you?"

"No, not at all," Terri straightened up her mess and scooted over. "No word at all on the toes. Nothing. No one is missing a foot, no one on this whole island. Have you heard anything yet?"

"No. That's strange."

Paula walked over and put two cups of coffee on the table, not bothering to take any food orders because she knew exactly what they wanted.

"You're up early." Mitch stirred his coffee, privately glad to see her without Darren.

"I know. I was anxious to read the paper to find out who was missing a foot. Weird, huh?" She looked over at Melvin. "Don't get mad, but do you think anyone can tell me if John's dead guy yesterday had both his feet?"

"I was hoping we were past that subject, Terri."

"But?"

"You saw him, I didn't.... And I'm about to have breakfast served." Melvin stared at Terri until she stared straight back into his eyes. His look told her to drop it. She fidgeted and tried to look away, but she knew he really did have her best interests in mind.

"Breakfast is served." Paula walked up carrying the two orders at once, gracefully laying each plate in its appropriate place. Same thing she had been doing for years, almost every morning for Melvin and Mitch.

"Melvin? Do you mind if I slip out before you begin? I want to get in early."

"What can I say to that?" He sat up straighter and Terri quickly squirmed to stand up. She was finished with both breakfast and the day's paper. She paid Paula and was right out the door.

"Where do you think she's off to? The shop doesn't open for another thirty minutes."

"Don't worry about it, Melvin, she can't get into too much trouble."

"It's her going out and starting trouble that I want to squash, but I don't want to overstep my boundaries as a friend. Mitch, do you think she'll ever get over me hiring John and Kathy?"

"Hmm. She's one stubborn girl, that's for sure. Hopefully things will turn around at the shop. Kathy seems real nice."

"She's a real asset." Melvin looked at his plate. "John does seem stressed out, and I think he'll get worse with Terri constantly riding his back." Melvin paused, seeming to want to hear something from Mitch.

Mitch just listened and nodded, not sure what to say. He of course didn't want to say anything too negative about Terri, who he secretly adored. It wasn't so secret, everyone could tell. *Except for Terri*? Mitch wondered again and again.

Melvin shook his head and took another bite. You know what I mean about Terri. You do. … I'm hoping things will blow over."

VOLUME ONE: RAPTIS TRILOGY

****

<u>10</u>

Down the street, Terri ran into Clift. She said hello and they started to talk. Right away, she asked him if he thought the severed toes and foot might belong to the dead man from two days ago.

"Terri, ah well mon, I tell you I don't know. I'm sure that firs' guy had bot' his feet mon. You saw him dead too, you know. Dey took him away anyway, we can no check."

"Who took him away?"

"Da ship, you know, took him back home."

"No investigation?"

"Terri mon, we been over and over all dis' now. Accident, was an accident." Clift slapped the inside of his hand with the other as if to spank it, emphasizing his point.

"And you think those sea urchin pricks all over him were an accident, too?"

"Oh yes, da was bad."

"Now I find these toes. And I told you I saw the foot."

"Yes, in da grouper's mouth."

"And no one, anyone, is missing a foot anywhere."

Clift rolled his eyes back in his head as he looked upward and shook it in disbelief.

VOLUME ONE: RAPTIS TRILOGY

****

He then looked her straight in the eye and said, "Nowhere here, Terri. Maybe that foot and toes floated here, from another island."

Terri believed him. He didn't know anything. Letting out a deep sigh, she leaned over and gave him a quick hug.

"Thanks Clift, I appreciate your help. I've got to get to work in a hurry now."

"I let you know if I hear anyting, Terri."

No answers. Terri went on to work.

All day, in between her own tours, Terri watched John and Kathy, pretty much Kathy doing most of it, running the beach. As they strapped tourists into diving equipment, the pair struck up conversations with the tourists, relieving any anxieties the novices might have about their upcoming adventures. Fortunately, Kathy did most of the talking.

Watching Kathy and John, Terri sensed some animosity between them. Once again, Kathy was doing much of the work and the decision making, and John was acting as her grunt. It almost appeared as if Kathy didn't really want John there at all.

The sun was out in all its fury. White skin quickly reddened on a day like this. And the blazingly brilliant setting was amplified by the beautiful, picture-perfect sea: rich blues lining up against bright greens, coming to a crescendo, lapping up on the white sand. The contrast of colors in the Caribbean was worth the price of admission. The air temperature was close to ninety degrees, making the cooler water a welcome relief.

Groups of beginner divers were waist deep at the shoreline, practicing a few skills before their decent into the sea. Other groups were out in the shallows of the bright green water. An early group was already leaving the surf, greeting gravity's heavier effects as they walked up onto land with a combination of grunts and smiles.

DIVE TOUR

****

******

Later in the day Terri found herself alone with John.

"Hey, John."

He looked around nervously upon hearing his name, fumbling with something in his hands. He hadn't heard Terri walk up.

"I'd like to see some of your underwater photography sometime. I would love to see your take on Aruba underwater, not to mention what you did the other morning here." She pointed out to the water.

John looked at her with confusion written all over his face. Reality was, he had never shot a roll of film underwater in his life. Captain Jerry simply thought that underwater photography was a good excuse to go diving once a week early in the morning.

"You did have a camera around your neck the other morning. You said you guys were out taking photos." Terri tried to jolt his memory in a sarcastic way. She could see his mind clicking as if to find the right answer. His forehead broke out in a sweat and he looked around as if to find an escape route. Terri took an aggressive half step forward. "You *were* taking pictures out there, right?"

"Well, yes, of course we were. That's what I said," John finally spit out.

"I think everyone's having a great time!" John's shoulders jerked in surprise, and Terri turned around. It was Kathy walking up to the two of them.

"You really keep things moving on the beach there, Kathy. I think everyone is enjoying it." Then Terri looked straight at John with a devilish grin. "I was just asking John about his underwater photography."

"What? Underwater photography?" Now Kathy had a look of confusion on her face.

"Yeah, I'm an underwater shutter bug, the ah—"

"Can you help me?" A voice right next to them gently begged.

The two women swung their attention around to a middle-aged man standing next to them with a broken mask strap. John slunk off, thinking no one would notice. In the background, all Terri could hear was John clearing his nasal passages. Terri couldn't wait to tell her best friend, Mitch, about all this.

****

That night, Terri didn't bother calling before she started to drive over, even though Mitch was one of the few people she knew on the island who had a phone.

She swung by the small market at the bottom of the hill to pick up a six pack of beer. The sun had begun to set, but the air was still and hot. There was very little air circulation inside the market—well, very little of anything for that matter. A small oscillating fan blew a small breeze across the lady behind the counter as she slowly fanned herself by hand, using a folded piece of newspaper. Gazing out the front door, the cashier seemed completely uninterested in her potential customer. This lack of attentiveness completely irked Terri.

Picking out a six pack there was never difficult; the selection was sparse. The lady looked over as Terri set her selection on the counter. Recognizing her customer, she sucked on her teeth loudly and rolled her eyes a little. Terri stood there and smiled as the attendant slowly pushed the keys down on the old cash register, then the total popped up at the top.

"Tree-aity five," the lady barked.

Terri handed the money over with a smile. The lady handed back the change without a word, and Terri gave her a big "Thank you!"

Someday she would get that lady to say thank you. *That would be no small feat*, and that thought made Terri giggle.

****

Mitch and Terri sipped their beers out on the back porch. The last sliver of sun tucked neatly into the sea. A light show of colors began: deep oranges and yellows cast from the sun quickly turned to reds and purples as the light slowly diminished. Mitch and Terri had named this part of the day "the encore." There was no music in the background, just silence broken only by the occasional mosquito landing on the glowing bug terminator. *Sizzle.*

"I'm telling you Mitch, I feel I'm onto something. It's just that I don't know what."

"Let's look at it, Terri. It's possible John is doing a lot of coke. We've seen what it can do to people and how it can affect their careers."

Terri looked down and shifted her feet.

"John's behavior was probably off-base. But as far as the drowning incident goes, there wasn't anything there to support more than an accidental drowning—"

Terri shot a quick look Mitch's way, but before she could open her mouth, he continued. "—even though you 'thought' everyone was acting suspiciously. And as for the discrepancies about who-knows-who, or lack of photography knowledge ... who knows? People lie about stranger things. So what if he's not a photographer?"

Terri sat there and took a long drink of beer. She didn't want to hear this from her friend; she wanted him to agree that there was something going on. Agitation crept up on her. She started

VOLUME ONE: RAPTIS TRILOGY

****

shifting, trying to get comfortable in her skin. *No one is seeing it, no one but me.*

"Look, I don't know how to explain it, Mitch. Call it a hunch, intuition, anything! I just know those two are trying to hide something." Without leaving a moment for rebuttal, she went for her big ask: "What we need to do is get up early next Wednesday morning and watch those two."

"I can't believe what you just said."

"Oh come on Mitch, humor me, just this once!"

"Just this one time? Are you serious?" Because of all the times he'd humored Terri in the past, Mitch let out a heartfelt laugh.

"Just this once, and if we don't see anything unusual, I'll shut my mouth and never mention it again. Please?" Terri looked over at Mitch and gave him the biggest puppy dog eyes she could muster. "Besides, you know I'll go by myself…."

Mitch was starting to give in to her. "God, I'm such a sucker! If we don't see anything, then for sure you're going to let all this go."

Terri eagerly nodded, "Yes."

"You'll let go of this whole John and Kathy thing?"

"I promise! Who knows, maybe the Captain is giving John photo lessons or something, and John's too much of a know-it-all to admit he's a beginner at something. Some guys are weird about things like that, you know, don't you?"

Mitch rolled his eyes. What he wouldn't do for this "friend" of his. *Terri,* he said to himself, *so difficult and beautiful. Impossible to tame. Fascinating.* He kept trying not to adore her.

Terri was still going on and on, "But, well, if we see anything suspicious…."

"I know, I know, you'll get to the bottom of it." Mitch took a drink of his beer. "I'm sure of it."

"It's a deal." Terri shoved her beer over to clink glasses with Mitch, sealing the deal.

The sky was growing darker now. The bug terminator stepped up its zapping beat. Together, Terri and Mitch watched the lights turn on in the town below. Familiar blasts filled the air: a cruise ship was ready to maneuver away from the dock. They watched it gracefully pull out from the dock and point its way to the next destination, traveling the water in the night while passengers dined and danced in their own floating city.

The two relaxed. Never feeling pressure to have to talk about anything, they enjoyed each other's company and the silence of just "being" that came with their close relationship. Mitch longed for more, but never quite said so. *Waiting for her to grow up a little more. Eventually.*

******

After some time had passed in this pleasant way, Terri drove home. It wasn't much, but it was her own space. A collection of tulip and trumpet shells mixed with other finds from her travels on her patio. Down below her little bungalow was a young papaya tree. It had four of those delicious golden globes hanging from it. Every time Terri looked at this tree, it made her smile. It always reminded her of how much she'd had to learn back when she had first moved here.

Her first week, the papaya tree had been overflowing with large, ripe, orange papayas. Terri, accustomed to scaling trees in eager search of fruit, began to scale the papaya tree as if it were a pole—one hand over the other as she swung her body for momentum. Though she successfully shimmied up the bottom of the trunk, the top of the tree wasn't strong enough to hold her, and her weight began to bend it over. Frustrated and so close to the fruit, she kept inching her way up.

Just as she was reaching the top for her reward, the tree snapped in two and Terri fell straight onto her heels, then down to her butt with a humiliating thump. When it was all over, the top of the tree lay on top of her. Not sure what was hurting more, her tailbone or her ego, Terri quickly tugged then scrambled to her feet and looked around for a possible witness. None.

So she plucked the tree of its fruits and then pulled the top half across the road, tossing it down the hill into the jungle. This way she could get rid of the evidence, even though papaya juice was everywhere.

DIVE TOUR

****

11

Another beautiful morning at the beach. The water was that turquoise blue and today exceptionally calm, the air temperature mild though warm enough to bring beads of perspiration to the brow.

Terri's mood bordered on obnoxious.

Darren was talking with Terri. Young girls walking by did their best to make eye contact with him—he fit right in. Clearly they found him irresistible. Terri didn't care about this. She was looking forward to spending some professional time with Darren. She wanted to see if his finesse, his ability to connect with people, followed him under water. She tried hard to ignore whatever else she might also want with him, whatever personal feelings she might have for him. But it was difficult to stay away as he kept signaling he was ready for more.

Darren was going to represent the dive shop at the upcoming instructors' training course. The master instructor, Robert, had certified John and Kathy some time ago. Terri was suddenly curious to see how Robert would respond to John's changed behavior, and thoughts about John crowded into her mind. At least John wasn't at the beach this morning to ruin this great day.

"Come on Darren, you're diving with me today. We're taking the first group right now. Pay attention and I'll answer questions after the dive. First lesson: Make them comfortable, get them underwater, and go. Never turn your back. Keep it like a Disney ride." Terri had backed up to her scuba tank and slipped it on as she was talking. Now she grabbed her mask and fins and walked away.

Darren imitated her organizational moves and followed her, privately eyeing her body as he did. He liked what he saw.

****

"OK! Group number four! Your wait is up, you're diving with me!" She walked over to the group and signaled with her arm for everyone to follow. They all slowly leaned forward, feeling the weight of the scuba tanks for the first time.

Terri entered the water and everyone waded in behind her. She turned around at waist deep and faced everyone, gesturing them to form a half circle around her. Darren was helping a beautiful twenty-something find her spot in the circle. Terri avoided noticing. Terri's first ritual upon entering the water was to dunk her head back in the water to cool off, get her hair wet and out of her face. Darren watched her. Terri noticed and nodded just a little.

"Alright everyone! Good morning, my name is Terri! This handsome young man right here is Darren. He will be hanging around watching today." She looked over to the first person on her right and asked, "And you are?" As they all went through their names, Terri glanced up at the beach to see where John was. *Please not so many trips to the truck today dude*, she thought.

After the last person had finished her name, Terri picked up where she had left off. "OK, everyone, in your hands you have two items. For those of you leaning on your neighbor, three. Let's all put our fins on. Start by leaning on your neighbor with your left hand while you put your left fin on with your right hand." Half the people nimbly put their fins on as they had practiced on the way out. The rest giggled and got them on with some fumbling.

"Next, everyone look into your mask." A chorus of "Yuck!" and "Eww!" followed. "Rub that blue stuff around everywhere and then rinse it off in the ocean. Then put the mask on like this." Terri quickly had her mask on and the learners did their best to follow.

"Breathe in and out through your mouth." Everyone was quick to learn. "OK, down on your right side—yes, there—reach down and find your regulator." She grabbed hers to show them what it looked like.

With just a few training drills, Terri had each one sitting on the bottom, deep water breathing and giving each other the OK signal by making a circle with the thumb and index finger touching.

Slowly Terri started to back up into deeper water.

Her entourage followed. Before they knew it, they were fifteen feet underwater feeding fish with a small amount of dog food doled out to them. At this point, some people would realize they were actually under the water and panic, trying to shoot for the top. Terri would always be aware of the potential "poppers," as she liked to call them. She tried to make them comfortable about their surroundings by having as much direct eye contact with them as possible while still showing everyone the wonders of the world beneath the water.

As she swam backward to keep a close eye on her underwater wards, the group swam in a large circle around the top of the reef. Terri watched every one; each had his or her own way of adapting to and enjoying the diving experience. Some had wanted to walk on the bottom of the ocean, and Terri would help them learn to hover above the ground in a state of neutral buoyancy.

******

Thirty minutes later, they were guided back toward shore, stopping back at that same chest level water where they had started. There, Terri made that one last underwater signal for everyone to stand up and surface.

"All right! Great dive! Great bunch of divers!" she applauded them.

Everyone started removing their masks and talking at the same time, telling each other all about all the different things they had seen.

Terri glanced up the beach, where John looked over his shoulder as he slunk toward his truck.

"That was really cool, Terri." Darren beamed, "I could do that all day!"

"Great. Here comes George with his group. Go dive with him and watch him teach." Terri patted Darren on the shoulder as she pointed him to George.

In response Darren turned to her, touched her gently on the arm and caught her eye. "Later maybe?" he whispered quickly. "Say yes."

Terri shivered just a little as Darren touched her. A momentary electricity raced between them. "We'll see...." She had to smile. *Am I going to resist this? Do I have to resist this? Damn, I have to be careful, this doesn't feel like a little fling, I'm kind of fond of him. What do I do? Nothing, try to do nothing. Try.*

"I'm ready when you are," Darren told her. "Spend some time with me, OK?"

"We'll see."

Darren grinned at her and then shuffled backward in the water toward George's group.

Terri turned back to her group of diving students. "OK, does anyone here know what reality is?" Terri looked around her group to see a bunch of bewildered faces. "Reality is leaving the weightlessness of the ocean and walking back up to the truck! Let's go." Making it look easy as she walked out, she turned around to see if anyone needed assistance. Several of them did. She looked up toward the trucks to get staff's attention, to wave someone down to help her group up.

****

John was watching Terri from the trucks. He reached up to his face and wiped his upper lip. He sniffed his nose. His other hand was shaking a small nasal spray bottle.

Terri was looking exactly his way for help with her group. For a moment they locked eyes. As she did, the intensity of her gaze was so strong that John looked away. It was as if Terri was seeing right into John's heart.

Kathy could feel the venom between John and Terri. With both of them doing this at the beach, it wasn't good for business.

****

That evening Melvin sat Terri down to discuss the personality conflict. He found himself reiterating yet again that Terri was neither experienced enough nor old enough to do the job he had given Kathy and John.

Every time Terri rose to the edge of her seat to say something, Melvin put his hand up, making it clear he didn't want to hear it. Then Melvin came right out and asked her to stop all this, to let what had passed between herself and John go. He asked her to do it for him, for Melvin. Anyway, Kathy and John were running the beach just fine—and, Melvin added, he needed harmony at the shop. So Terri and John needed to work out their differences somewhere else, not at the shop or on the beach.

That was that.

Terri was dismissed without a chance to speak. Although it was always hard for Melvin to speak the last word, this time he found it necessary. She solemnly walked out of the office. As soon as the door shut, he let out a heavy sigh. No sooner did the sigh leave his breath did Terri turn around and poke her head back into the office.

"But, you never—"

"Terri! I said I've had enough!"

She quickly shut the door and walked away, a curtain of frustration and defeat coming down on her. Everyone had left for happy hour at Frankie's. All alone on the sales floor, Terri looked around. It seemed that her small world was changing, and she didn't like it. Melvin was truly upset with her, which really hurt. She didn't like the way this felt, not at all.

"I'm going home." There wasn't anyone to hear, but she knew that Melvin would still have his new video monitor rolling to watch the sales floor. It was her way of saying goodnight to him.

Melvin was indeed watching his monitor out of the corner of his eye. A concerned smile spread across his lower face as his upper part still had a worried brow. "What am I going to do with her?"

12

Kathy was silent most of the way home that evening. "I keep seeing Terri come up to you at the truck."

"I told you she's a bitch," John interrupted.

"Why do you hang out at the trucks so much, anyway?" The tone in Kathy's voice was a little suspicious.

He wasn't sure how to respond. "I'm working, doing everything you're telling me to do."

"And why again are you supposed to be the big underwater photographer? I can't believe I lied about such a stupid thing. What are you and that Captain up to? There's something you're not telling me."

"Nothing Kathy. I—I don't know why ol' Captain says such things, but I just go along with what he says. I guess he thought it would help us get this job. He gets so much business over to Melvin's dive shop. And look, it did help us get this job. So let's not try to figure it out." John thought he was about to babble and stopped talking. He didn't know what was going to come out of his mouth next.

Kathy chose to ignore him, as she doubted that the Captain had gotten them their jobs. Still, Kathy worried a moment, *do we actually owe this Captain Jerry something?*

They both looked ahead as they rode up the tree lined driveway and parked.

Kathy went straight to the shower to rinse the day off. She didn't even want to look at John. His once sexy body was deteriorating. Clothes were drooping now instead of fitting on him. Dark circles had set in under his eyes, and now his eyes

VOLUME ONE: RAPTIS TRILOGY

****

somehow appeared to be receding even deeper into his head. His scent—she cocked her head and grimaced as she realized it—even that had changed again, gotten worse.

Frustrated, confused, and lonely, she sat on the edge of the bed. Her world was changing and she didn't like it. Her husband was changing and it didn't feel good at all.

Laying her head down, she closed her eyes, wanting it to all go away. Soon she dozed off.

****

John whiled away the evening hours pacing around outside, filling his glass with ice and vodka again and again until the sun went down. For the longest time he didn't even realize Kathy had gone to bed. He was all alone now, with nothing to do but get higher.

Kathy was asleep. He looked in one more time then snuck into the kitchen. Like a thief in the night he walked with great care, exaggerating every movement very slowly so as not to make a sound.

John wanted something different from the nasal spray concoction. He wanted to feel the powder rushing up his nose; it would be a better, stronger high. Looking over his shoulder for movement and seeing none, he opened the refrigerator, reached in and grabbed the box of baking soda which kept the fridge fresh. He pulled out a baggy that had been carefully hidden in the box and examined it under a small light. Looking at the amount he had left, he was in disbelief. That disbelief was followed by a brief moment of despair, which turned into an unexplainable urge to do more.

He carefully removed some of the precious powder from the baggy and laid it on the Formica countertop. Slowly, very slowly, he chopped it, trying not to let the knife make a sound as it sliced through the powder. Admiring his work for a brief moment, he leaned over and stuck a rolled up dollar bill to his nose and quickly inhaled. He leaned his head back and inhaled again, not wanting a speck to drop back out. Immediately he decided to do another line since, after all, the bag was out and right there.

He put the box away, carefully placing it back into the refrigerator. His supply was low and he wasn't going to see the Captain for days. *Will he have another bag for me?* John wondered, worried. A flood of sweat broke out across his body as anxiety began to rush through him. His nasal passages gave way and a steam of mucus flowed out his nostrils. He leaned his head back and snorted it all in, not wanting to lose a drop. As he looked forward, he sensed something behind him.

It was Kathy. "John? Are you still up? What are you doing?

He looked to the countertop before turning around or answering. *Evidence, evidence.* He didn't see anything. "I couldn't sleep."

"Are you sick? You sound all clogged up."

"My allergies." His face was devoid of emotion.

"Allergies? Why the sudden allergies? You never had them on Aruba."

"Hell, I don't know. What are you doing up, anyway?" John stood as his quiet mood quickly shifted to agitation. His solitude had been invaded. *Questions, questions, always the fucking questions.*

"I had to get up and pee and saw the refrigerator light on. I didn't know it was after two in the morning. I thought you were cooking dinner. What did you eat?" Glancing at the knife and spoon on the counter top, Kathy opened the fridge, hoping for a taste of a leftover or something. Her stomach was beginning to growl from going to sleep without any dinner or snack.

John put both his hands to his face and looked up. He began to draw his hands down with his fingertips clinging to his skin, pulling hard on his face as if trying to hurt himself. "Stop with the questions!" he shouted. He dropped his arms down at his sides rigidly straight, to the point of shaking, with both fists clenched tight.

Kathy stepped back in disbelief. Who was this person? His paranoia seemed to be getting worse. Frightened, Kathy glanced down at the counter to reassure herself the knife was still there. At the moment she didn't know what John was capable of. She looked back at him.

He was moving his head around, rolling into different positions as if to work out a kink. He was in a daze, talking to himself.

"I'm sorry." Kathy tried to jolt him out of it. "Hey, I'm sorry."

John looked at her with an expressionless face.

"I—I'm sorry I interrupted you, I didn't mean to ask questions."

Never changing his expression, his fists slowly relaxed.

"I'm going back to bed." Kathy continued to face John as she spoke and backed out of the room. Wondering if she should fear for her life, she looked over at the knife on the counter one more time.

John just stood there as she backed up into the bedroom and shut the door.

PART TWO

ENIGMA

****

<u>13</u>

The next morning, a slight trade wind blew in as Kathy approached the cruise ship, pausing for a moment to enjoy the sweet breeze brushing her face. She was on her way to pick up forty-three scuba divers and snorkelers. She had two buses arriving any moment to take them all to the dive shop.

"Kathy! Kathy!" Everyone was gathered for the scuba/snorkel tour, and from the group, three girls shouted and waved.

Kathy turned when she heard her name. Those voices, she recognized them. Looking through the crowd she saw her best friends in the whole world! There they were—Rachel, Patty, and Laurie—coming toward her, weaving their way through the crowd of tourists. They had managed to totally surprise her.

Kathy was speechless and broke into tears as her friends reached their arms around her. She closed her eyes with joy. This was the first time Kathy had seen any of her friends, let alone family, since she married John.

The crowd standing around them was a cross section of the more adventurous tourists, dressed in different selections of attire. Each them knew they were witnessing an emotional moment. Clapping and cheers erupted as the crowd helped to celebrate this lovely reunion. Kathy didn't want to open her eyes. She was at work and she was having difficulty finding her composure in front of all these strangers. Someone from the group of tourists handed her a Kleenex. She wiped her eyes and blew her nose. With a sheepish smile, feeling everyone's eyes on her, she introduced herself.

"Hi! My name is Kathy. I hope you're all here for the scuba and snorkel tour!"

VOLUME ONE: RAPTIS TRILOGY

****

The crowd responded with a cheer.

"There are two buses out front. In the bus in front, I want the scuba tour. The second bus, you guessed it, the snorkelers. Don't worry, families, we're all going to the same immediate destination."

Everyone started to shuffle away from the ship to their buses.

Kathy turned to her friends. She was pale as if she had just seen a ghost. Her hands were clammy and shaky.

"Are you OK, Kathy?"

"Oh my God, yes! You guys gave me the surprise of my life." They had a lot of catching up to do. They had a year and a half to catch up on in one short day.

"Patty is teaching high school already, can you believe it?"

"I've almost got my master's degree completed!" Patty added.

"Anyway, when some of her senior students told her about this trip they were taking, she agreed to chaperone!"

"We wanted to come, too!" Laurie added, trying to get a word in edgewise.

The four girls walked out to the buses with Kathy.

Everyone had already found seats on the bus. Now it seemed that all eyes were on the girls as they boarded. Everyone stopped talking and looked at Kathy.

Kathy was still in a state of shock, she felt a little as if she was dreaming. A combination of the heat, the silence, and forty or so strange faces staring at her brought her back to reality. She cleared her throat and looked at everyone.

"My name is Kathy...."

DIVE TOUR

****

Everyone stared back.

Realizing she had already introduced herself, Kathy felt like an actor who'd forgotten her lines. She wanted to burst into tears again. But she just froze, at a complete loss for words, as her friends and the tourists stared, surprised. Kathy silently berated herself a moment. This was what her life was. Somehow she felt very small.

Putting everything she could into a little smile, Kathy shouted, "Let's go diving! First stop the dive shop!"

The crowd revived again as if on cue and everyone cheered. Conversation was restored. The bus started with a loud growl and lurched forward. Kathy was glad to escape the spotlight.

Suddenly she became aware of her appearance. *Damn, no mirror.* She looked down at herself as she bumped along on the bus seat. Her skin was tan, and she had definitely lost weight. *I look like such a rag doll; they all look so good, so put together.* Kathy reminded herself that she had chosen the island life, that she loved it. She kept telling herself that.

Kathy's confidence shot up as they rolled to a stop in front of the dive shop, the place where she worked. There she could show off. But her confidence quickly deflated when she looked through the window and saw her husband slinking away around the corner to the bathroom. He looked over his shoulder, glancing at every angle in a paranoid way. He was avoiding everyone.

****

From her seat, Kathy fixated on her husband's strange behavior a moment—until the familiar jingle startled her. From inside the shop, Henry jerked opened the front door and stepped out, as if to save Kathy.

"Scuba divers! I've been waiting for you!" Henry shouted to them.

VOLUME ONE: RAPTIS TRILOGY

****

That was all it took for the crowd to abandon their leader, Kathy. They scrambled off the bus as Henry herded them inside. Ricky jumped up and started giving instructions to the snorkelers, directing them to follow him. Terri could be heard barking other instructions further inside.

"Hey, girlfriend, you seem dazed. Wow, we didn't mean to throw you over the edge." Rachael came up next to Kathy as everyone moved inside.

"Where's John? Doesn't he work here too?" Patty questioned Kathy.

Kathy felt her stomach start to twist into a knot. How was she going to keep these three from him?

"How long are you staying?" Kathy was looking at them like a homesick puppy. For a moment she had completely forgotten about work.

"We have to get back on board late this afternoon, honey. We just have the day to see you." Rachael stroked at Kathy's hair maternally.

The shop door popped open again. This time it was Ricky carrying out two scuba tanks at once. A glimmer of perspiration covered his fine muscles.

"Wow, do you get to work with him all day?" Then Darren came out, also carrying two tanks. All three girls turned their heads.

"I forgot how nice island life could be—you know, the attraction!" And the girls giggled in unison.

Kathy tried her best to laugh along, feeling a little pinch in that remark. After all, Kathy was the one who had stayed behind on the girls' last vacation together in Aruba. She had met John and it had been love at first sight.

****

"Are these guys taking us diving?" "Where do we begin?" "Are we missing something?" The girls started to get excited and move toward the door.

Kathy stopped them; she didn't want to go inside, dreading that her miserable life would be revealed. John. She didn't want her friends to see what her life had become. "Wait, I have a better idea! I'm going to take the day off and give you guys a personal tour!"

"But we already have our tickets, and this will be fun!" Again the girls were determined to go inside. The front door kept opening and shutting as Henry, Ricky, and Darren kept parading back and forth with the tanks.

"Hey, Kathy, where's John?"

"I don't know, guys." Kathy started looking over her shoulders; she wanted to get out of there before her friends saw him.

"Don't worry about the tickets girls, I'll get your money refunded. I have strings to pull. I've missed you guys so much, so please?" It was almost as if she was pleading with them.

The girls looked at each other and then gave their silent nod of approval.

"Sure, why not," Rachael spoke up. "The whole point of today was to see you!"

"Can we still go snorkeling?" one asked.

"Absolutely! In fact," Kathy motioned Ricky over to her. "Ricky, these are the three best friends I have in the whole world, here for the day."

Rick teasingly smiled and kissed the back of each girl's hand.

"Are we sure we want to let this guy out of our sight?" Patty was winking at Ricky.

VOLUME ONE: RAPTIS TRILOGY

****

"Down, girls—besides you're here to see me, remember? Ricky, can you please personally assist these ladies with some snorkeling gear? I'm going to play hooky and take them over to Pelican Bay for the day."

"Follow me, ladies." The three were at Rick's heels, asking him question after question. Kathy slipped in behind them to maneuver them away from John if he appeared.

****

Kathy made a beeline for Melvin's office. Melvin looked up.

"Melvin?" she said in her most sincere voice. "My best friends just surprised me on the cruise ship! A visit, a visit for the day. I had no idea, I...." She stumbled to find the right words.

"Would you like the day off?"

"Can I, please?"

"Sure, John will be staying here though, right? He can handle the beach without you, yeah?"

Probably not, Kathy thought. But she didn't care. She felt as if she could go totally AWOL from this island life, from her life— and today, if given the right push.

"He'll have no problem, and besides, Terri will be here." Her voice tapered off thinking maybe that wasn't such a good thing to say.

"You're right. Maybe this will help them find some common ground without you there, no offense. Go have fun with your friends. I'll see you tomorrow."

Kathy practically ran out the door after bending over and giving Melvin a big hug and thank you.

****

DIVE TOUR

****

"Kathy! Look who we found!"

Kathy's pace came to a standstill as her heart began to race. There was John, in the middle of her friends. She began to blush with humiliation. John's baggy shorts were cinched up on his waist and his wrinkled shirt hastily tucked in. Drips of perspiration were rolling down his face and neck, his shoulders were hunched over.

"Are we going to the beach today, Kathy?" John asked as he walked over to her. His eyes were looking everywhere but at hers.

The girls watched him with that same distrustful look they had had before, back when Kathy had fallen in love with him. This was definitely a different man now; another side of him Kathy hadn't seen. He looked weak, broken down. His face was pale and sunken, and the light made his sun drenched wrinkles look like long trenches. Somehow, his facial expression seemed childlike.

Kathy spoke to him in a mother's tone. "No, John, I'm going to the beach with my friends. I haven't seen them in so long. You need to stay here and run the beach with Terri."

"But—" John started to protest. Kathy could hear Terri in the background wrapping up her talk. In one minute a flood of people was going to rush out. Kathy ignored John and looked at her friends. They knew the look.

"Let's get going while the going's good! Are you ready, girls?" Kathy didn't wait for an answer. "I'm ready, let's go! Bye, John." Kathy couldn't stand to look at him right now. And his breath. It was so bad.

John reached over and grabbed Kathy's arm. He leaned over to whisper in her ear, "Don't leave me here. Don't leave me here alone with Terri." His grip was tight and his facial expression reeked of desperation.

Kathy wanted nothing to do with it. She acted as though John was whispering sweet nothings in her ear. She turned him around to put his back to her friends. Leading him away, she didn't even give him a chance to say goodbye to her friends as she whispered back to John, "You'll be fine. Ask Henry about getting a ride home, 'cause I'll be late. I want to spend the whole time with my friends, since their ship sails this evening." She didn't wait for a reply. Instead of a kiss, she patted him on the arm, turned around and left him standing there. She hustled her friends out the door, masks and snorkels in hand, before anyone could say anything else.

John stood there stunned. He needed a blast of cocaine and a shot of vodka to level it out.

"John's not coming with us?" Rachael asked outside.

"No! No men, just us girls, OK?" Kathy looked back over her shoulder to see if John was following.

"Are you OK, Kathy? You seem a little tense."

"Oh, I'm fine. I will admit, it's been an adjustment. This island is a different pace than Aruba."

"John looks so very different from how I remember him. Has he lost weight or something? And you, are you OK?"

Kathy felt her eyes welling up with tears again as she listened to her friends direct questions about her life. "I'm fine, I'm fine! Let's stop talking about me ... and about him."

Her friends understood there was trouble in paradise. They didn't know what it was, and weren't going to give up so easily. For a while, though, they'd stop, and come back to it later.

"What about you guys? Laurie, are you dating anyone yet?" That was enough to completely change the subject. Kathy knew it would be. Laurie was constantly searching for Mr. Right and ending up with Mr. Wrong.

DIVE TOUR

****

The girls jumped into Kathy's jeep. Before she started the engine, she looked around at her three friends. She was so emotional, tears were running down her cheeks. "I'm so glad to see you guys, you have no idea what this means to me."

Rachael leaned over from the back seat and patted Kathy's arm. "We came all the way down here just to see you."

Patty and Laurie reached over and put their hands on Kathy's shoulder. "We'll always love you, Kathy," Laurie assured her. "Now let's go have a 'coco-loco' or whatever the favorite drink on this island is!" Giggles broke out, the engine started, and the four girls took off down the road.

****

John was still standing where Kathy left him. Ricky walked up to him, smiling. "Those four girls look like trouble! Trouble I wouldn't mind being in!"

"Who? Those bitches? They're going to try to take Kathy away from me," John moaned.

"You think so? Give her a break, dude. I know how it is to miss your friends. What a great surprise for her."

"That's what they're here for, right now, I know it. They're trying to take her away."

"Hey, hey, whoa boy, calm down. You're getting a little too paranoid for me. They're just excited to see each other. You know how girls are." Wanting out of this conversation, Ricky walked away.

John didn't even notice Ricky leave. His nagging inner voice took over. *I know how girls are; they talk behind your back, and they secretly hate you. Kathy can't tell me what to do. She will do what I say. She's starting to act like—*

"Right this way folks. Line up here for your mask and snorkel, these folks will make sure you find one that fits properly. Then over here for your fins." Terri's voice startled John out of his thoughts as she walked right past him with forty people anxiously tailing behind her. "Store your clothes under the benches."

John was just standing there in the middle, not participating. Perspiration dripped down his face as he clenched and unclenched his fists.

"OK, John, wake up. I've got them all ready for you and Kathy."

"Kathy's gone." His face was blank.

"What do you mean Kathy's gone? Where did she go?"

As soon as Terri had asked the question, the office door opened and Melvin stepped out.

"Terri, I gave Kathy the day off. You will run the beach today with John." The door shut as quickly as it opened. Melvin didn't want to hear one word of protest out of Terri.

"Great." Terri had a knack for sarcasm with a smile.

John had slipped away while her back was turned.

"Shit, where did he go?" Terri asked as she walked over to Ricky and said, "I need you on that first bus with me and John, and John just did his usual disappearing act." Terri went outside in search of him.

People were making their way onto the bus. They climbed aboard in their bathing suits and scooted across the vinyl benches. Jimmy the bus driver walked around, alert for dirt and scratches at all times. He prided himself in a clean bus. Waiting for the bus to be 'full up', as Jimmy would say, Terri walked about, impatiently searching for John.

John reappeared from around back. His lips were moving as he talked to himself.

Terri, trying her best to keep her cool, was nevertheless ready to poke John.

"Come on!" she said in a low, terse voice, not wanting anyone to overhear. "Let's go, we've been waiting for you. You stay with me here on the first bus."

"But that bitch left without me."

"Sheesh. Let it go, you weirdo. So what? Is she your mom or something?"

John looked back at Terri and locked his eyes on her. The depth of his focus on her eyes and the scowl on his face caught Terri off guard.

"Who told you about my mother?" John growled. He put his face right up to Terri's and towered over her.

"I didn't mean...." Very rarely was Terri at a loss for words. "What I meant was—"

"You keepin' us waitin' mon," Jimmy's voice broke in. "Da people are getting restless you know."

John took a step back from Terri.

She seized the opportunity to take back control. "John, I can't believe I'm having this conversation with a grown man. We need to get on that bus now! You ride in front with jumpin' Jimmy and by the time you reach the beach, fifteen minutes from now, you will have your shit together. Got it?"

Terri sat in the back of the bus. Ricky was in front, milking the tourists for all the laughs he could get. The crowd was laughing and having a good time as the bus bumped and turned its way to the beach.

VOLUME ONE: RAPTIS TRILOGY

****

Terri watched John up front in the cab with Jimmy. Usually it was Jimmy doing all the talking. This time it appeared Jimmy couldn't get a word in edgewise.

DIVE TOUR

****

14

It was eleven o'clock and the girls were already spread out on a long sandy beach. Tall coconut trees provided a cabana effect. The water was so clear, and on top of the white sand it was the lightest of shade of turquoise. Out toward the horizon, the turquoise color abruptly changed to deep blue. It was as if God drew a line with a huge magic marker a hundred yards offshore. That was where the depth dropped to fifty feet down. It was alive with schools of fish and large colorful coral heads stretching upward toward the sun.

The girls were into their first six pack of beer.

"I can't believe you guys are here with me! This is my favorite beach and getaway here." Kathy took a long sip of beer and wiggled her toes deep in the cool sand.

"This is perfect." Rachael was still lathering herself with sunscreen.

Laurie, already bored with sitting still, busied herself taking pictures and recording the moment. She was almost done with her first roll of film.

"This is like something out of an exotic beach magazine. You're never really sure if it's a special lens or if something this beautiful actually exists." Patty was having a moment. Back at home, her job kept her inside at a computer in a cubicle all day. Her days off were always planned out. First day off, clean house; second day, getting ready for work the next day; and so on.

"It is beautiful, isn't it." Kathy was proud to be able to show this to her friends. "Of course you do remember the four-wheel-drive excursion it took us to get here!" She smiled.

VOLUME ONE: RAPTIS TRILOGY

****

"Oh, and that 'little hike!' It was supposed to be 'just around the corner now,' until suddenly it was a damn-I-forgot-my-machete hike!" Rachel burst out in an uncontrollable laugh. "Should we be checking each other for leeches or something?"

The girls howled. It was just like old times.

"Hey now, I thought you were all just telling me how exquisite this place was. That's all a small price for such paradise, don't you think?"

Without a word, in unison, the girls all tipped their beers toward each other for a toast.

DIVE TOUR

****

<u>15</u>

"Grrroup number five! Let's go!" Terri shouted out toward the beach. A family of four climbed out of the surf, where they'd been wading with two middle-aged men who'd taken the day off from their respective wives. Terri shouted, "John! Wake up! I need six setups on the table, now!"

John was at the truck cab, busy. *Busy doing nothing*, Terri assumed. He had a way of looking busy without accomplishing anything.

"OK folks," John said as he put a tank up on the table. "Stand next to a tank and we'll come around and strap you in. Does everyone have a mask and fins?" He droned on like a disinterested recording.

The divers checked their hands to ensure they were still grasping their own masks and fins. A brother and sister stood with their backs to their parents. The boy was around eleven, the girl an overdeveloped fourteen-going-on-twenty.

"Shut up Becky, I am not."

"You're embarrassing to be around, you little dork." She was self-conscious and having a hard time. With all these men running around everywhere without shirts on, she wanted to impress them all.

"Then why are you standing next to me!" her brother retorted.

The girl rolled her eyes as if she had the sophistication of a supermodel. "You," the young girl emphasized with a point of her finger, "came over here right next to me. Now leave me alone." As she turned around she came face to face with John and let out a slight gasp, he was so close to her. A shiver ran down her spine as she couldn't help thinking he was staring right at her.

"Here, put your arm through here." John said. He was doing his best to get through the motions of work.

"Eww, has anyone else used this thing today?" A disgusted look crossed the girl's face as she held up the regulator mouthpiece with one hand and picked at the straps with the other.

 John squinted his eyes tight and pulled the straps tight to her shoulders.

"Ow! Does this have to be so tight?" the girl complained.

John tried to put two fingers between her straps and shoulder blades. A slight grin cracked out of the corner of his mouth as he realized he had caused her some slight discomfort. John picked out a piece of lead to weave onto her waist strap.

"Do I have to wear one of those?" Her complaints were in that young, whiney voice.

I'd like to tell you where I really want to put this piece of lead, you stupid whiney girl. John shut his eyes. He shook his head as he tried to fight off the voice and the violent, twisting images in his head in which he saw himself smashing this girl's face. Everything, images of all kinds, were swirling through his head. Swirling everywhere.

"Ohhh, gross!" the girl exclaimed as she started wiping at herself with another look of disgust. "You flicked sweat all over me!"

Her brother started laughing loudly.

John stood there looking right through the children, as if he didn't see them at all for a moment.

"Hey, you going to strap me in next?"

The boy's voice sounded tinny, hollow, and far away. John turned to him. This kid had already put his arm through one of the straps and was waiting for John to help with the other. The boy whispered to John in a low voice, as he didn't want his parents to overhear, "She's a slut."

The words reverberated in John's ears. *Slutttttttt.*

"Shut up, you faggot!" the sister shot back at the brother.

Now John looked over at the sister and saw his mother's face instead. *Mother! Go away!* John rapidly covered his eyes with his hands and screamed in his head for the image of his mother to go away. As he did, his mouth made the motion of a scream. Then John heard the voice again.

"I said, shut up!" a voice said. But this time the voice was different. It wasn't in his head now. Surprised, John uncovered his eyes and looked down. This voice was the boy's sister, and she was very confused.

Both kids' mouths were gaping. They couldn't believe how this adult had just acted. John turned to the boy and started fumbling with his strap. The girl let out a nervous giggle.

"Do you think that was funny?" John shot her an angry look.

"Uh, no, I uh...."

"Hey, lay off my sister," the young boy piped in, now protective.

"I'll tell you something funny. You want to hear something funny?" John was transfixed on this young girl suddenly. "Those bitches are trying to take my wife away! Right now. You're one of those bitches, aren't you?" John was talking in a low, monotone voice with an anger in his throat, a growl waiting to sound out.

Strapped onto the tanks, the kids were trapped and apprehensive.

John went on. "I know why they came, they can't fool me. Oh sure, they all say they love me, they're doing this for me. First she goes with them, and then they'll come'n take me! They will, you know!" John's voice was getting louder now.

People started turning their heads toward the commotion.

"John?" Terri was not close enough to hear what it was John was saying, but she could make out the unusual tone he was taking. And the undercurrent of anger.

"You kids OK?" Mom asked from a distance. She could sense something was going on over there.

"They're hiding her from me. I can't—" John's sentence cut off in the middle when Terri, who had now come up right next to him, grabbed at his arm and started pulling him away from the kids. Then Terri kept walking, holding on to John's arm with a death grip.

"Let go of me." John tried to jerk away.

Ricky came over and stood nearby. He sensed Terri might need him.

Terri did her best not to draw further attention. "What in the hell, John? I knew you were a whack job."

John looked at Terri. His eyebrows were drawn downward with a bizarrely menacing look. "I'm not a whack job." John's voice was on the edge of trembling.

Terri wasn't sure what John would do next. For a moment, she herself was afraid of him. His behavior was clearly agitated and unpredictable. She tried changing the tone in her voice; she lowered it further and mustered the best maternal voice she could manage. "Look, I don't know what's going on with you. But you know better than to talk like that here, especially

****

around the kids. We're halfway through the day, an easy day. Go for a walk, a swim, do something for the next hour then you can go back to the shop. Maybe then Kathy will be back with her friends." Terri emphasized the word "friends" to see if it would sink into John's shrinking brain.

****

Right then, as if a lightning bolt had stuck there, Terri remembered the tourists! She had left them standing there! She turned around and was relieved to see that Henry had had the good sense to lead group number five away, to get them all down to the water.

John's stomach turned inside of him. He needed a fix. Terri had rushed him away unprepared for the day, and now he couldn't think.

"John, it's time to go." Terri woke him out of his trance. He looked up at her. She saw how his hollow eyes looked, as if they had sunk back into his head.

"I haven't eaten in a while," he said to her quietly. "It's my stomach." It was the only excuse he could offer. One minute he felt like an adolescent with uncontrollable emotions and then in a brief moment of sanity he realized he was a grown man with not much to say.

John was afraid to look at Terri, afraid of the image of his mother appearing again.

He's losing it, really losing it. For the first time since they'd met, Terri felt sorry for him. He looked so pathetic now, especially without Kathy around. Now, with the moment to completely squash him, to blow his cover right there on the beach, Terri backed off and let him off the hook.

"John, I don't want you around any more people until you get some rest. You look like shit and your behavior is out of control."

John couldn't even look up to acknowledge her.

"You have your own friend coming soon, remember?"

"Bullshit, I don't have any friends."

"Yes you do! Uh, Robert, he's coming to town to run the certification course. He's your old friend from Aruba. Melvin is counting on you to help make Robert feel at home for the week. Robert gave you your instructor's certification, didn't he?

"Yes. And Kathy got her certification from him too, and …."

Terri could see John's face begin to lighten up. He was holding on to the vision of his first dive with his brother. Robert had made that work.

"I miss my brother." John's eyes were shut as he spoke, as he didn't want to let go of the vision.

"Brother?" Terri had no idea how to respond to John's pain. She was trying to remember more of what she knew about John and Robert and all. But there wasn't much she knew.

"My brother was Robert's best friend. I miss my brother."

"I'm sure you do," Terri mustered in response. "Go lie down in the cab of the truck. We're leaving the beach soon." As badly as she had wanted to kick John for days, she couldn't kick a man while he was so down.

John headed off for the truck.

Ricky came up to Terri once she was alone. "What's wrong with him? He's been acting off-base all day," Ricky said.

Terri shrugged and then Ricky and Terri moved over to the table and put up tanks for the next group.

Terri scanned the beach for damage control, seeing just how much attention they had drawn. "If he's not tweaking, Ricky, I'll eat my visor. I've never trusted that guy John."

Terri knew there was something much bigger going on. She just didn't know what all was involved. But she suspected *at least cocaine, lots of it. That,* she said to herself nervously, *and murder*....

VOLUME ONE: RAPTIS TRILOGY

****

16

Rachael looked down at her watch. It was two o'clock. The girls were dozing in the sand, limp from the day of sun, swimming, laughter, and a cooler of beer.

"I don't want this day to end," Kathy said when she saw Rachael sit up and look at her watch. Kathy was dreading discovering the time, as that would only bring her back to reality.

"Our ship sails in two and a half hours. Do we have time for a quick walk through the town? I heard it's really cute."

All the girls were sitting up now. All except Kathy, who was once again fighting off tears.

"Kathy, you sure everything is OK? I don't want to sound like a broken record but—but are you really happy here?"

Kathy didn't want to lift her head out of her arms without her sunglasses on. She was afraid of them looking into her eyes and knowing what she really was thinking. "Yes! I'm happy! For the hundredth time, yes, I'm happy here!" She put on a gregarious smile, overplaying joy.

"So we can tell your mom everything is fine? We hardly saw John." Laurie was determined to get a response from Kathy.

"We were hoping to see more of him. You know, get to know him more." Rachael wouldn't let the subject go. "When I saw John this morning, I was shocked. He looks so different from how I remember him."

This time Kathy did cringe. "Come on guys, what exactly is it you're fishing for here? Did my mom put you up to this?"

"No, of course not."

Kathy went on, feeling she needed to give them something. "I'm not saying it's been easy. John lost his brother. We relocated to this island and this job is higher pressure. It's different here. The politics at the dive shop where we work are sticky, it's hard to explain. Things are pretty intense, but you all are here today, and next week we have an old friend of John and his brother's, a guy from Aruba, coming over to see us for a week! He is teaching a diving instructors certification program while he's here. We're both really excited." Kathy had been feeling so down lately that she had forgotten Robert was coming. "Other than the work stuff—well you see, life is good!"

All three of Kathy's friends just sat there, shifting their feet back and forth in the sand. They were just listening, realizing that life is pretty much the same everywhere, that paradise has pressures just like they experience back home.

"I'm sorry Kathy, we didn't mean to push you. I'm going through my own shit, too." Laurie stood up as she spoke.

"You're always dealing with shit, Laurie," Patty teased.

Rachael looked at her watch. "Let's get out of here, girls." That was Rachael's way of dropping a subject and moving on: you just do so.

And they did. They packed up and left the beach.

****

At home, John had spent the rest of the day walking about, often in circles, back and forth and round and round, from the kitchen to the outside, underneath the house and back, again and again. He was searching for a secret place, some sort of secret place, a place where he could be all alone. He wanted to be alone. Finally, he found such a place below the house. It had been built up on stilts to house a cistern underneath to collect rainwater. He worked the door open and began cleaning up. Every ten minutes, he ran upstairs to look out for Kathy and to lay out another line of coke to keep himself going.

His nasal passages constantly dripped. Watery mucus flowed from his sinus' inflamed cavities. The tender membranes inside the passages burnt from cocaine and all of the chemicals they use to cut it into a powder. A red rash had appeared under his nose from wiping the drip over and over.

The colors in the sky had long faded now. The only sounds were the frogs, croaking to each other in the dark. John found a shoebox to store his drugs in and took it down to his secret place.

This will be the last one tonight, John shut his eyes and told himself. A moment of sanity hit him as he walked back to the refrigerator again. He was finding it harder to tell the past from the present. His head swirled, yet he continued to open the baking soda box and pull out the baggie so he could go through the ritual all over again, and again and again, all following a voice in his head.

Now he stood there looking at the small bag. And he remembered the deep, dark abyss of pain and emptiness that never left. "The abyss" was his name for it. "Illness," the doctors, court, and hospital had said. But he didn't feel sick. He just woke up one morning and his sister was dead. He only remembered the nightmares he'd had that night. The trail of blood to his bed, his clothes drenched in his sister's blood, and the knife, all told a story he didn't remember.

John looked up as if to have a realization and spoke out loud, "I hated her." He tried to envision his brother. *If only he were here, he could help me. Brother, help me.* John needed his brother.

He ran to the bedroom and opened up the bottom dresser drawer, reaching way back, and he found it. Here was his medication bottle, only it was empty. It had been empty for some time now. Yet he still shook it as if somehow something might be just stuck. He didn't have the prescription to get it filled, his brother did. Kathy couldn't help because she had no clue about the medication—nor of John's past. His family had shunned him, never forgiven him. But once John turned twenty-one, his brother had signed all the papers to get him out of the hospital. There had been a big push to release some mental patients and John became one of the "lucky" ones. With his brother's guidance and help down in Aruba, away from the past, John had managed to lead a normal life.

But all that was all gone now.

Here he was right then, all alone without Kathy, and his compulsion took over. He opened up the baggie. He dished out a little bit with the edge of the knife. And then a little bit more because he knew he would just do this again in three minutes. *Hurry, hurry, she'll be home any minute!*

****

Kathy didn't want to go home that night but had nowhere else to go. This was her life. She had chosen it. She told herself this again on her way home, while she couldn't stop crying. She had stayed out as long as she could, waving to her friends until she couldn't see them anymore. She then stayed and watched as their ship pulled away from port and into the night. She fantasized about shouting to her friends, diving off the pier, and swimming after the ship, being picked up and rescued from this place, this place she called her home now. She wanted out. Or did she? Or should she?

Pulling up the driveway Kathy noticed John's silhouette walking to the back of the house. Her dread deepened as she walked in the front door and saw a startled John dashing past her into the kitchen, just moving by as if he didn't notice her. "What are you doing?" she asked.

John was fumbling around inside the refrigerator, and then stepped back empty handed. "I'm out of fucking vodka and you're home late!" John stepped toward her, his eyes wide open, pupils as small as pin heads locked on to hers as if to penetrate her thoughts. She looked away and took a step to the side, out of his path.

"You're a pathetic, disgusting mess, John. I know things have been rough; you're still mourning your brother, and this whole move down here...."

John reached over and grabbed her forearm, staring intensely into her eyes.

"Don't you ever talk about my brother like that again." He squeezed her arm tighter to emphasize his point. "You hear me?"

For a moment, she felt her power being drained away as if he was just sucking it out through his wild eyes and intense grip. She looked away again.

He threw her arm away, as if to push her.

"What is wrong with you? You're not the John I married. You're turning into a monster!"

"I am not a monster!" he screamed back.

Kathy froze again as John towered over her. She cowered, waiting for the strike.

Instead he stopped and stared off into the distance as if he were seeing something in his head.

She slowly stepped back, watching John as he stood there, gazing at something, somewhere.

Looking at the counter, she saw an empty vodka bottle. Surely the alcohol was at the root of his emotional turmoil. He was drinking every day now. She walked over and threw the empty bottle away and opened the refrigerator. It was basically bare, a half dozen eggs, some half eaten fruit, and a box of baking soda. It was clear they weren't taking the best care of themselves.

VOLUME ONE: RAPTIS TRILOGY

****

John was still standing there. He was docile now, approachable by comparison to the person he had been just two minutes ago. Kathy looked at John's face. She thought she noticed a dry streak left by a tear. This vulnerable moment, a moment of compassion for John, caught her off guard. It wasn't how she had been feeling toward him lately. She reached out and gently touched his arm.

He stood there motionless.

"I'm sorry," Kathy whispered as she gently rubbed his arm. Then she gave him a light squeeze without saying another word.

He couldn't look at her or speak.

She wasn't sure what to say, not knowing how to discern what had just happened between them.

DIVE TOUR

****

<u>17</u>

"I'm telling you Mitch, I know it's weird but I really think this has to do with cocaine. They're doing something at the beach on the mornings that the *Captive Sea* is in. John and the Captain of that same old *Captive Sea*, maybe they're meeting a boat or something." Again Terri looked at the map she had placed on the table between them. "We'll be waiting for them over here. They'll never see us," she said as she pointed to a place on the map.

"They'll recognize your car on the way in for sure," Mitch worried.

"Ah, but Mitch, we'll be in your car, so they won't recognize it."

Mitch rolled his eyes and took a drink.

"Look, just humor me, OK?"

"I have enough humor in my life, Terri."

"Well, I'm going to do this with or without you." She looked away, taking a sip of her beer as she pondered the thought that Mitch wasn't going to be of any help.

"You're putting me in a weird position, Terri. Melvin is my close friend too, you know, and as much as I trust you, I trust him, too."

Terri was still looking away but she was listening, her brow furrowing as she did.

The sun had set long ago. There in the dark, they sat in the reflection of the tiki torches that helped ward off insects.

"I just don't want to be a part of this drama. I... I think you're way overreacting, Terri."

Terri's could feel her teeth starting to clench with tension. This was not what she wanted to hear.

"Melvin thinks you're putting unnecessary stress and responsibility on yourself. Really, it's time to lighten up now. You used to enjoy your job."

Terri stood up. "You know Mitch, I'm getting real tired of this being blamed on my hormones or on my being just a plain sore loser. Last week you said you'd go with me."

"Yes, but Terri, it wasn't your job to lose...." Mitch thought to himself. Except he'd said it aloud.

"Yeah, yeah. I've heard it five hundred fuckin' times," Terri interrupted. "Terri, you're too young. Terri, you're a girl." She scrunched her face and used a voice to mock Melvin. She was angry and wanted to lash out. She was hurt. She wanted to hurt Melvin back but couldn't. "Never mind what I'm up to tomorrow, Mitch. I'll be fine alone. Not a word to Melvin."

Mitch wasn't sure if this was a trap, because now she was letting him off the hook too easy. *Now she doesn't want me to be there?*

Terri shrugged. "OK, well, I've got to go, big day tomorrow."

"Terri, I thought this whole thing would have blown over by now."

"No, look Mitch, I get it. This is my problem, not yours." Clearly hurt, she left in a hurry, no small talk. She was done for the night.

Mitch watched her leave. He was irritated with her, but wished she would turn around and fix things with him. She didn't.

****

****

Five o'clock. Terri's alarm went off and she woke with a jolt. But it didn't take much to wake her this morning. She been half awake all night waiting for this very moment. She pounced out of bed and went into the kitchen to make herself a shot of coffee.

Terri looked out the window at headlights coming up her driveway. It was Mitch after all; she knew he would come through for her. Besides, if they did see anything, she sure wanted a witness.

They weren't sure what they were looking for. They knew the *Captive Sea* would dock at five o'clock and it would take at least thirty minutes for John and the Captain to get to Coconut Beach. Terri and Mitch would be perched to watch their moves.

Terri was packed and ready to go. She headed straight down with an edge of excitement.

"Hop in, we should be out there in time to find a great seat and watch the sunrise!"

Terri opened the door and tossed her pack into the back seat. "I know right where we're going to sit. I brought binoculars! And Mitch?"

"What now?"

"Thank you!" She patted Mitch on the arm and gave him a huge smile.

"And Terri?"

"Yes?"

"If we don't see anything out of the ordinary you are never to mention John's name or the Captain again, got it?" Mitch had both hands on the wheel and his eyes focused on the road. Terri didn't need to see his eyes to know he meant it.

"Fair enough. Thanks again." She sat upright and looked forward. The turn-off was just up ahead. The reddish hues of dawn were beginning to fill the sky. Looking at her watch, she sensed John and the Captain were on their way. "Go up past the entrance and around that corner," Terri pointed. "They should be arriving the other way so there shouldn't be a chance they'd see us parked here."

Mitch pulled over and stopped. There the two of them got out of the car without saying a word. The sky was beginning to light up on the horizon. Before their eyes, the colors of the water and sky separated, announcing the sun's first rays.

"We'll follow this path down," Terri said as she pointed. "Then we can sit behind the cover of the mangroves and watch."

Mitch scrambled, trying to catch up to his dear friend, Terri. She never looked back, assuming Mitch was right behind and following her. At first Mitch had thought his car was a bit obvious parked there, but then he had shrugged it off. After all, this was Terri's hunt. But he did make sure everything was out of sight and locked up.

The sun was well on its way up now, providing plenty of light to see the path. Morning light meant morning feeding time for insects.

"Damn it! No-see-ums, biting up my legs." Terri was slapping away at her legs as if to shoo them away. "How could I have forgotten my repellent?"

Mitch reached into his pack and pulled out a large bottle, handing it to Terri.

"Thanks again, Mitch. I really don't know what I'd do without you." She squirted a big dab into the palm of her hands and started to apply it immediately.

"There's really no telling how much trouble you could get into without me." Mitch grinned. He knew he was Terri's main man, her much needed mature, solid, honest, caring man, whatever this meant to her, and to him, he was never quite sure. *But someday*, Mitch told himself. *Someday she'll see I'm the one.*

As they walked on, the mosquitoes were lifting up from the mango leaves in swarms, as if they were a squadron preparing for attack. They began to swirl around Mitch and Terri's heads, searching for an inch of raw skin to attach to.

"Shit, I need that cream again, Mitch!"

Mitch was already lathering his head and face.

Terri put even a larger squirt on her palms and began massaging it onto her face, neck, and hair. "This must be where all the mosquitoes in the fuckin' world live!" Terri looked at Mitch and started to laugh.

He had so much cream applied that his face was white. He looked like a cartoon character. "This can't be healthy, Terri. You should see yourself. What a sight! You look like a wild woman from the jungle!"

"Oh, I am!"

"Yep, one that can't be tamed." *Darn it*, Mitch thought to himself.

Terri giggled as she walked further down to the perch she wanted to sit on. "Mitch, I am a wild woman. And you kinda like it." *Don't think you can change me, no one can,* she told him without saying it.

The two sat down on their respective choices of comfortable rocks. They looked over at Coconut Beach. Terri eagerly pulled out the binoculars and began scanning the roads and viewing the horizon. She had one hand on the binoculars while the other swatted bugs away.

Mitch pulled a thermos of coffee out of his own backpack and poured not one but two cups of coffee.

"Coffee, wow. You're incredible!" Terri told him.

"That's what they all say," Mitch chuckled.

"All the women?"

"Yep."

The two sat there and sipped their coffee for what seemed to be an eternity.

"Maybe they're on to us, Mitch. They're not coming today."

"Or maybe there's nothing to be on *to*... and the novelty of getting up this frickin' early to go diving has worn off!" Mitch swirled the last sips of the remaining coffee in his cup.

But suddenly Terri's attention was at full focus on the entrance.

"It's them!" Her eyes were big with excitement. She was whispering, as if there was a chance they could hear her. She followed them with the binoculars as they pulled up to the parking lot and stopped. John was driving the company truck and Jerry sat in the passenger seat.

The two men exited the car and went to the back of the truck, each pulling out his own equipment and setting it up.

"Looks like they're getting ready to go in. Hmm...." Terri was not ready to share the binoculars, although Mitch could see everything just fine. "Well, there goes John into the cab of the truck again, sheesh. Look there! I can't see with his back to me. What is he doing?"

"Shhh, the less talk the better; it's so quiet out here."

Mitch's whisper was so low Terri could hardly hear it herself. She wasn't sure what he had just said, but never mind, she

DIVE TOUR

****

wasn't about to look away for a moment. Terri went on as if she were talking to herself, "He's bending over, like he's sneaking. The Captain is pulling out another box, it's camera equipment...." She watched as this Captain Jerry pulled out two underwater cameras from the box and then tucked the box away in the cab. John shut his door and returned to the back to don his tank. The Captain leaned into the back of the truck and pulled out three more scuba tanks. It seemed that the two men never said a word to each other.

"What are they going to do with those tanks? I don't recognize them." Terri strained her eyes and tried adjusting the focus on the binoculars to see if she could make anything more out. Each man put a camera around his neck. John grabbed one extra tank and the Captain grabbed the other two. "They're going to take them into the water. Do you see that?"

"That's strange," Mitch said a little more audibly now. Terri could tell Mitch was taking this a little more seriously now.

"What would be strange is if those tanks were full of air and not cocaine." She took her eyes away from the binoculars for one quick second to give her companion an I-told-you-so look. She turned back just in time to see the two men enter the water and quickly slide underneath. In silence, Terri and Mitch watched their bubbles as they swam out, then as they swam around to the right. By then, the sun was reaching a point where the glare made it hard to see.

"Well Mitch, that was interesting, don't you think?"

"Stop gloating. It's so ugly."

"I told you something was up." Terri stood up to see if she could get a better view, trying to find their track of bubbles.

"Sit down! What if someone is watching them—or worse, us."

She sat down. "Good point." She looked at her watch every minute. Fifteen passed. "Wait, are those bubbles out there?"

She lifted the binoculars up to her eyes. "They're coming back already? They haven't been out very long."

Mitch strained his eyes to see the bubbles, since Terri seemed completely unwilling to share the binoculars.

"Yes, they sure are bubbles. Look at that, they're coming in already!"

Mitch and Terri watched as the men swam up to shore and exited from the water. The cameras were still strapped around their necks but now they had no extra tanks. Without saying a word, the two men walked up to the truck and began to take off their equipment. John gave his camera to the Captain.

"I bet those bastards never even took a picture." Terri watched as John sauntered off to the cab. The Captain pulled out a blue box and put the cameras away. Taking no time for small talk, they were in the cab almost immediately.

"Let's get out of here." Terri, now satisfied she'd seen all she needed to, was anxious to leave the swarming bug hotel.

"Wait, stay down, we'll let them leave first."

"I don't care if those bastards do see me, their butts are mine now, you saw it."

"Wait a minute now, Terri."

But Terri was stubborn and already hiking upward.

"Terri, wait, just cool your jets. We're not sure what we saw, and—"

"I can't believe I'm hearing this!" Terri interrupted and looked back at Mitch, shocked. "You saw those tanks, what do you think is in those tanks? Air?" Turning around she started walking back up. She was fifteen feet from the car when the dive shop truck flew by. She froze. "Shit! Do you think they saw me? They're not supposed to leave this way."

DIVE TOUR

****

"Well, they did leave this way. And who knows if they saw you."

****

"Whoa, whoa! Watch the road!"

"Some bastard parked his nice car half way out in the middle of the street! Did you see that?"

"What I think I saw were some people."

"Maybe someone stopping to take a piss."

"Hmm. Stop the car. Turn around, we need to find out who that was."

"Are you serious?"

Captain Jerry reached into his bag on the floorboard in front of him and pulled out a handgun.

"Yes I'm serious, now do as I said."

John stopped the truck. It took him three turns to get it turned around. The sight of the gun made John so nervous his leg began to shake uncontrollably as he let out the clutch, and the truck lurched forward. "Look, they're going the opposite way. Catch up with them." John's hands began to shake as he focused on the road in an effort to catch the BMW.

"I said catch up with them, damn it!" The small green dive truck and John's driving was no match for the BMW with Mitch behind the wheel. And John was beginning to crave cocaine as each minute passed.

Jerry was beginning to scare John with that pistol waving in his direction. *What is going on? Why is he aiming at me?*

"Forget it John, we'll never catch them like this."

John let out a noisy sigh of relief as he let up on the gas.

"I think that was that nosey bitch you work with."

"No way, she drives a total beater of a car." John wiped the sweat accumulating on his brow with the back of his hand. He sniffed his nose hard, as if to capture a speck of cocaine he might have missed earlier in his clogged nasal passages.

The Captain glared at John in complete disdain. "I'm hoping I didn't make a big mistake with you, John."

"What do you mean by that? It's cool, it's all cool man." John began sniffing again and fidgeting in his seat.

Jerry clenched his teeth and winced. The sound of John sniffing his nose had become screechy like nails on a chalkboard.

DIVE TOUR

****

18

Terri and Mitch pulled up to the deli and got out of the car. As they walked, the dive shop truck drove by on its way to the dock around the corner. "There's the car! And the driver's going into the diner," the Captain quickly noted.

John's fears were realized when he saw Terri accompanying Mitch.

"Do you know these people?" Jerry asked as he looked over at John who was now slumped against the steering wheel in defeat.

"Yeah, that's Terri, the girl from the dive shop. And her friend Mitch. The guy's kinda dull, straight up boring if you ask me. And she's wild, crazy, and a real bitch. What are they doing together, I don't know."

"The question is, what do you think they were doing at the beach? Are they watching you?" The anger was rising in the Captain's voice.

"No, they don't give a shit about me. Probably they parked for sex. She's always running around with some guy. Slut." John could feel sweat dripping down the front of his chest and soaking his shirt. He needed some cocaine, now. His head swirled. His stomach felt as if it was beginning to lift up into his throat. He went on, "If they're not doing it, they're probably just checking the conditions out for a dive today." John doubted it.

"Let's hope so, John. You'd better be keeping your cool. And a low profile."

VOLUME ONE: RAPTIS TRILOGY

****

The very words made John fidget more. He wanted to reach for the handle and open the door. The heat was suffocating him.

As he looked wistfully toward the door handle, the Captain snapped. "Look at you! You look like you've lost ten pounds in the last week; you're clearly addicted to the stuff." The gun sat on his lap and he stroked it before putting it away. "And this Terri girl, she's proven to be a big problem. I want her taken care of."

"What do you mean 'taken care of'? … Don't worry about her, she's an idiot. I'll take care of her."

"Hmmph. You're drawing too much attention to yourself. You're nothing like your brother, are you? Big mistake, giving you that coke. You used to be quiet, hardly said a word. Your brother did all the talking."

John pursed his lips together; he didn't want the Captain to bring up his brother. "Look, the owner of the dive shop likes me, and he thinks Terri's a bitch. Besides, I have an in with Melvin right now; he's depending on me to entertain a bigwig next week. And the woman out there, Terri, and my Kathy, and everyone, they'll be there."

"A bigwig, huh? Well, it better not interfere with next week. I'll have three more tanks next week."

"Don't worry. Same time, same place." John jiggled the watch on his wrist trying not to sniff his nose.

"I'm not going to worry, John. It will go like clockwork. If a thing gets in my way, I have means to get it out of my way."

John reached up and clenched the steering wheel so tight his knuckles turned white. He couldn't get comfortable in his seat. *Ask him, ask him!* John shook his head while he listened to the voice inside it. Sweat flung like a dog drying itself off. *He won't say no!* John cleared his throat. "Did you bring me another package?"

"Shit, really, another one?" The Captain looked over at John in amazement. "I gave you enough to kill a horse!"

Don't let him talk to you like that! "I need more, every week, that's just my side of the deal."

"Why you—" The Captain took a deep breath in and held it. He slowly let it out and looked over at John. "You're going to get us both killed, I just know it. I told him you were a bad choice."

John was sweating profusely and needed to get out of the car. He turned to look long and hard at Captain Jerry, squinting his eyes. His mouth thinned. He needed more cocaine. Needed it big time.

"Look at your nose! It's a running faucet, a billboard: 'Look at me, I do coke.' "

John leaned closer and stared the man in the eye. And the Captain noticed this was a slightly different John speaking now.

"I want more and I get it now." *Tell him what you'll do! Tell him!* John closed his eyes, trying not to let the voice talk over him. "You'll go get it for me. Now."

The Captain's silence was long. He sensed John's desperation. "Grab my bag and the camera case, follow me to my room, and don't look at or talk to anyone! No one. You got that? And next week when I see you, if I so much as hear you sniff once...." The Captain puffed up in his seat and looked John back in the eye. He had to take command again, gain back the upper hand.

This sent a chill down John's spine.

"You'd better make this last, or we might have to replace you...." Once again the Captain reached over and touched his gun, "... or maybe your wife."

John tried to hide his gulp.

****

****

The tense pair walked up the gangplank and wove their way through the interior of the ship. The Captain's companion was an obvious contrast to the typical tourist, waking up and heading to breakfast in newly purchased resort wear.

John, feeling as if all eyes were on him, couldn't look up at anyone. He stared at his feet and focused on staying in his skin.

The Captain had gone a bit ahead. John had to knock when he got to the room because the door was locked. Barely opening the door, the Captain stuck his hand out with an envelope as if he wanted John to mail it and said, "Very good, John, we'll see you next week." That was all. Then the door shut abruptly, giving John no time to respond.

It took John two stops to get high before he could find his way off the ship.

With only twenty minutes before the shop would open for the day, he had a problem to solve. His mouth watered and his spine tingled at the thought of what he was going to do. Looking down at his forearm, he flexed the weak bit of muscle he had left. His tattoo of a satanic marking had been transformed into a colorful tropical flower. His brother had taken him to a tattoo artist right away to have it covered. Now, if John stared at the tattoo, he could see his old marking. He had done it himself using a needle and india ink. And now there it was, coming through to him; his past mocking him, daring him. John closed his eyes trying to get the images in his head to go away. His face twitched as he opened his eyes.

****

John was slightly shaky as he walked into the dive shop ten minutes late. The doorbell clanged, drawing attention.

Terri was standing on the sales floor, half waiting to pounce. She had promised Mitch she would behave and not say a word

****

until after the instructors' training course. They didn't want to distract the ones who had worked so hard to get there.

"Good morning, John!" Terri was practically singing the words out of her mouth. "How was your dive this morning? Any good pictures?"

"Oh, pretty, un—, uh, uneventful." John stumbled for words. "We looked for the school of grey angel fish."

"Did it work?"

"Did what work?"

"You know, did you find the angels?"

"Angels?"

"Hello, Earth to John, the angel fish? You were photographing the angel fish?" She said "angel fish" so slowly she almost spelled it out.

"Yes, we photographed angel fish." John's voice had the intonation of reading a flash card.

"Hmmph. How unusual for the early morning. I'd love to see your pictures. Where's your film?" With everyone bustling around him while Terri grilled him, John's nerves were winding tighter and tighter by the second. He fidgeted the watch on his wrist and stared at Terri with a blank face.

But Terri had to get on with her day, so she'd be leaving it to the rest of the crew to deal with this guy. Terri lowered her voice to make John lean in to hear her. As he did, Terri could hear every inhale of his nose and wanted to shove something up it. "You should get ready, John."

A streak of paranoia hit him and his head darted around looking at all angles. "For what?"

Terri had a hard time keeping a straight face; she couldn't believe his reaction. "For the day, John, people will be here any minute."

She walked away with a shake of her head, wondering what conversation was like between John and his wife. Just then the door rang open; it was John's wife Kathy with a bus load of tourists behind her. Showtime.

Out of the corner of her eye, Terri saw the office door open. Melvin stuck his head out. "Kathy, can I see you for a minute?"

Terri kept smiling, looking over at Melvin, trying to catch his eye. He was careful not to look her way. Kathy entered the office and the door quickly shut behind her. Terri felt left out, but more importantly wanted to know what was going on in there. This was even more important than the fact that she had to tend to her people.

DIVE TOUR

****

19

Mitch looked at Terri as she got into the car. There was a scowl across her forehead and it was obvious she had a lot on her mind. Her lips moved at the speed of a one-way conversation, but no sound came out. She was totally unaware of this silent mumbling. "Who are you talking to?" Mitch inquired as Terri settled in.

"No one yet, Mitch! It's just you and me." She inadvertently looked over her shoulder to see if anyone was there.

"Never mind." He started the car.

When Terri was this deep in thought, talking to herself trying to figure something out, she had a tendency to overlook things. Losing interest in buttoning up her shirt halfway through was a pretty common thing. Mitch would gently encourage her to take better care of her appearance, at least when around the tourists. He did wish she would at least wear a bra more often. Terri's seeming lack of modesty and absent mindedness had caused more than a few embarrassing moments with red-faced tourists.

Terri was a particular mess tonight, and Mitch noticed. "Hey Terri, do you need a hairbrush? There's one in the glove compartment."

"No, no, I'm fine. My hair is all tangled. That's all. So you don't like the way I look? Is that what this is?"

"I love the way you look. I think you know that. And you can get away with a lot because you're so naturally beautiful. But still, you might want to brush your hair a little more, like right now. That's all. So I offered the hairbrush." Mitch was sounding a little defensive; he realized and stopped. He had just gotten off work himself, and looked sharp, dressy casual and very neat. He and Terri clearly contrasted in style. "Just run a brush through your hair and take a peek at your buttons, they're a tad askew."

Terri scowled at Mitch, saying to herself, *who does he think he is telling me how to look?* But then she looked down the front of her colorful Hawaiian shirt, one she still savored from a great time over five years ago. She had buttoned it one hole off, where she had buttoned it at all. "Hmm, I wonder how long it's been like that," she said as she fixed her shirt. "Thanks for telling me. … Anyway, I had a frustrating day today. Kathy's Melvin's favorite now, and Melvin forgets she's just there because of John, who shouldn't be there. And John, well, he's sure up to *something*. Really Mitch, we're on to these guys. These guys are definitely up to no good. I bet Jackie can fill us in on the Captain."

"Slow down there now. Remember, you told me you wouldn't rock any boat right now. I don't want you to go anywhere with this until after the instructors' course. You promise?"

"Yeah. Yeah."

"Terri, look at me."

"Yes! I said I won't, OK? Sheesh."

"I don't want any more stress on Melvin, he has a lot on his plate hosting this course. Half his instructors will be gone to help run the program. Or taking the program, like your what's his name."

"You mean Darren?"

"Yep, your wonder boy."

"He's not my anything, Mitch." Terri heard herself say this and realized she hoped she was wrong. *Darren, what am I going to do about you?*

"OK well, forget him. Anyway, on this other stuff, slow down. Hang tight a few days, maybe a week, OK? Let's see how things look then."

They headed for Jackie's office.

"Come in, come in!" Jackie looked up and smiled as she greeted her friends. She pointed to the chairs in front of her desk. "Sit down and let me finish this transaction, I'll be right with you." She quickly went back to doing what she did best, counting cash.

Terri fidgeted like a little kid with news about to make her head explode. She sat on the edge of her chair and started to open her mouth, only to be met with Jackie's index finger waving her back without even looking up. Terri looked over at Mitch and he motioned for her to calm down. Reluctantly, she sat back and folded her arms to keep them to herself.

Jackie finally completed her task. "OK. Now your turn." She reached her hand out with a big smile. Terri handed over the wad of tickets they had collected for the day. Again Jackie started her magic, counting the tickets, then counting out cash and traveler's checks in exchange. Five minutes later business was complete. Terri liked having Mitch with her, he was like her private security guard. He made her feel safe and grounded.

****

The three walked upstairs for cocktails, picked out a table and sat down. "There now, isn't this better?" Jackie got herself situated and looked at Terri. "Now, what is it you're so anxious to talk to me about?"

Terri looked over both shoulders before responding. "We're on to something, Jackie. I'm telling you, I have proof!"

Jackie didn't say a word as the waitress stopped by.

"Cocktails? Hi, Mitch!" The waitress placed a bowl of nuts and little signature cocktail napkins on the table. She flirted just a little, trying to get Mitch's attention.

"The usual, please." Mitch smiled back at the young lady, whom he knew only as Carol. He was always surprised she remembered him and what he ordered. But, he wasn't interested in Carol. He was more and more fixated on Terri as the days went by. *Is Terri just playing hard to get, or is she just plain hard to get?*

Terri continued the minute the waitress turned away. She lowered her voice as she leaned forward. "You see, this guy John who works at our dive shop, you remember him?"

Jackie nodded her head and glanced over at Mitch.

"Well, he's been acting very strange lately. Stranger than usual. So Mitch and I decided—"

"Luuucy," Mitch did his best Ricky Ricardo imitation: Terri was getting it wrong.

"OK, *I* decided. And Mitch reluctantly decided to join me." She turned to Mitch and gave him a look that asked, *Happy now?* Jackie remained silent, and Mitch cocked his head to return Terri's look with a stern one of his own.

"OK, whatever. Don't ask me how I know, but something is up and I think the Captain is involved."

Terri watched as the friendly expression on Jackie's face began to tense. "I really don't want to hear about any of this. He is the Captain of this ship," Jackie whispered harshly.

"But Mitch was there too, he saw."

"I'm sorry, I don't want to hear it. Mitch, you know how I feel about gossip. It's been hard to avoid ever since—well, you know, the drowning." She almost whispered the word "drowning." She stopped talking as the waitress brought them their drinks.

Jackie was not going to reveal just how well she did know the Captain. Jackie would never share the story, not in full. She figured that even the Captain did not know how much she knew. Her deceased husband had known this Captain Jerry when he was simply Jerry, the son of a high-ranking Naval officer. Jerry and her husband had been on a ship together in the Navy. Jerry had been accused of running gambling and prostitution rings in many ports, and it was also rumored that drugs were brought back to the US from these exotic ports of call. With Jerry's father's connections, he was never accused, just excused with an honorable discharge.

"Well besides the drowning—let's say we forget about that—well, there's something else that's suspicious. "

Mitch was giving Terri some sort of signal now, tilting his head some.

"What is it?" Terri looked up. The Captain was approaching the table.

"Well, what do we have here? Hello, Jackie." The Captain gracefully took her hand and acknowledged her. He turned to the others. "Terri," he nodded. "Do I have the name correct?"

"Yes, you do. This is my friend, Mitch."

Mitch gave a nervous nod.

Terri was shocked to see how much affection the Captain showed for Jackie, obviously trying to mark his territory. Terri had heard nothing about this from her friend Jackie.

In fact, the Captain had had his eye on Jackie for quite some time. It was he who'd suggested she apply for her current position on this ship. Captain Jerry and Jackie had happened to meet at one of his mid-cruise Captain's cocktail parties. Actually, that meeting had not been a total coincidence. She

VOLUME ONE: RAPTIS TRILOGY

****

had just lost her husband. He recognized her last name and mentioned that he had known her husband. He had no way to know the stories Jackie's husband had shared with her, stories about a shipmate named Jerry and all the trouble that man somehow dodged.

But Jackie had been grateful for the opportunity to work on the ship. She loved the sea, the routine, and the ports they visited. In a way, she had created an extended family for herself, one that didn't know her or about her past. It was a complete change of scenery, and it had been the best way to grieve the loss of her husband. Because of all this, she had always been cordial while keeping them all at arm's length. This included the Captain.

Now is the time to test him, right in front of his Jackie, Terri thought. "Mitch and I are going on a little night dive tonight, down at Coconut Beach. Too bad you can't join us."

"You are, are you? Sounds intriguing, but I must be at the helm shortly."

Terri pressed. "Maybe I can join you guys some morning for a dive. I love underwater photography."

"Well if it's underwater photography you like, we must visit about that sometime in the future. Perhaps you and your friend would like to join us on a cruise. I can arrange for you to teach underwater photography at a port, to say, get you a complimentary cruise. We can do some diving then." Without giving Terri a chance to respond, he dismissed himself and quickly moved on.

"Now, don't you feel silly Terri, he has nothing to hide. He invited you on a cruise, for free! That was very generous." Jackie was hoping this bit of news would lighten up the whole evening.

Instead, Terri sat there and brooded to herself, knowing the man was up to something. Mitch and Jackie chose to ignore her and chatted away. Then, out of the blue, Terri sat straight up and declared out loud, "Let's go next week. Let's cruise next week! I can get the time off. The instructors' course will be done and I'll deserve a break. Let's do it! Can you do it, Mitch?"

"Yes Mitch, say yes," Jackie added.

He was caught in the middle of these two women who apparently both wanted him to say yes now; he felt he had no choice but to agree.

This was not exactly how Terri had anticipated the evening would play out. She had thought everyone would be on her investigative bandwagon once she laid it all out for them. But Jackie didn't even want to hear it, which was too bad, because Jackie could be Terri's most valuable watchdog, or so Terri thought. And Mitch…. *What's with Mitch?*

Frustrated but not willing to give up, Terri was going to go on that cruise and find the answers for herself. *What was in those tanks? And where were they going?*

****

Leaving the lounge, Captain Jerry walked down to the dock. He couldn't risk communicating from the ship for fear of being traced or overheard, but a payphone was on the far side of the dock. He dropped in his coins and dialed.

An older man with a smoker's rasp picked up the phone and answered with a simple, "Yes?"

"The woman I spoke of earlier, her curiosity has peaked."

"How unfortunate. It was curiosity that killed the cat."

"Yes."

The two men hung up. They never spoke long enough to be traced.

VOLUME ONE: RAPTIS TRILOGY

****

Later, under Captain Jerry's direction, the *Captive Sea* quietly slipped out of its formation on the dock and into the night. The sound of a calypso beat trailed from the back of the deck as the drummers danced to the rhythm, pounding steel drums.

DIVE TOUR

****

<u>20</u>

Jackie was alone in her room. She was indulging in another drink before retiring for the evening with a good book. Pouring herself vodka in a short glass, she splashed some tonic in it to assure herself that it was a drink and not a shot. To most outsiders, Jackie's life appeared small—her work, her room, a handful of ports week in and week out. But that suited her: she'd already had a full life, and she wasn't ready to let herself live again. That would mean opening her heart up and she was not ready for that. She wanted life light and easy, no responsibility other than for herself and her job.

She sipped her drink and thought about her friendship with Mitch and Terri, that odd duo. Somehow Mitch and Terri were good together. Part of that duo's attraction was the way they approached life. No land anchors, nothing ruffling them. Life was easy for the two of them, just the way Jackie liked it, except for this kink in the Wednesday evening flow. She could sense a change in Terri's energy.

She took a long sip, giving it some thought. She really hadn't known Terri all that long or all that well. There was obviously another side to Terri—the one she saw tonight. Of course, Terri's ego had been severely bruised when the new help arrived at the dive shop. So she could see how Terri might be prone to act out right now, *she's under stress*. But tonight, this thing about the Captain, this accusatory behavior, was more than Jackie had wanted to listen to. Jackie did not like having her boat rocked.

****

A knock on her cabin door startled Jackie. She was not expecting anyone, nor did she ever encourage anyone to just stop by. She walked over to the door. "Who is it, please?"

"It's the Captain ... Jerry." The sound of his voice was followed by a long pause, without an explanation for the intrusion.

On the other side, Jackie was hiding her drink and looking into a mirror to see if she looked presentable for unwanted company. She opened the door.

"Yes, Jerry, what can I do for you?" She was friendly but wanted to remain on opposite sides of the door.

"May I come in?" Glancing down, making sure her robe was secured, she slowly and reluctantly opened the door.

The Captain stepped in. It was nine thirty in the evening, but he was still crisp in his uniform and his usual cool charming self. He had an air about him, as if he could do no wrong. "Jackie, I fell a bit awkward about knocking on your door like this, but I was hoping we could chat for a moment."

"Well actually, as you can see, I am in my robe. I was retiring for the evening."

"Hmm, yes." Jerry stopped for a moment to admire her night wear as if it were an invitation, never thinking about what she had just said. "Sorry about that. I wanted to ask you if you could have a talk with your friend, Terri."

"Jerry, I have no idea what transpired between you two, but I will tell you the same thing I told her. I prefer to stay out of your business, as well as hers."

"So, she asked about me?"

"No." Jackie felt flustered and somehow in the middle. She didn't want anyone in trouble and certainly didn't want to be a part of it. "Don't read into my words."

He wasn't sure what type of response he was going to get, but this was a bit icier than he'd hoped for. He tried a different approach. "Well Jackie, it's not me I'm concerned about, or

Terri for that matter. It's my friend John, he's not doing so well. Poor guy, he's been under too much stress for one man to take." The Captain looked away and shook his head slowly as if he was having a moment of compassion. "Terri has been picking on him, making matters worse. Jealousy, I think: she apparently wanted his job and didn't get it."

"Hmm. I see." Jackie didn't know what to think. "Well it's not my place to talk with anybody. Perhaps you've misunderstood my friendship with Terri. We are more acquaintances than friends, I would say. A good acquaintance. I don't particularly want any relationships deeper than that right now." She looked right at the Captain. "Was there anything else? I'm sorry, but I was about to retire for the evening."

"I'm sorry to have troubled you, Jackie. I did misunderstand. I was just hoping you could reach her." He locked eyes with her. "I hope Terri doesn't come between us."

Her eyes did not leave his as she tugged her evening robe tighter together. "There is no 'us,' Jerry."

"I mean, Jackie, I was hoping."

"Jerry, please, that's nice, but I'm not ready. You know I'm not, it's too soon."

Her frankness always left him at a loss of words. For Jerry, Jackie was going to be a challenge to obtain. "Of course. I'm sorry. I like you, you know that. I didn't mean to complicate things. I know you still miss your husband, of course you do." He could see her face soften as he spoke. "And I've been real worried about my friend John, so I'm distracted. So excuse me for not thinking before speaking up here."

"Thank you for explaining and for understanding."

The Captain smiled as he turned and left.

Jackie found herself smiling, too. He was a perfect gentleman, a perfectly handsome gentleman. She hated the way she would

VOLUME ONE: RAPTIS TRILOGY

****

unconsciously quiver inside when he looked her in the eye and smiled. But she knew he was charming like a beautiful spider enticing his prey. And she did not want to get tangled in that web. Not now. Or ever.

But Captain Jerry didn't need to know the never part of it. Not now. Someday was enough for him for now.

<u>21</u>

"No!"

"But—"

"No!"

"Melvin, you haven't listened to me! If I'm on the cruise ship I'll do slideshows, talk it up to the crew. Not only help sell tours, but teach the crew how to dive. We'll double our profits; long term clients, right?" Terri was giving Melvin her best sales job because she wanted to go on that cruise.

"I like the way you think, Terri, but no! Not now. Robert is coming tomorrow night to get ready for the instructors training course. I want you here to be of assistance. OK? Make him comfortable. We'll look at that cruise for you next month."

"I thought that was John and Kathy's job. He's their friend. Tomorrow night is the big party."

Melvin ignored her and kept talking. Terri was a gem, he was quite fond of her in a paternal sort of way. She had her own sort of beauty. She was raw, wild, independent, brave, talented, but she was too much sometimes. Probably for herself as well as for him. "I want you to be here for Darren, too. I want him to pass this course effortlessly."

"He'll pass, no problem. I'll only miss the last two days, anyway."

"If I have to say no to you one more time today, I'll probably say things I'll regret later. I want you to get to know Robert. I said next month we'll look at it, and if that's not good enough you can go on your own vacation time, four months from now. Got it?" Melvin was staring right at her and meant business.

"Oh, Melvin! You are so frustrating to me sometimes." Her face began to pout.

Melvin couldn't help but let out a small chuckle.

"I'm sure I frustrate you when you don't get your way. But I'm the boss. Grow up, Terri. … Now get to work, OK?" He looked back at his desk, doing his best to ignore her as she stood there. "Go!"

She reluctantly left the office. Darren came up from behind and surprised her by tickling both of her sides. "Hey, Terri, great day for a dive."

Terri jumped and looked back with a scowl on her face. But the scowl melted when she realized it was Darren. "Sure, but I can't go. Work. You go, have a good time Darren, dive away. I'll be thinking of you." She turned and walked away, needing a moment to herself.

Darren stood there and his face went from total enthusiasm to hurt and abandonment.

Ricky walked up after witnessing his brief encounter with Terri.

"Don't worry Darren, it wasn't you. She's a hard woman to win, many've tried. All have failed. But maybe you're the one, who knows. Hang in there."

They both watched Terri reach the front door. At the same time she pulled, Kathy pushed from the other side. Terri's firm tug just about flung Kathy into the shop. Although a bit surprised, Terri ignored the other woman and kept walking.

"Sorry, Terri," Kathy spoke up. "Didn't see you in such a hurry."

Terri couldn't resist shooting back. "Yep, that's me, in a hurry. To go nowhere." Terri walked away.

"Did I say something wrong?" Kathy wondered out loud.

"Don't worry, it wasn't you," Ricky said again. "She's an intense lady."

"She does seem unusually upset today. Everything OK?" Kathy glanced around to see whether everything was in order.

"I really have no idea what happened," Ricky admitted. "But my best guess is that someone told her no to whatever she wanted."

Henry walked up on the tail end of the conversation. "It's such a nice day and someone told Terri the 'no' word? That could be worse than a day with six-foot swells and a twenty-knot current!"

Henry and Ricky started laughing out loud. Darren and Kathy didn't know what to think.

Darren wanted to protect Terri from this gossip and declare her his territory, but he didn't see a moment where this would work. So he just said, "Come on, she's not that bad."

"The last time someone told Terri no, she didn't speak to anyone for three days."

Melvin unexpectedly opened the office door and poked his head out. "You've all been warned," he said in a serious tone that caught everyone's attention. "I was the one who said no." Melvin started to laugh out loud and everyone joined in.

John walked up in the middle of this and worried the laughter was directed at him.

Melvin looked at him. "I need to talk to you." He was pointing at Kathy too.

John started to shake his wrist uncontrollably as he entered the office. Kathy stepped in before him. His eyes began to dart around the room as if Terri or someone was going to pop out of a corner. *Keep it together, keep it together!* "I—I've got to go to the bathroom!"

John didn't wait for any response to his announcement. He turned and almost bolted out the door. In a brisk trot he walked through the sales floor, out the front door. Melvin and Kathy watched him leave on the camera monitors. They saw him step up his pace as he headed for the detached bathroom.

****

Once inside the bathroom, John latched the door and tried to calm himself. *We're safe, we're safe.* He grabbed at the toilet paper and wiped at the sweat on his face. His wet and shaking hands ripped through the toilet paper. Reaching high up on the window sill, he found the small package of wrapped newspaper he'd hidden the day before. He unraveled the newspaper to reveal a half dozen diabetic syringes, some cotton swabs, and a small container that a roll of film had come in. *You're home free now.*

****

John moved swiftly through the motions, motions he was all too familiar with. A dark past medicated away. Ten years of his life in a mental institution. Undiagnosed, explained away mental illness had led him into a heroin addiction as he tried to numb the voices. His parents were staunch fundamentalists who refused to believe his psychotic behavior was anything more than a lack of self control. The only thing they could see was the drugs.

His family had woken up one morning to the horror of their eldest daughter lying in bed, stabbed countless times apparently while she was sleeping. John lay in his bed, covered in blood, curled up in the fetal position with his arms wrapped around himself. His eyes were wide open but he had lain there unresponsive to his family's terror. Despite the prosecution's best efforts to try him as an adult as his parents wished, he was found insane and sent to a psychiatric hospital. After his high-profile crime in their small town, his parents denounced him as the devil himself and cut all ties, never to visit again.

John sat drugged beyond memory in an asylum for nine years. Medicated and docile, he was a ward of the state until released to his older brother, Bruce, who was the only one who ever came to visit.

Bruce was ten years older. He had been in the Navy when John killed their sister, and only came back to town when their parents had died in an accident, to help with the estate. It was only then that he realized that his kid brother still sat in an institution, rotting.

With a scuba diving business in Aruba, Bruce had offered to help his brother regain a stable, medicated life in the Caribbean. It afforded a pace much slower than in the United States—and a place far away, where no one would know of John's past.

A year after John started living on Aruba, Kathy showed up on a two-week vacation with her friends. Kathy asked the shy John out for drinks on the second night, at the urging of her friends. They had all gone snorkeling with John and Bruce earlier that day. Bruce offered to cook dinner for all four of the girls, and he himself thought Kathy attractive.

But it was John that Kathy wanted. She found his quiet demeanor intriguing and different from the rest of the men she knew. She quickly fell in love with both the island and with John. Her friends were stunned when she told them she was staying.

John had begged Bruce not to tell Kathy about his medication or his past. John swore he wanted to reveal that information to her himself, eventually. Bruce had agreed. Kathy never had a reason not to trust John completely. Things went alright until Bruce died. Bruce had been John's way of living OK outside the mental institution, and had been John's access to the meds he needed to function sanely and safely.

But the prescriptions for his meds that his brother had provided him and paid for had run out. Now, without his medication for over a month, John's mind was swirling with old thoughts and new ones. Emotions he hadn't felt in over a decade, and sensations in his body he had never felt before, rose in him. John's self-medication via cocaine and alcohol seemed to help at first but actually was acting as fuel for his mental illness. Now the voice in his head was getting stronger. John wasn't used to making his own choices without running them by Bruce. But Bruce was gone.

****

Now John found himself in a trance as he stared at the small diabetic syringes trying to choose one. *Hurry up! Hurry!* He did as the voice told him and quickly picked one up. His nose was going to heal now. He poured cocaine into a film canister and without thinking of the consequences dribbled water into it from the makeshift sink in the bathroom. He swirled it around and stuffed a cotton ball in there to prevent any undissolved crystals from going up the needle. Holding the needle up, he tapped it to release any trapped air bubbles upward.

He looked down and smiled at the hula girl tattooed on his arm. One of those old tattoos he'd scratched into himself was disguised with a hula girl. *You'll never stop smiling at me, will you?* He poked her in the eye with his needle and smiled as the cocaine quickly took effect on his mind and body. He felt like a new man almost instantly. He pressed down on the hula girl's face to keep the spot from bleeding, imagining he was squashing Terri's head. He saw his brother's face float through his vision. He stared at the face, trying to keep it focused as it drifted away.

****

There was a loud knock on the door. Almost jumping out of his skin, John shrieked back, "There's someone in here!" He rolled up his goods, tucked them away, and opened the door.

George was standing outside waiting. "Sorry man, I didn't know anyone was in there."

John's eyes were glazed over and he smiled as the cocaine rushed through his body. "No problem." He was relieved to know it was George and not Terri. ... But then John ran into Kathy.

"Where the hell have you been?" Kathy looked stern as John walked back into Melvin's office.

John looked at his watch, realizing more time had passed than he had thought. *Stand up straight, don't look at her.*

"My stomach is not cooperating today. Sorry." His eyes darted around the room as if he didn't know where to look first. Melvin did not appear to be in the mood for any excuses, stories, or problems. He wanted the dive shop to run harmoniously, like it used to.

"I'm counting on you to pick up Robert at the airport and take him to his hotel. His instructors' course starts in two days. Make sure you get him any assistance he needs from the dive shop. Tanks, air, anything. Got it?" Melvin looked at John and cocked his mouth to the side. "I want you to be rested, neat, and clean. Make him feel welcome. Now: Terri should be here any minute with a busload from the *Sea Dancer*. Kathy is leaving to do pick-up; John, make sure everything is ready out front." Melvin had pretty much spoken directly to John the whole time, trying to engage him in eye contact while John avoided it. Finally, Melvin shrugged and turned back to his desk as if to dismiss them both.

Kathy looked over at John. They both walked out.

Once outside the office, John looked over at his wife for some kind of acceptance.

Instead he was met with a cold stare from Kathy who said, "Let's just try to get through this day without any more drama, OK?"

John blinked and dared to look Kathy in the eyes. *Fuck her drama. We know what real drama is*. He looked over at the wall for something to grab while inhaling deeply through his nose. Then quickly he closed his eyes and winced.

He wanted the voice in his head to go away again. It was back and had to leave.

****

Back out front where everything was going on as it should, Terri ignored all this the rest of the day. She was all business. She put the people in the water and lead her tours. The tourists didn't know her otherwise, so they didn't miss her contagious personality. But her coworkers did. They knew enough about Terri to stay an arm's length away, at least until after work. With a drink in her hands, she'd figure things out and come back to reality. And Melvin trusted Terri to do the right thing. She'd be there for him.

DIVE TOUR

****

22

Friday morning, Terri strolled into the dive shop ten minutes late. She wanted everyone to be aware that she still had a bad attitude. However, if she could just get through the day, tonight she could cut loose.

"Hey Terri, we were wondering if you were going to show up today. Tonight's the big night!"

Henry, Ricky, and Darren were putting together the setups for the day.

Donna was busy behind the counter putting underwater cameras together for people to rent. "Did you go out and party last night?"

"No. Just hung out with me, myself, and I. We three had a few beers and a few laughs."

"You're not going to miss the party tonight, are you?" Darren looked at Terri with his usual bright face. "I'll drive you if you want!"

Terri laughed as she picked up a box and carried it to the back room.

Darren picked up another box and followed. "Hey, today's my last day of being an assistant instructor!" Terri had been short with Darren for days, very busy, and he missed her. "So we can go on dates now."

"Darren, you're going to be great at the certification course. I understand Robert's a real nice guy. And you're right, you'll pass the test. No more assistant instructor for you."

Darren found another moment he could say something to her and not be heard. "So, I'll be running my own tours. You won't be as much my superior … if you know what I mean. So let me take you out to dinner some night soon."

Darren touched her arm a moment.

Sparks flew.

"Hmmm, dinner, well, we'll see. And thanks for the offer of a ride. But I'll just meet you there, at the party tonight." *I can't be seen walking in with him. What am I going to do with him? He's darling, gorgeous. Damn. And then there's Mitch.*

****

George and Pam were throwing a party and everyone was invited. Potluck and all the booze you could drink. Anyone who had ever been to a party those two threw knew not to miss another one; they were too much fun. They featured a green concoction rumored to mix four different alcohols: If you weren't in the mood to party before, you definitely were after sipping on that elixir. There were always a few newcomers at these parties, and you could pick them out by the expression of disbelief on their faces. Soon they'd get those green drinks in their hands and blend right in.

That night, Terri showed up already intoxicated. Then she laughed away with a handful of her friends. They were already skinny dipping in the swimming pool, and telling their funniest stories about the times when they first moved to the island.

Terri secretly hoped Darren would keep his own funny story to himself. He had walked out to the back at one point and was startled to see the four girls naked in the pool. Terri caught his eye and laughed; he blushed. Terri's friends laughed as he turned around and exited quickly. These women didn't work at the dive shop, so they didn't know anything about Darren. Now they wanted to know who that handsome guy was.

Terri found herself wanting to reserve Darren for herself. "He's innocent and too young for you girls. Anyway, there're a lot of cute guys on the cruise ships, let me tell you! In fact, I think I'm going to get on that ship and get me one. Some real cute guys. This Wednesday, I'm at 'em," Terri warned. She was drunk and talking out loud about stowing away on a cruise ship to catch a guy.

Terri wanted to see where Darren was. She told her friends, "Oops, I've still got some work to do. I'm going to go out to that ship and collect the day's money. Hey, maybe I'll just forget to disembark the ship. That's the plan."

Her friends just listened. Each one was afraid to say anything for fear Terri would translate their words of apprehension into words of encouragement.

******

"Thank you for taking me out tonight." Robert was in the front passenger seat while Kathy drove. She could see John in the back moving his lips as if he was talking to himself. Every five seconds he cranked his neck as if to get a kink out of it. What he really wanted was another fix of cocaine in his blood.

Kathy and Robert were getting along like two lost friends. She was so hungry to talk to someone who paid any attention to her. John sat in the back seat, sweating, he couldn't think of anything to say. They were taking him to George and Pam's party against their own better judgment. They had no idea why John wanted to go. Nor did they know why he had brought a small duffle bag. He had told them it was to carry his swim suit and towel.

"There are going to be some people there tonight that you'll want to meet. I'm sure Darren, who has been training with our shop, will be there. I know he's looking forward to meeting you." Kathy started looking for a parking space, rounded the corner, and saw cars lined up all along the side of the road. Finally, she found a spot to park. "We'll have a little walk. It looks like this is as close as we're going to get."

John did not want to go in. "You two go in, I'll catch up. I'm going to change my shirt. I think I have one in my bag. Wow, I've sweat through this one." John indeed had soaked his shirt with sweat.

Kathy didn't care. She had Robert by her side and wanted to get away from her husband. Her response was a quick, "We'll see you up there." Then Robert was whisked away before he realized they were leaving John behind.

****

Up at the party, the two were greeted with excitement and welcomed in. Kathy felt special for the first time in a long time. She mingled with the crowd, introducing Robert to everyone. A rhythmic calypso beat thumped in the background. The crowd unconsciously moved with the beat. Most people were finding it hard to keep their feet still. Robert panned the crowd, taking in the many different faces. His own hips started to sway as his feet began to tap to the music.

"Darren!" Kathy called out and waved him over. "I'd like you to meet Robert, the certification course instructor."

The two men shook hands.

"Heard all about you, Darren, I'm looking forward to this week. Is Terri here? I'd like to meet her."

"Oh, she's in the back, but I don't think she's—" Darren realized he didn't want anyone else to see Terri's wet body.

"What did you say? In the back? Thanks, Darren, we'll catch up with you in a minute." Kathy looped her arm around Robert and took him through the crowd. She spotted George. "Where's Terri?" He motioned to the back, toward the swimming pool.

"Hey, look! More company!" Terri was pointing at Kathy and Robert as they walked up. Kathy, nervous about how Terri was going to respond, didn't notice that the four women in the pool were naked, and walked Robert right over to them. Terri, with nowhere to hide, decided to shrug it off.

"Terri!" Kathy was red faced and embarrassed. Robert smiled, as he didn't know what to say.

"What? I was here first! You must be Robert." She stuck her hand out.

"Yes I am, and you must be Terri. Very nice to meet you. What a party!"

"Yes well, some of us have a little more steam to blow off than others, you know. These parties get pretty crazy." The swell of redness and steam on her face (and other parts) caught her by surprise.

From the other side of the fence they heard John calling over the music. His voice had a high-pitched, nervous tone, and he was looking for Kathy. Terri sensed a good out. She didn't feel like talking to these people right now. She especially didn't want to talk any kind of dive business. "Oh, that's John. You guys go catch up with John. I'll find you later."

They had been dismissed. Kathy, dreading having to go find John, looked at Robert with a somewhat apologetic expression. "We better go find him."

Terri sprung out of the pool so fast she almost lost her footing. She grabbed her towel and wrapped it about her like a sarong. "Hmm, I think my butt was starting to shrivel."

"Probably not a bad time to cover it up." Mitch walked over to her and handed her another towel for her hair. He hadn't been too far away, and had been keeping a watchful eye on her. He hadn't seen her this drunk in a long time. *All this drinking is getting out of hand*, he thought, wondering whether Terri would listen to him if he said so. He wanted so much for her to get past this phase of her life, but he would wait until she was ready.

"Let's go get you something to eat."

The duo walked through the gate and into the central gathering of people in the big back yard. Terri saw John standing there like a scared deer caught in headlights, appearing totally uncomfortable in his skin. He just couldn't stop fidgeting. She thought she noticed Kathy veering Robert in another direction to actually avoid John.

Terri looked over at John, accidently making eye contact. Looking him straight in the eye, she reached up and scratched the side of her nose with her middle finger, giving him a very pointed message. He turned and walked away. Mitch still wasn't sure what to think but led Terri into the house before she could start in on John.

Pam was busy putting out more hors d'oeuvres. "We're almost out of ice. We've been through almost a hundred pounds!"

"I'll go get some, Pam," Terri quickly offered. "I'm parked for easy in, easy out."

"Oh no missy, you're not driving anywhere, not tonight." Mitch was firm with Terri, putting his arm around her as if to hold her still.

Darren, who had also been keeping an eye on Terri, headed over from the side door. "I'll drive, what do you need, Terri?"

"Ice, Darren, thanks so much. Here's a twenty, get as much as you can."

Darren didn't need the cash, but he took the cash just to touch Terri's hand.

Terri felt the touch and said, "Thank you for taking care of this ice problem."

"Sure. See you in a few minutes with ice, tons of ice." Darren headed out the door.

DIVE TOUR

****

But Darren was back in the room within two minutes. "Sorry, I'm blocked in by I don't know who." Darren, so eager to help out, so eager to please, looked at Terri. "Mind if I take your car? Did you say it was 'easy in easy out'?"

"No problem Darren my dearrrrrr." Terri was slurring her words. "Just drive the ice back up here and park my car anywhere you can." Terri walked out of Mitch's hold and gave Darren a hug. "You're such a nice guy. I think you're my new best friend."

As Terri handed Darren her keys, he touched her again. She felt the energy. She told him. "Here, use this. No key required. Just get in and go for it."

Darren murmured in Terri's ear, ""I will. I'll be back in a few minutes. Stick around, OK?"

Terri nodded yes, quite subtly.

Darren left.

Terri looked at Mitch and grinned. "So there, I'm not going anywhere."

"Ouch, don't hurt my feelings now, Terri. I thought that best friend was my job," Mitch laughed.

"You're my number one man, Mitch, you know that." She walked over and gave Mitch a big hug. She did love Mitch, she did. But Terri's mind was on Darren. She really wanted him. What's more, she really was growing quite fond of Darren, *darn it.…*

VOLUME ONE: RAPTIS TRILOGY

****

DIVE TOUR

****

23

Darren had watched Terri start her car more than a dozen times. He reached under the dash, flipped the switch and pushed the button on the front dash. It started right up. He concentrated as he pulled out, being careful not to scrape the front bumper on a tree. Pulling out into the road, it was all downhill, and the car quickly gained speed.

It was dark, and the only surroundings he could see were what the headlights illuminated directly in front of him. They began to reveal one sharp turn after another. The mountain went straight up on his right side with the incoming traffic lane in between. On his left side were steep and narrow crevasses leading to the bottom of the mountain. He approached a tough turn and pressed on the brakes. His foot hit the floor with no resistance.

"Shit, Terri!" Grabbing the wheel with both hands, he pumped the brakes hard, trying to get them to grab as the car continued to gain momentum. A red light suddenly came on, lighting up the dashboard. The red glow eerily cast around him warning of imminent danger. "Come on baby, come on baby!!!" He tried to remain calm as he spoke to the car, hoping it would respond to his command.

With finesse, he moved his right hand off the steering wheel and reached for the emergency brake. Pulling with all of his strength, he gave one quick jerk. The cable snapped with little resistance.

The right bumper crossed the incoming traffic lane and careened into the side of the hill. It scraped along the edge of the mountain, slowing the momentum. With a sharp left curve coming up, he pulled the wheel hard to the left to avoid ramming straight into the mountain. The wheels on the right

VOLUME ONE: RAPTIS TRILOGY

****

side dislodged from the side of the road, throwing him into the incoming traffic lane on a blind curve.

Trying to maneuver left out of the incoming traffic lane, he came dangerously close to the other edge. He could feel the gravel under the wheels on the left side now, and jerked the steering wheel to the right. He overcorrected, came back, and scraped the hill on the right again. His palms were sweaty which made it harder to keep a firm grip on the wheel. The car was beginning to shudder in duress.

A tear ran down his cheek as he screamed for help, trying not to panic. There was no one but the darkness to hear. Another sharp right turn caused the left front wheel to drive off the edge of the road. He pulled hard to the right again, but it was too late. The car twisted and somersaulted down the ravine.

Darren's screams into the night were hushed by the explosion as the car burst into flames. His life was quickly extinguished.

****

It took ten minutes for another car to drive by and see the fire. The passer-by stopped and looked for the source, then had to drive down to the market, Darren's intended destination, and hope the phone there worked. In another five minutes, the wail of sirens could be heard streaming up the hill.

It wasn't the approaching sirens that caught the attention of the party-goers; it was how near the sirens stopped. People couldn't help but wonder what could be going on. Looking east not far away, they could see a black plume of smoke. The party gathered on the east side of the property, everyone looking at the horizon and speculating what the source of the smoke could be.

Terri walked over to the crowd and asked, "What's going on here?"

"Not sure. Sirens, smoke, could be a number of things," someone said.

DIVE TOUR

****

Terri froze. The hairs on her neck stood on end and her heart sank to her stomach when she realized the direction they were looking.

"Mitch? Where's Darren? Is he back yet? We've got to find Darren." Her voice was sharp and sober as she tried to keep her composure. They walked quickly, almost jogging into the house. They opened the door hoping to see Darren putting the requested bags of ice in the freezer.

Pam, having the same thoughts, came into the kitchen behind them. "Oh my God, where's Darren? Is he in here?" Her voice was cracking as she tried to control herself.

"I didn't see Darren out there, he's not back yet."

The three of them knew Darren was on that road with nothing between their house and the market but a dark winding road.

"Mitch, please, please take me to the market, I've got to find Darren." Terri was holding back tears. "He's in my stupid car. That stupid, stupid car." Her mind swirled with bad thoughts.

"OK, no problem. Just because we see smoke, it doesn't mean Darren is in the middle of it." Mitch was doing his best to calm the girls. "I'm parked just down the hill. Let's drive down and we'll investigate." Even Mitch couldn't keep the concern out of his voice.

Pam's eyes welled up with tears.

****

Terri was already outside. She was walking down the road at a fast pace, almost jogging. Mitch ran to catch up with her.

They could see the empty spot where her car had been parked. There was a large puddle of oil with a bolt lying in the middle of the black liquid.

Mitch saw this bolt.

"Look, look at that. … Oh my God, what has happened? Mitch—I'm scared."

He had never before heard those words from Terri's mouth: "I'm scared."

They drove down the hill slowly, but as fast as they could. They knew how hazardous this road could be, especially at night. Within a couple minutes they could see flashing red lights and men scrambling. Some were shouting down a ravine where the black smoke was still rising.

"Pull over!" Terri shouted. Her hand was on the door release, ready to jump out as soon as the car slowed. She jumped out.

"Terri, wait, stop!" Mitch shouted as he parked. "Terri!"

"Ma'am, ma'am! Stand back!"

Terri didn't listen.

The rescuers were confused about what to do next. They tried to hold Terri back from the edge.

Terri ignored them and walked right past them over to the edge of the ravine. She looked down: her car, twisted and charred, burned at the bottom. "NOOOOOOOOO!!" she cried out.

"Ma'am, ma'am, I tell you, you must stand back." The speaker was pulling on Terri's arm.

Mitch came up behind her, turned her around, away from looking down, and held her tight as he moved her further away from the edge. She sobbed uncontrollably in his arms, clinging to him.

DIVE TOUR

****

"Terri, Terri!" her friend Clift called out as he walked over. "Mon I was afraid! Afraid dat was you, you know mon? Dat's your car!"

"Oh Clift, I know," she managed to answer between heaving sobs. "My friend, Darren, he was driving."

Clift looked down and away. Someone had to tell her. "I'm afraid … your friend … he … he didn't make it."

Terri was silent a moment, stunned, horrified, trying to understand what Clift just said, while trying not to know what Clift just said. Then she started to shout:

"WHAT?!?!? … NO!?!?! … OOOOOOOOOOO!!!!!!! … That should be me!!! I should've gone! I should have gotten the ice!" Terri was shouting, mad at herself for being too drunk to drive.

Then she began to pound at Mitch's chest with both of her fists. "I should have gone! You wouldn't let me go!"

Mitch tried to hold her still and just hold her tight, tried to bring her in closer, but now she pulled away.

She stood there alone and shaking.

Pam was walking up from behind with two others; they couldn't take the suspense any longer. More rescuers arrived. They all looked down the ravine waiting for the flames to subside. A generator roared awake and floodlights flashed on.

Terri stood there, away from the others. She didn't want comfort, she wanted solitude. She prayed for this to be a dream. In the generator's bright lights, all she could see was the darkness.

Mitch came back closer to her and again tried to comfort her. "Terri, Terri."

She grabbed his hand. Now her voice was merely a whisper. "Oh my God. That was meant for me. … Someone messed with

VOLUME ONE: RAPTIS TRILOGY

****

my car, Mitch…. This was meant for me, it was. Oh my God. Someone just tried to kill me."

Mitch wanted to calm Terri down somehow. "Terri, no, it was an accident. An accident. It has to be an accident."

"No Mitch. Listen to me. That was meant for me. Can't you see this? Now that bastard is trying to kill me."

"Terri, no. No one wants to kill you; this was an accident. Terri, really, an accident." Mitch desperately wanted to believe this himself. He was going to believe this. That was that. An accident.

Terri again pushed away from Mitch and looked down the ravine. She watched as the men draped a yellow sheet over Darren's remains. She turned away once to puke, her body convulsing as it purged the contents of her stomach onto the ground. She turned back, almost frozen in shock, her eyes stinging as she watched them prepare to bring Darren up.

PART THREE

ABDUCTION

DIVE TOUR

****

<u>24</u>

He hovered over "Captain" Jerry, growling: "You've muddled my plans with your own agenda!"

Jerry was looking up, trying hard not to shake.

De Gerlick's eyes were locked like a rifle sight on Jerry's pupils. A drop of sweat let loose from De Gerlick's brow. It fell onto Captain Jerry's neatly pressed khaki pants, but Jerry did not look down. He put all his focus into hiding his fear as he returned the man's death stare.

The whir of the fan above was off beat. Slightly swaying with each rotation, it was gnawing at Jerry's concentration. "Sir, your plans would have worked if someone else didn't drive the—"

"Yes, my plan was perfect, but I'm talking about your man, John. He is clearly unstable."

"So."

De Gerlick continued as he circled around Jerry like a vulture honing in on its prey. "Your theory was that a slight dependence on cocaine would keep him quiet and loyal to you."

"Yes, I—"

"Shut up! You ignored my directions completely." He stopped in front of Jerry and leaned forward, looking him straight in the eye. "And you never checked his background. How can you be so stupid?"

"His brother was a straight arrow. Navy guy."

VOLUME ONE: RAPTIS TRILOGY

****

"Yes, who turned out to be untrustworthy, as you know. We had to deal with that because of you, and now we have to deal with his brother because of you."

Jerry shrugged this off a bit.

"I said and now we have to deal with John."

"But sir, one more death, don't you think that would be so obvi—"

"Shut up!" The sound of De Gerlick's voice reverberated throughout the room. "You're going to deal with John, and I'll tell you when!"

"But sir, I can't risk—"

"I said, *shut up*! It's your poor judgment that got you into this." De Gerlick was leaning over Jerry now, one hand on each arm of the chair, trapping him with nowhere to look but up.

Jerry's face began to redden. He was unconsciously holding his breath.

"You will leave here with these three tanks and we will move this plan forward. And if I find out you are still giving that psycho cocaine, you will be the next one I deal with."

Jerry nodded and began to exhale.

"I will contact you if you fail to please me. There will be four more tanks next week, and they will be waiting for you here in Caracas. You will not disappoint me again, yes? Correct?" De Gerlick lifted his cane and jabbed the end of it into Jerry's chest, worrying Jerry that the concealed blade would come out and pierce him.

Captain Jerry nodded to agree as he remained in eye contact, swallowing slowly to keep his body from visibly shaking.

DIVE TOUR

****

Without saying another word, De Gerlick turned and walked out, the scent of antiseptic trailing him….

******

Captain Jerry sat there, watching De Gerlick leave. Jerry's head was spinning, he was so lightheaded from holding his breath.

Jerry lingered in his chair until he was composed: he knew he was being watched.

VOLUME ONE: RAPTIS TRILOGY

****

<u>25</u>

Wednesday, in the late afternoon, Mitch pulled into Terri's driveway. The gravel popped as his wheels drove over it. Usually she'd hear the sound of the gravel and come down to meet him, but this time she wasn't out.

"I didn't think this was going to be easy," he said aloud to himself. *I have to get Terri through this, have to, she's not doing very well.* He climbed up the stairs to Terri's house and peered in through the sliding glass door. Terri was there, lying on the couch with her eyes closed.

"Hmm, I didn't think it was going to be this hard, though...." Mitch knocked on the sliding glass door to get her attention. She turned her head, opened one eye, and waved him in.

"You didn't have to knock, you know that." Both her eyes were shut again.

"I wasn't sure if you were awake."

"Mitch, I can't wake up. I haven't slept in for I don't know how long."

Mitch wasn't sure what to say.

Terri couldn't take the silence. "I never knock at your house, you know. I don't know why you knock...."

"Terri," Mitch interrupted, "are you packed? We have to go now."

"You'd think I'd be jumping up and down right now, wouldn't you? But I'm paralyzed."

"Let's get your stuff and go, OK?" Terri opened both of her eyes and looked at Mitch.

"Mitch?"

"Yes, Terri?"

"Will you carry me?"

He looked at his closest friend. He had never seen her look so pathetic. "No, but I'll carry your bags. Let's go."

****

The two stopped at the dive shop on the way. Mitch insisted they stop and get her diving equipment. He was bringing his. He managed to physically pull her out of the car and walk her into the shop. She had not stepped foot inside for several days, not since Darren's death. As soon as they walked in, Terri winced. John was standing right in their path.

John looked over and almost gasped out loud as he saw her. He wasn't expecting to see her at all today. He'd heard that Melvin was sending her away on the cruise she'd asked to go on, hoping it would help snap her out of this deep depression.

Sweat began to pour off John's forehead as he looked for a place to run and hide. He jangled the bracelet on his wrist and broke out in a whistle in an attempt to act like nothing was wrong.

But it was.

The police had found the bolt lying in the puddle of brake fluid. How the bolt had worked its way off and how the fluid had leaked out was suspicious; they'd announced an investigation.

John knew it looked bad for him. He'd stayed behind at the party that night, hadn't gone out to see what had happened. He had needed another fix of cocaine in his arm. No one would be

DIVE TOUR

****

able to account for his missing time, if they asked around. He felt so alone. And Robert was gone. The instructors' training course had been postponed for three more months, so Robert had packed his bags and left. And Kathy—John's own wife—would hardly look at him or talk to him. She would shut and lock the bedroom door at night when she got home, isolating both of them. John would spend his evenings sitting in the kitchen, regularly walking down the outside stairs to the cistern where he'd shoot up more cocaine under the house.

For her part, Terri felt the inquiry would consist of a bunch of men in uniforms scratching their heads. How were they equipped to deal with such a charred wreck? She immediately offered her help in the investigation, because she knew exactly where it was going to lead. They refused her: she was hysterical, they said, and upset—one man mentioned she might be starting her period. They sent her away.

So when Terri passed John, it was with a blank stare on her face. She couldn't take another emotion. All she could feel was pain. *Why can't anyone see what is so obvious about this guy?* Something wasn't right with John and she had tried to explain this to whoever would listen, but no one would. Now they wanted her dead—whoever "they" were. She was positive John and the Captain were part of it, whatever "it" was.

****

Mitch led her into Melvin's office. "So, *now* you want to send me on a cruise." Terri had her mouth halfcocked; she couldn't manage any pleasantries at the moment.

"Terri," Melvin was as serious as he sounded. "Darren's death has affected many people."

Terri looked down and kicked the ground with her right toe. She didn't want to hear about any more death. A tear ran down her cheek and she quickly wiped it away. "Would it be possible to get my check?" She spoke in a monotone, as she was being careful not to show any more "attitude" to Melvin. Melvin

VOLUME ONE: RAPTIS TRILOGY

****

opened up his desk drawer and pulled out an envelope that had her name on it. He handed it to her.

"You go now and take care of yourself. Get some rest and we'll talk when you get back."

"I see John's still here." She couldn't help herself.

"Terri, I meant what I said, go and get some rest. This place will still be standing when you get back."

Mitch grabbed her hand and left Melvin's office. He was hoping John, this apparently questionable (according to Terri anyway) dive shop manager, had left the sales floor.

****

John had gone into the bathroom as soon as Terri and Mitch were in Melvin's office. Without Terri's constant monitoring, no one was paying much attention to John now. His own wife hardly spoke to him. No one else cared.

Now John sat on the toilet, flexing his wrist as he watched the tattooed hula girl's hips sway on his forearm. *Maybe someone will finish her off, finish her off, finish her off.* He laughed to himself; it sounded like a familiar nursery rhyme tune in his head. John finished shooting up and began fantasizing about news of Terri's death. He didn't want to leave the safety of his small confines. He watched the motions of his hula girl as he flexed his forearm with different rhythms. *Dance, dance, dance and sway. They'll never let Terri get in their way.* The voice in his head was content for now.

DIVE TOUR

****

<u>26</u>

Mitch walked up to the *Captive Sea* with Terri a half step behind. She had stopped to take it all in, as if for the first time.

Jackie was coming down the plank to meet them. She gave Mitch a squeeze then wrapped her arms around Terri. "I'm so glad you can join us, honey. I'm so sorry to hear about the other night. Are you OK?" Before Terri had a chance to respond, Jackie continued. Jackie was polite enough to ask, but really didn't want to know how Terri was feeling. "I've got your rooms all set, right next to each other. Come with me."

Terri wanted to lie down on her tidy new bed. As soon as Jackie and Mitch had left her room, she shut the door and turned the lights off. The air conditioning in the room felt unusually cool. She slipped under the covers and shut her eyes.

"Terri! Terri! Wake up!" There was a knock on the door.

She awoke from her deep slumber disoriented and confused. Now her cabin was completely dark.

It was Mitch's voice calling to her from the other side of her door. "We're getting ready to set sail. Come on, everyone's on the dock waving goodbye."

Suddenly it all came back to her. She was on his ship, Captain Jerry's ship. She got up, went to the door, and opened it.

"Jackie has saved a place on the rail for us!" Mitch was all excited. It was obvious from the smell of his breath and the grin on his face, the vacation had started.

"All your friends are out there. Come with me. OK?"

"I'll be out in a minute. I have to pee."

"Good idea, meet me out here in a minute." The faint sound of steel drums could be heard in the background.

****

Terri joined Mitch in a few minutes and they headed up to their spot on the rail. Terri had never witnessed St. Todos from this view before. As many times as she had been on a cruise ship, she had always disembarked before it set sail. So now, here she was. She had slept through the cocktail hour and everyone had let her. The drums clanged their rhythmic beat while people ordered more bright, slushy tropical drinks. The crowd erupted in cheers of excitement as the ship let out two long blasts followed by a shorter blast to signal it was leaving the dock.

Looking around, Terri realized that but for a few people, no one there knew her. And now there were no tourists to take care of. In fact, she was one of them now. She nonchalantly wondered whether she actually looked like one.

****

The ship reversed itself out of the harbor on its journey to another island destination. Terri welled up with emotion as she watched the details of the landscape fade away with distance. She unexpectedly felt a teardrop roll down her cheek and quickly wiped it away, hoping no one noticed. She wanted to run away but she was flanked on each side by Mitch and Jackie.

"Have you ever been at a point in your life where everything is smooth, I mean perfect? Then, *bam*!" She threw her arms up in the air to emphasize her point. She was beginning to feel anger. She knew how to transform pain into anger all too well. "All of a sudden everything around you turns to shit and you sit there, frozen in it."

Mitch squeezed Terri closer to him. "You'll be OK, everything will be OK. You'll see. I'm right here."

"I love you, Mitch. I love you so much, Mitch." The tear in Terri's eye turned into a stream. "I'm gonna go to my room now."

"Get all the rest you need, sweetheart; you know your way around this ship. Get some rest. Mitch is right next door to you." Jackie gave her a short hug.

Terri didn't want Jackie's hug to stop. What she really wanted was a hug from her mom. She walked away into the crowd.

"She doesn't seem at all herself, Mitch. Do you think maybe she should go home? Like to her mom or someone…."

"Melvin tried to talk her into a trip home, but she didn't want anything to do with that. She said she'd be fine after some rest."

"Well, maybe she's right."

"The weird thing is, she's been so numb she seems to have sidelined her witch hunt. She said she's 'given up,' that she doesn't want anyone else to die."

"She really thinks Darren's accident was her fault?"

"She thinks that the accident was meant for her," Mitch lowered his voice, "and that of course somehow, John and the Captain were behind it."

"The Captain? Again? But we were at sea!"

"I know, everyone knows. And John was with Kathy and Robert all night. That bolt they found must have somehow worked loose and just dropped right where she was parked, along with the fluid."

"Hmm."

"We'll, I'd much rather have the feisty Terri back, any day. I hope she snaps out of it soon."

******

Terri lay on the bed, staring at the four white walls that caged her, at least for the moment. The cabin, neat and tidy, somehow gave her comfort. There with the lights on, her eyes half open, she wondered whether this cruise was the right thing. She didn't want to be around people, even if they didn't know her. She thought of Darren's mother, devastated by his death, mourning somewhere in the middle of the United States. Terri couldn't even remember the name of his hometown. How could she enjoy herself? She felt like crying again.

Her tears began to slow when she tried to move on in her head. She thought of the Captain. Here she was, on his ship. What was he doing right now? Her thoughts began to spin as she felt her anger rearing its ugly head once more. She knew Jerry had the perfect alibi—he wasn't there when Darren died. *Darren.*

Terri asked herself, *Is John in any way together enough to even think of a plan like that? Would he be stupid enough to try it? No. He's too much of a moron to come up with a simple dive plan, let alone a plan to kill someone. The Captain is surely behind it, but what is "it"... and who else is involved? Smuggling cocaine in scuba tanks? And maybe smuggling other stuff as well? This is big business. There must be other people involved somewhere along the line. Who?*

A light bulb went off in her head. *Aruba! It must be Aruba! Someone in Aruba!*

Terri got up and went over to the tiny desk in her cabin where she'd tossed all her things. She shuffled through the papers to find the activities for the week. She scanned the page and found what she was looking for. Scuba tours. They offered one in St. Todos and one in Aruba.

Of course! John and Kathy are from Aruba. That must be what they're doing. Something with someone in Aruba and this ship. Who would ever suspect the Captain of a ship like this? Hell, they won't even listen to me! I'm sorry Darren—I'm all alone in this, but I will figure it out. Somehow. I owe it to you, and to me, and to the rest of us.

Terri was sitting on the edge of the bed looking at herself in the mirror. She had to do something. Somehow, she had to turn this pain into action. She began with a plan to watch the scuba tanks. It should be easy, since the Captain's tanks were unmistakably marked. *I've got to find that Jerry and keep my eye on him. And when we dock in Aruba, where does he go there? Does he go on an early morning dive there, too? Where does he fill his tanks?*

She realized that this trip on this ship could be her chance to finally find out what Jerry was up to. Her stomach started to growl as visions of opulent cruise ship buffets appeared in her thoughts. She opened up her suitcase to see what she had brought to wear, knowing that she hadn't put much thought into packing. After some rummaging, she realized just how little: three bathing suits, a towel, two pairs of shorts, and numerous t-shirts. There was nothing to wear to dinner. *A pair of clean shorts and shirt will have to do.*

DIVE TOUR

****

27

Terri changed her shorts and shirt and ventured out of the confines of her cabin. The ship was cruising out in the open sea, causing a gentle to-and-fro motion. She felt quite obvious and underdressed as she passed others in the narrow hallway, and this brought back uncomfortable feelings of her past. Still, she held her head high and tried to exude confidence. Besides, who should care if she was dressed the way she would dress on her way to the beach? It wasn't like she was meeting her mother or something.

She took a short stumble as her mind drifted. Standing herself back up, she looked behind to see if there were any witnesses. None. Gathering her sea legs, she started to search for her friends. She looked in their usual place, the lounge. They were having a drink before dinner. Mitch was in his suit and Jackie in formal dinner attire. She looked gorgeous; Terri had never seen Jackie out of uniform before. There were other people at the table she had never seen or met before.

"Terri! Terri!" Jackie was the first to spot her and waved her over. "Honey, come join us, we're having a drink before dinner." Terri felt like a fish out of water as she walked over.

"I was on my way to have a casual buffet dinner tonight." Terri tried to explain away her casual attire.

"That's OK, come on, sit down and join us."

Mitch stood up, found a chair for Terri, and put it next to his. "You look fine, always lovely whatever you wear," Mitch whispered in her ear, although he secretly wished he could see her all dressed up and made up once in a while. *What a sight she'd be, stunning I'm sure. Oh well, someday….*

Jackie introduced Terri to everyone at the table and made an attempt to include her in the conversation. Terri spotted the Captain across the room; he was working his way toward them.

"Well, Terri and Mitch, nice to see you." He reached his hand out to Mitch without even looking at Terri. He acknowledged the remaining couples with a nod. When his eyes met with Jackie's, his face immediately softened. "Good evening Jackie. May I say you look exceptional tonight."

"Thank you, Captain."

Terri thought she saw Jackie blush as she replied and did not the like the looks of that at all. Terri began to wiggle in her seat.

"Terri," the Captain turned his attention to her. "I'm sorry to hear about your friend. He saved your life."

"Yes, I suppose you could say that." Terri looked him straight in the eye. "I'm not sure I could have gotten myself out of that situation. It appears the brake fluid was drained. And if they would let me within five feet of my car, I bet I could show them the emergency brake cable was compromised, too."

"Well," Jerry kept his cool at all times, "I'm sorry to hear that, I'm sure the police will sort that all out."

"Are you going diving in Aruba?" Terri continued.

"I'm not sure what my schedule will be that day. I thought I might offer you two a special tour the next day."

"Sounds dangerous."

"Terri!" Mitch scolded her then turned his attention politely back to the Captain. "That sounds like a possibility. It's the day after tomorrow?"

"Yes. Think about it." He looked over at the rest of the group seated around the two small tables pushed together. "I must move on now." With one quick nod of his head as if to dismiss the whole group, he walked across the room to converse with another table.

"Hmmph. Won't that be a grand day." Terri shot Mitch a look of disapproval. She decided to stop there, feeling she had already attracted way too much attention. "Thank you for allowing me to sit in, but I must bid ado for now." Terri stood up. "I'm famished and not quite dressed for dinner, now am I?" With a quick goodbye, she didn't allow anyone to respond as she exited the same way she had come in.

DIVE TOUR

****

<u>28</u>

Terri woke up in the middle of the night. Her bed was swaying with the ship's gentle sway. Her eyes adjusted to the bright red digits on the clock display. Four o'clock in the morning. She opened up the shade over her cabin window and looked out. The ship was moving slower, as if they were approaching a port on the other side, but she couldn't see anything but darkness from her view.

Turning the lights on, the remnants of a party for one lit up, all of her favorite foods, brought to her room. She started snacking. Once her stomach was full, she lay back down on her bed and fell asleep.

****

Terri didn't hear the faint knock on the door the first time, or perhaps she vaguely incorporated the noise into her dream. Then, the second time, a knock jolted her awake. This second knock was louder, more demanding.

"Terri!" Mitch's voice was on the other side of the door. She slid out of bed and opened the door. "Aren't you coming? Jackie has the day off, she was going to show us around today."

Terri was confused. Looking out her window, she could now see a lush island. The sun was up and it was bright out, without a cloud in the sky. Glancing at the clock she could see it was ten. "I'm sorry, I forgot."

Mitch looked in and saw the trays of empty plates.

"You two go, I'm staying here."

VOLUME ONE: RAPTIS TRILOGY

****

"Don't you want to go into town? With Jackie?"

"I'm tired."

"You can't just eat and sleep the day away."

"I won't. I'll catch up with you two when you get back." She began to shut the door, not wanting to hear another word. She could hear Mitch on the other side.

"We won't be gone all day."

Terri looked out the window again. It was inviting, this island, and she had never visited it before. But tomorrow was Aruba, and today she wanted to scout around this ship, find out if there was a diving department on board.

****

"No madam, we do not have a diving department on this ship. I'm sorry. We do offer diving tours on two of our destinations. Tomorrow there will be an underwater tour on Aruba."

"No, no thank you, I was hoping to have my tanks inspected and filled with air on board, are you sure?"

"Yes, I am sure we do not offer any of those services on board. I will be happy to find a dive shop at our next destination for you, though!" The concierge was trying to be as helpful as he could.

"No, no thank you. How about the Captain? Where does he hang out? Does he go diving tomorrow?"

The concierge tilted his head and looked at her a little more closely now, with a little suspicion. "Excuse me? The Captain? Of the ship?"

"He goes diving with a friend of mine on St. Todos."

"Madam, I am not at liberty to discuss any officer's schedule, let alone the Captain of this ship." His head remained cocked, his eyes narrowed.

OK, now you're waving a big red flag. Walk away, walk away! "Well, thank you for your help." Suddenly flushed with embarrassment, Terri looked the other way as if spotting someone she knew. "Oh, I've got to go now!" Practically sprinting away, she was hoping the concierge would forget her face and the conversation.

******

Descending down the sterile white stairway, she pushed her way through a door that signed *No entry: Employees-only.* Asking an officer about the Captain was risky, but maybe she could find out more about Enrique from someone he used to work with. Her lips were moving silently as she tried to come up with a reason to be down there in the first place. At the bottom of the steps was a long corridor. She looked down each way and then went to the right.

A door swung open in front of her. Two men stepped out almost coming face to face with her. Terri was the most surprised.

"Excuse me." She looked down and kept walking as if she were going somewhere. The men stood in the hallway and chatted to each other. She strained her ears to her what they were saying. *Spanish, damn. Wait—maybe....* She turned around and approached the men.

"Hello, I'm looking for Enrique, my friend. Well, I don't know his last name, so he's not a last-name kind of friend, but he's a friend of mine. We've been diving together." She was so nervous she couldn't stop talking.

The men stared at her.

"Enrique? Do you guys know an Enrique?"

They looked at each other before one slowly responded.

"We didn't know Enrique. Who are you?"

"Oh, just a friend. A diving friend looking for Enrique." She didn't know what else to say.

Now the men were facing her and blocking her exit. *I don't belong in the detective business.* "I'm sorry, I must be lost, I thought this is where I met him before."

"Who?"

"Enrique! I'm looking for Enrique."

"Only Enrique I know died. Just a couple weeks ago. Diving. Was he diving with you?"

Now they had a suspicious look in their eyes, and one of them crossed his arms.

"Nooo, no! He died? Wow, I didn't know! What happened?"

"We don't know. Went diving and came back dead." The man whose arms were crossed scrunched his face as he looked at his companion, obviously displeased he was divulging information. The voice was low but direct. "We don't know anything; you need to leave this area." He looked over his shoulder to make sure no one was there. "Let's go," he directed the other man and then spoke in Spanish as if he didn't want her to understand. They turned and went through another door.

That was enough for her. Her nerves were on edge; it was time for a beer by the pool while she planned her next move.

****

Mitch found her on a chaise lounge by the pool. She was sound asleep on her back, mouth wide open and snoring, loudly. He

DIVE TOUR

****

couldn't help himself; he stepped back and took a picture with his camera before waking her gently.

Opening one eye, it took a minute for her to focus. She smiled.

"OK, I'm drunk. But...." She raised her index finger in the air to make a point. "I'm out of bed." She started to laugh out loud to herself. "That wonderful man over there has been taking good care of me." She turned and waved to him, slipping halfway off the lounge. She giggled.

Her friend said, "You must have booze to cruise, they say! And I must say, I agree."

Mitch picked up the drink on the table and smelled it. His body shimmied from head to toe. "Whoa, what's in those drinks?!"

"Taste it! I don't know what it is. He said it's special, just for me!"

Swirling the drink around in the glass, Mitch lifted it up to his lips and sipped. "Hmmm, intriguing. Whew— strong!" He shook his head from the lingering aftertaste. But he was warm, and the drink was cool, so he had another swallow. "Wow!"

"See what I mean? Want one?" Retrieving her drink from him, she drank the rest.

"No thanks—wow, I'm feeling that already."

"We gotta learn—we gotta learn how to ... how to make those. Mitch? I'm ah, I'm umm, want to pass out, I'm not sure if I can ...walk."

Mitch sat down next to her. "I'm feeling buzzed, and I just had a sip. Come on, I'll help you while I can."

<u>29</u>

Terri tossed and turned all night while restless, anxious dreams haunted her sleep. The ocean's slow rhythm was working against her. She was fighting a losing battle, one on one with the ocean in her dreams. Her head swirled, feeling the realness of sea sickness as her stomach moved closer to her throat. She was alone on a life raft in twenty-foot seas, with no horizon to focus on. Her insides were tossing to and fro when she bolted awake. This wasn't a dream; she was going to be sick, really sick.

Running to the bathroom in this tiny cabin didn't take much, two steps and a dive. Relief came, but her body shuddered as she tried to ward off another convulsion to no avail. With no energy to move, she lay down on the tiled bathroom floor. The tile felt cool on her hot, sweaty skin. She looked up and saw a washcloth which she then made a half attempt to reach without lifting her head. Too sick to even keep her eyes open, she quickly gave up and lay still.

In the silence, she thought she could hear the same scenario being played out next door. She slowly rolled over and knocked on the wall.

"Mitch? Mitch, is that you?"

"Terri?" Mitch did not sound well.

"We've been had, Mitch ... I'm sicker than a rabid dog ... Oh my God." A wave of nausea hit Terri like a fist plunging into her stomach.

Lying back down, she just wanted to pass out. Pulling the soft luxury towels down, she pulled one over her body and used the other as a pillow. This was where she was going to spend the night.

On the other side, Mitch dug into the cornucopia of medical supplies he traveled with. Vomiting, diarrhea, gas, even a sprained ankle; he was ready.

******

Terri woke up to a pounding headache. Glancing at the clock, she was surprised to see it was eleven. Next to the clock was a tray of some different foods. As she sat up to further investigate, her head spun. She shut her eyes, laid back down, and tried to relax.

When Terri next opened her eyes, the clock read three-thirty. She sat up and swung her legs off the bed, trying her best to ignore the pounding in her head. Next to the breakfast goodies there was a note which read, "Hope you feel better. Jackie." There were several opened over the counter medications lying next to the tray.

I must have really been out of it. I don't remember any of this. I've slept away half my vacation. Someone made me sick. That fucking Jerry, he ditched me so I couldn't follow him! There was that anger again, suddenly there inside her; it was never far away. She tore the head off a muffin and crammed it into her mouth. She looked at herself in the mirror. "I look like Rumpelstiltskin: too much sleep." There were big dark bags under her eyes. She took a shower.

Stepping out of her cabin, her first stop was Mitch's room, to see how he felt. After numerous attempts at knocking to either get his attention or wake him up, no one answered.

She went out to see the sun. She climbed the stairs to the pool deck. The sun felt good on her skin, although her insides were still not one hundred percent better. She looked around and spotted Mitch at a table sharing a laugh with Jackie—and the Captain? *I can't believe Mitch and Jackie are so cozy with that guy!*

Terri's rage began to build inside as she marched over to their table.

"Hey! Terri! Welcome to the land of the living." Mitch lifted his glass to toast her wellness.

"I see you feel better, Mitch, no thanks to the Captain here." Terri looked directly at Jerry as she spoke.

"Hey now honey, let's settle down." Jackie shifted her chair as if to be in a better position to defend her boss.

"Jackie, can't you see? He made us sick. Or at least me. Mitch was an innocent bystander." Terri's voice was escalating and starting to quiver.

"Terri," Jerry sat up on the edge of his chair. Upright, he was a sizable, well built man. "I'm terribly sorry you were sick yesterday."

"Yesterday?" Terri looked out at the horizon. They weren't in Aruba. "I missed a whole fuckin' day? Where are we?" Terri wanted to scream. Her guts churned as desperation began to well up inside.

"Yes, a whole day." Jerry kept his cool. "I assure you, Terri, I had nothing to do with that. And we are not in Aruba, we are in Caracas now."

"The hell you didn't have anything to do with it. You wanted me sick in my cabin or what—maybe dead? Well, here I am." Terri was reaching her maximum capacity for frustration and beginning to spin out of control. She narrowed her eyes. "Something went down, I can feel it." She had caught the attention of everyone around them.

The Captain stood up and towered over her in an attempt to quiet her.

Terri leaped at him with her hands, arms and fists flailing. He was quicker than she was. Grabbing both her fists he pulled her up and very close to himself. She could feel his hot breath on her face as the scent of medicinal mouthwash filled her nostrils. She shut her mouth as if she were a paralyzed animal. Holding her tight in place, a steward rushed over to help.

"I'm OK, Washington. I'm going to let go and she is going to sit down."

"Let me go!" Terri tried to tug away.

"You're attracting a crowd, young lady. You do this again, and I will have you removed and the police will take you away on our next stop."

Terri gave a half cocky smile and didn't say a word as she loosened the tension in her body. Jerry slowly released his grip as he felt her calm down. The small crowd of people watching the scene diffused just as quickly as they had gathered.

"Thank you for your company as usual, Jackie." He looked over and acknowledged Mitch with a nod. "She's some pistol," he winked at Mitch as if sharing an inside joke.

"Captain, I'm sorry, I...." Jackie was standing next to him as she apologized.

He smiled and without saying anything, walked away. Jackie just stood there with Mitch in the aftermath. She turned her attention to Terri. "How dare you!" Jackie did her best to contain her volume but couldn't contain the anger and humiliation.

She stepped next to Terri, and right then, Jackie's five-foot-three frame felt six feet tall to Terri. "You have crossed my line. I graciously invite you on this ship and the Captain, despite his opinion of you, agreed to have you and Mitch aboard. He could have just as easily said no. And here you have done nothing but humiliate him, and in front of his passengers no less!" The pitch in her voice had been rising even though she was trying to control herself.

DIVE TOUR

****

Terri was speechless.

Mitch didn't want anything to do with this. He thought Jackie was doing a fine job.

"I—I just can't believe you two are so blind." Terri was not going to give in.

"So far as I'm concerned, young lady, you are the blind one. You are blinded by your own self righteous and kind of crazy agenda."

Terri was again rendered speechless.

Jackie turned to Mitch and held his right hand lightly. "I'm sorry it turned out like this." She walked away in the Captain's direction.

Without lifting her head to look around, Terri could feel people's eyes on her.

"Sit down, Terri." Mitch's voice was unusually firm. "I went diving with the Captain yesterday on Aruba. Jackie went with us and sat on the beach the whole time. The three of us actually had a good time."

Terri could not have felt any smaller as she tried to ignore all the people staring at her. "I—I didn't know." She was trying her best to keep from crying.

"Maybe if you had simply asked a few questions like 'How was your day?' instead of just barging over and starting your accusations, you would have known."

Terri had been testing Mitch's patience for some time now. It was hard for him to keep the sarcasm out of his voice. "We all left together. Jackie, me, and Jerry, the Captain."

"Yes, I know who he is. Sheesh, Mitch, I can't believe you went diving without me."

"Are you going to let me finish?" Mitch was beyond irritated.

She could tell he meant business, so she shut up.

"I had my equipment, he had his, Jackie watched."

"Where did you get the tanks?"

"Jerry brought them, they had his name stenciled on them. We stopped at a dive shop on the way back and had them filled. No hanky panky. We all left together and returned together. He was in our sights the whole day."

"What about today?"

"I was just saying hello for the first time today. I didn't pay attention to him. Jackie had to work, I went into Caracas to do a little sightseeing by myself. Interesting, a very busy city. You missed it."

Terri's head was really spinning. She didn't know what to think or believe. "Well, now I really feel like shit."

Mitch didn't answer that. He just let her sit in the thought for what seemed to be an eternity.

"I want to go home, Mitch."

"Home?"

"Yes, St. Todos."

"We'll be home in a couple of days." Mitch wanted to lighten up the conversation. "Look, over there, Caracas. Ever been there before?"

Terri was sinking further into herself. "Jackie must really hate me."

Mitch looked at her and shrugged. "I don't think she hates you, but I do think you really pissed her off. You put her in a tight spot with her boss. He's not a bad guy, Terri."

"Hmm. I'm going to check out the port for a minute. I've got to get off this ship, this air conditioning is too much for me."

"We're outside now, and besides, the ship is leaving soon. In three hours, I think. I could show you a cool spot I found."

"Yeah, well, I want to go alone." Terri couldn't look at Mitch as she spoke. She felt totally defeated by her best friend, her only ally. *Jerry has Mitch fooled, too.*

She couldn't even hold her head up as she stood and walked away. She just stared at the ground.

"Terri," Mitch tried to get her attention but she didn't bother to turn around. "Just remember the ship sails at six thirty!"

"I know ... I know ...." She didn't bother turning around as she mumbled. Choking back tears, she went to her room. At the moment, her life seemed a living nightmare and it just kept going from bad to worse. She couldn't prove anything. By the time she had reached her cabin door, she was convinced she knew what she had to do.

Terri nonchalantly walked off the ship, bag in hand. It was a small bag, so no one noticed. She walked up to a cab driver in line.

The Captain watched from the deck with binoculars, smiling as he recognized the driver.

****

Minutes later the Captain was conversing on the dock with a waiting taxi driver. "I want to know where she went, who she talked to, and what they talked about."

VOLUME ONE: RAPTIS TRILOGY

****

"Si, Señor, I understand." The driver paused to light a cigarette. "Don't worry, I will find out what you need to know."

Jerry felt he had the driver's loyalty. He discreetly handed him cash for his day.

After several long drags of his newly lit cigarette, the cabbie extinguished it. He sat in his car and adjusted himself before turning over the ignition. His movements were slow and deliberate, as if he were turning on a woman. The taxi was his, his prized possession. He pulled away from the dock without passengers.

DIVE TOUR

****

<u>30</u>

The familiar jingle of the bell at the front door announced Mitch's entrance. Mitch had watched Melvin, his closest friend, build his business all the way up from what was once just a good idea.

Mitch knew what time to stop by to avoid the crowds. "Good morning, Donna."

"Hey, Mitch. I thought you and Terri were on a cruise or something?"

"Yes, we were on a cruise but we both got off early. I was hoping Terri would be around here today."

"Gosh no, haven't heard from her or seen her since last week."

"Is Melvin in?" Mitch asked as he walked toward the office. He had seen Melvin's car parked outside.

"Sure, go on in." Mitch stopped and looked back at Donna.

"Say, if you do happen to run into Terri, tonight or out somewhere else, will you tell her I would like to see her?"

This sounded a bit odd to Donna, who wasn't sure what to think as Mitch and Terri were so often together. "Sure, Mitch. If I see Terri, I'll tell her that." With a shrug, Donna went back to straightening up behind the counter.

Mitch gave Melvin the courtesy of a knock on the door.

"Come on in, Mitch." Melvin had watched Mitch come into the shop on his video cam. "This is a surprise. Should I be afraid to ask?"

Mitch sat down in the chair across from Melvin.

"I take it you haven't seen or heard from Terri either."

"No. Now I'm bracing myself for the reason why you haven't seen her, when you two are supposed to be coming home from your cruise together. Tomorrow morning." Melvin looked at the time on his watch. "I've got less than an hour before everyone starts arriving back. Let's go get some lunch."

"Sure, I'm right out front. I'll drive." No one ever argued with Mitch when he offered to drive, not even Melvin. Walking onto the sales floor, Melvin told Donna he was going to lunch.

"Have a good lunch, and bye, Mitch." Donna promptly went to the back to turn the background music up. John was in the repair room, sitting in a corner. His arms were crossed with scowl lines etched across his face.

"Aren't you supposed to be at the beach?"

"Mind your own business. Melvin knows I'm here. I'm supposed to be repairing this fuckin' regulator. ... So hah, I'm supposed to be at the beach later."

"Oh well. Lucky you get to go to the beach. I have to stay here all the time. Someone has to mind the store. You haven't seen Terri, have you?"

"Seen Terri? Why would I want to see that bitch. At last she's gone."

"Guess so. No one's seen her."

****

As soon as Mitch and Melvin closed the doors of the car for the half mile drive to the deli, Mitch began his story. Melvin had begun to feel a bit hot under the collar, and the car's air conditioner was a luxurious relief.

"Terri just got completely out of control on Sunday, on the ship, in front of passengers."

Melvin reached both hands up to his face and covered his eyes as if to make the visual go away.

Mitch continued. "She accused Jerry of making both of us ill. She was so sick she missed a whole day and night holed up in her room. Once she got out of bed, she attacked him."

Melvin shook his head in disbelief. Mitch opened the door up for him as they walked into the deli. Paula, the waitress, smiled and waved from across the room. This was the second time she had seen Melvin today.

The fans whirling above were a far cry from the comfort of a BMW's climate control. Melvin's face was pale and he was visually upset. They sat down in a booth away from the others and Mitch continued his story.

"The Captain handled it well. He pulled Terri right up to his face. She didn't know what was going to happen. He kept her flailing arms at bay, he stopped her from more of it. He then completely ignored her and walked away."

"Wait till I get my hands on her. If we lose that ship's business because of her antics, I don't know what I'll do. I guess a humble visit to Jerry tomorrow morning when the ship comes in will be in order."

"Not a bad idea. I tried to apologize the best I could to Jackie. I was so pissed, I didn't even realize Terri was gone 'til we were at sea the next day. She must have gotten off on Caracas."

"And of course, no one knows where she is now? She could still be in Caracas, for all we know?" Melvin groaned. He cared about Terri, a lot, but she was wearing on him.

"I was hoping she flew home and went back to work. You know how she is about her work. I flew home last night from Miami after we came into port."

"Can't stay away from this place, huh, Melvin? The Blue Plate Special for the two of youse, right?" Paula's Jewish ancestry showed all over, from thick, black curls to a beautiful olive completion. She had moved from New York to St. Todos with her parents, some seven years ago. Her mother, Millie, swore the weather in the Caribbean beat a hot New York summer day anytime.

"Yes, Blue Plate. I'll have the usual ice tea with that, please."

"Blue Plate and ice tea for me, too," Mitch added. "Thanks."

"So, you two in a hurry today or you gonna sit and try to relax?" Paula inquired. She sensed she had interrupted something on a serious note. Her ears had caught a few phrases and now they were burning for all the details.

"We always have time for you, Paula."

She quickly blushed and gave Mitch's arm a light squeeze. She walked off with their orders in her head. It was never difficult as they always ordered the same thing.

"Terri has taken on way too much for herself." Mitch didn't know what else to say.

"Yes, she takes everything on at once and tries to juggle it all. When she drops a ball, she's harder on herself than anyone else could be. But the thing about Terri, she usually learns from her lessons, comes out better, stronger."

Mitch cocked his head in thought. He was rethinking all the events of the last couple of weeks. "What lesson do you think she going to get from all this?"

"Maybe trust? Or delegation. Or relaxation. Perhaps she takes her job and herself a bit too seriously."

DIVE TOUR

****

Mitch slowly nodded in agreement. "Maybe you're right. Her whole life is about diving, and about your shop. She doesn't have much else in her life to round her out.... As a person, I mean."

The two men smiled, both of them envisioning different experiences with Terri and her gregarious personality. Melvin started to snicker to himself.

"What? What's so funny?" Mitch had to know.

"I was just thinking of this poor guy a couple of months ago, he was here on vacation. He tried every which way to get Terri to go out with him. The funny thing was, Terri was oblivious to all of his attempts. Do you think she's even interested in guys?"

"What? Where did that come from?"

"Well, Mitch, you're perfect for her, and does she even know this?"

Paula walked up and placed two ice teas in front of them. She quickly reached over and put an extra sugar on the table for Mitch before he could ask. She liked Mitch, he was the most eligible bachelor on the island. She left the table smiling, leaving them to their conversation.

"I knew Terri would have some attitude adjustments to make after I brought in some help."

"She called it bringing in a slap in the face," Mitch couldn't help interrupting.

"No matter how many times I've told her, 'This is just business, it's not personal,' she still won't believe me."

The two men had discussed Terri's apparent attitude problem on several occasions. It wasn't the first time Melvin had sought out Mitch's advice.

"She's just so young. These continual outbursts of hers just prove it even more. She's simply not mature enough to handle all that responsibility all herself. Ever since Dick left, we've all been taxed around here trying to make it work seamlessly."

"How are those two working out? I mean right now, with Terri gone and all?"

"I've been relieved. Terri's been suspicious and hard to work with. Kathy's fantastic. But John has been a bit—" Melvin stopped talking, not wishing to be overheard.

Right then, Paula walked up with two Blue Plate specials. Meatloaf today. "Here you go, some comfort food today. Can I get you guys anything else?"

They both shook their heads no as they were busy filling their mouths.

Melvin looked at his watch, always aware of the time, and motioned for the check in between bites. He resisted the urge to look at his watch one more time. He knew it was time to go. That was that. He frowned.

Mitch asked, "You running late?"

"Yes, as usual. And, I'm both angry at *and* concerned about Terri. Where could she be, Mitch?"

"Not at home. Her car is at home and everything is just as it was left. I checked. I'm sure she hasn't been there."

"Well, I've got to head out, Mitch. I'll ask around the shop and see if anyone has seen or talked to her. Maybe she's staying at someone else's house for some strange reason. I guess we'll have to see where she surfaces."

Both Melvin and Mitch reached for their wallets and pulled out a predetermined amount of money. It was always the same amount.

31

Terri walked through the brambles very carefully, she didn't want to be followed. Stepping on the brush so it would fall away from her and not scratch her all over, she chose each footstep carefully. She held a large kitchen knife in her right hand, prepared to hack down anything that got in her way. Anything.

****

She had returned quietly, carefully unseen, and then she had stopped by her house to rest. But lying down didn't last long. Her mind was spinning; she had to leave early and was afraid she'd oversleep. She couldn't fall asleep anyway, so she changed her clothes and cleaned up a bit. She was careful not to move anything around, because she didn't want anyone to know she had been there. She knew someone would look, most likely Mitch, and he knew how to get into her house. *No one should know I am back.*

An unsettling instinct kept popping up: she felt as if she was being watched. She put her small bag away and changed into some dark working clothes. It was going to be hot, but she needed pants and long sleeves to protect her arms and legs from the brush and bugs.

She hitchhiked a ride in disguise, not wanting to be seen or recognized. It was hot and she stood out in long sleeves.

When she'd ridden far enough, she thanked the driver and got out. Next, she cut her way through what seemed to be the middle of nowhere. Less than a mile or so from a small back road, she arrived near John and Kathy's house. She wanted to get there while they were supposed to be at work. She couldn't risk coming up the front road as the driveway was steep, and if someone was home she would certainly be noticed. From the back, she could observe the home before anyone there could see her.

****

Sweat was dripping down the front of her face, mixing with the bug repellent she had liberally applied. Her hair was in tangles; she hadn't brushed it for days. She wiped her brow and tamed her mane with the back of her hand. A mixture of salty sweat and repellent stung as it ran into her eyes. "Ouch! Damn it!" She reached up with her other hand in reaction to the sting and almost poked herself with the kitchen knife. Throwing the knife to the ground, she grabbed at her shirt and started wiping at her eyes. She splashed some water from her canteen over her eyes for relief.

Hot, thirsty, and very sweaty, Terri heard a car pass on the road she had just left. Taking a big swig of water, she contemplated whether this was the smartest move, hacking through almost a mile of vegetation by herself. A sudden fear of running into a total stranger out in the middle of nowhere washed over her.

Holding the knife more defensively, she stepped up her pace, checking over her shoulder several times. The brush was heavy and pulling at her feet. She lifted her feet higher to avoid getting caught. The sun was up overhead now and the air was stiffening in the brush. She started to feel that she was competing with the plant life for oxygen.

Stopping to catch her breath, she took another long drink of water and enjoyed every moment of the relief. She pulled the diving compass out of her back pocket and checked her bearings. She was still on track.

She approached the back area of John's house. She ducked down low when she heard a large dog barking. She had not planned on any dogs protecting the premises. Terri listened for any movement. The bark disappeared as soon as it started. The dog must have been in a passing open jeep.

She proceeded to sneak up on the house as if it were a sleeping mad dog she was afraid to wake. She was more afraid of being seen or heard. Her heart thumped hard in her chest as she slunk from one tree to the next. The car was gone, and there was no movement or noise inside. She climbed the stairs up to the back door and slowly turned the knob as she put her eye right up to the crack to see in. She stayed focused on her full field of vision as she carefully opened the door. She held her breath and listened for any sound.

******

Inside and all alone, she stood frozen, looking around. She had never been inside their home before. She didn't know what she was looking for. It could be anything, any clue about what John and the Captain were up to. She began tiptoeing through the house as if she were going to wake someone. She ducked below windows, afraid of being spotted by someone outside.

Bored with how uninteresting the house actually was, she started peering into drawers. There was nothing to see. Kathy was neat and clean. The bed was made. She looked at the pictures in the room and noticed there were only photos of Kathy's family, none of John's. Looking harder, she wondered if John even slept in this room with Kathy; it certainly didn't smell like him—it was fresh, clean.

When Terri reached up and tugged on the cord attached to the fan above, it slowly started to spin into action. The breeze felt good on her wet face and clothes. Looking around to make sure no one was there, she tore off her shirt and pulled her pants off. Now she really felt better. The breeze caused a shiver of coolness across her hot back.

Walking back through the house she found an area where she figured John must sit. There were countless water rings left to dry on the table, never cleaned off. There was an area where it looked as if he had picked away at the cushion with a pen or some pointy object revealing the stuffing. It smelled like him, his pungent sweat. She looked at the refrigerator and walked over.

She pulled open the fridge door and her eyes zoomed in on three cold beers. "No, no, no…." Terri said aloud, scolding herself at the thought; they would certainly miss one of those. She swallowed as she looked harder. Warm water from her canteen was not quenching her thirst.

There was a gallon of cold water. She drank the last sip in the canteen and made a light mark on the water bottle so she would know how much to refill with the tap. She cringed at the thought of drinking tap water straight from the cistern. It should be boiled. Her stomach growled as she looked at the packaged lunch meat and bread. She wondered if they would notice if she had some, but decided she couldn't chance it.

She sat back down in John's space to see what he saw when he sat there. There was nothing else to look at in the house. She had opened all the doors, looked in all the drawers, and nothing, not even a stub of a straw was there to see. Where was the cocaine?

Looking again, she could see two points from his chair, the refrigerator and the back door leading down the wooden stairs, the way she had just come in. A thought hit her like a lightning bolt.

She got up and dashed to the refrigerator. She opened the door. The box of Arm & Hammer. *Oh yes, baking soda, that's where people put coke to keep it dry….*

Uhuh, I got you now, bastard. She practically tore at the box knowing his stash was at the bottom. *Nothing! Where is it? Damn it!* She reached into the box again and felt with her fingers. There was nothing there.

Frustrated, she couldn't pull up a visual in her head, a memory of exactly where the box had been sitting before she picked it up. She placed it on the top shelf, the far back left, where she kept hers.

DIVE TOUR

****

Sitting back down in John's chair, Terri nestled her head face down in her arms. Feelings of defeat were starting to creep in. Her eyes grew heavy as she tried to think of her next move. Move where? Prove what? She didn't have anything.

****

Startling herself awake with what must have been a loud snore, Terri bolted upright in her chair. Looking at the time on her watch her heart began pounding hard, it was five o'clock. John and Kathy would be returning home from work soon. Gathering her belongings and dressing, she took a quick look in each room making sure nothing was out of place. She was prepared to spend the night on the property so she could watch John all night. It was time to find a place to stay.

****

As she walked down the stairs to the back, the first obvious place to hide was right in front of her: there was a door that led beneath the house. She noticed the house was built up on concrete pilings. *This must be where the cistern is.*

The sun was going down behind the mountain and the backyard was shaded. It would be dark in a while. Reality set in. She realized she had made a conscious decision to sleep out somewhere tonight. How could she have done this to herself? She was afraid of the dark! Reaching down to the bottom of her bag, she pulled out a flashlight to have it ready, and walked up to the door.

The door opened with ease, no pushing or squeaking. She turned the flashlight on and looked inside. It was very dark, almost black, and the air had a dank smell. Her pupils started to dilate and adjust. Centered in the middle was a huge concrete cistern. She ran the flashlight beam across the length of the concrete structure.

Over in the corner she could make out a small table. It didn't fit in, it didn't look as if it belonged down here. As she pointed the flashlight down to the ground to check her footing, she noticed the path was worn. She continued to the corner and stopped. *Holy shit....* Terri moved the flashlight beam up and down the corner where she saw plywood walls. The light beam revealed ink drawings, scribbling, and words heavily inked and underlined, none of it making sense. Terri sat down in the chair, as she read the wall, trying to understand it.

Most of the drawings were stick figures with angry faces. The phrase "Make her stop" was written over and over down one wall, with some words bolder than others, some words underlined. As she looked at the wall behind her she could see her name underlined. Stick figures drawn one at a time looked like a stack of dead stick bodies with X's for eyes.

Panning the flashlight downward she saw an ice chest tucked on the other side of the chair, it was covered by a sheet of newspaper. She sat down and opened the lid. *Bingo!* There was a large plastic bag of what was surely cocaine centered in the middle of pounds of rice.

Her heart pounded with excitement as she unraveled the knot and stuck her finger in the middle of the white powdered substance. Without hesitation, she put the finger in her mouth. It immediately started to numb her lips and tongue. *This is some good shit!* She dipped her wet finger in again for another taste. She had never seen such a large amount of the flaky white powder before.

Terri reached down below the rice. She noticed another plastic bag. It unraveled as she held it up. Staring at the contents in the bag she couldn't believe what she was seeing, at least two dozen small syringes. She looked in the box further and found a large handkerchief. She rolled it up and put it back where she had found it.

That poor bastard's got it bad. He's way over the edge. She looked at the walls surrounding her and realized this was where John spent most of his time. Kathy stayed in her bedroom, John down here. Her heart was pounding so hard it was all she could hear in her ears. She held her breath and listened for any other sounds.

She grabbed at the newspaper and tore off a piece, folding it into a tidy little square. Opening up the bag to the powdery white substance, she began helping herself, filling up her homemade paper pouch. Sticking her finger in for one more dip she retied the knot and pushed it back down in the middle of the rice.

****

Suddenly the room under the house lit up, the light coming straight in and blinding her vision for a moment. She could hear the gravel popping under the wheels of a car as it came up the driveway. On the other side of the cistern was a lattice wall which let the headlamps shine through. She sat motionless as the car slowly passed by and parked.

She listened for conversation as the car doors opened. No one said anything. She strained as she leaned over, afraid to move her feet while the newcomers were right there on the other side of the lattice. Footsteps began ascending the front porch. Terri moved fast as she put everything back in John's corner as best she could remember.

Quickly retracing her steps so John wouldn't notice, she walked around to the other side of the cistern. The lattice wall made her feel a little vulnerable to the outside, but she was confident she could break through to the other side if she had to. Looking out, she recognized John and Kathy's car in the carport.

****

Dusk was giving way to sunset; the sky was glowing orange to the west with the darkest of blues slowly extinguishing the yellows, oranges, and reds. The bushes were coming alive with noises of the dark, frogs calling out to one another. Terri resisted turning the flashlight back on, although she hated the dark.

VOLUME ONE: RAPTIS TRILOGY

****

Out of the silence she heard a shouting match explode upstairs. She held her breath and listened. The tones were angry but the words were inaudible. The shouting match stopped abruptly. Terri heard the back door open and shut. Someone was coming down the stairs. She sat down and did her best to remain motionless.

The footsteps reached the bottom of the stairs and she could hear the door to the cistern swing open. Fear began to enter Terri's thoughts, fear of being discovered. She shut her eyes and slowed her breathing, trying to focus on her hearing. John was walking to his corner. She could hear him sit down and reach for his ice chest. She imagined John shooting up in his corner as she heard bags rustle. The motor to the water pump clicked on and started pumping, startling Terri.

"Didn't I tell you to stop looking at me?"

Terri opened her eyes. The voice was far away but she knew it was directed at her. There was no one else in room.

"Control yourself, I hate that bitch, control yourself, I hate that bitch. Control yourself." John was repeating the phrases over and over to himself. She didn't hear any movement, but she thought she could hear him scratching on the wall beside him.

Terri sat holding on to her legs and put her forehead down on the top of her knees. She was afraid of making any noise. John stood up and then she could hear footsteps. Holding her breath, she didn't move.

The door opened inward, then closed. She could hear John's footsteps going up the wooden stairway. She followed the path of the footsteps above until they stopped. *He must be sitting in his chair now.*

Slowly Terri tiptoed back over to John's corner, stopping at each footstep and listening for any movement from above. He left a needle on top of the ice chest with a glass of water. *This is going to be a long night. I need to be ready.* Terri lifted the lid

DIVE TOUR

****

slowly. The bag of cocaine was on the top, the knot was half tied for easy entry.

She put some of the powder on the lens of the flashlight then ground it to dust with the edge of a penny from her pocket. Balancing the flashlight between her legs, she snorted the powder up her nostrils through a dollar bill she rolled into a straw. Pulling out her homemade envelope, she carefully transferred more of the crystal powder. She included some grains of rice to help prevent moisture from ruining it.

The floor creaked above her. She heard footsteps again.

Quickly she replicated the knot in the bag and opened the ice chest. Her heart started racing as she tried to remember just how the bag was lying before. There were more footsteps above, too many; she couldn't tell the direction they were going.

The sounds of muffled voices began to filter through the cracks; she put her ear to the wall, trying to make out anything. They were arguing, or was Kathy just yelling? Terri listened hard, only being able to decipher bits and pieces.

****

Then Kathy's voice got loud and shrill. "You said you had stopped with the cocaine, but you're not acting like it. I've had it with your paranoia, it's making life more miserable than it already is. You're getting worse. Oh great—fix yourself another drink!"

Now the floor above creaked with footsteps. Terri envisioned John sitting in his chair while Kathy circled him.

Suddenly John's voice came in loud and clear. "You leave me alone! Right now!" John stood up and confronted Kathy one foot from her face. "You got that?"

John's finger was in Kathy's face as she tilted back. Mr. Hyde was back. Kathy never knew when he was going to appear or what he was capable of doing.

"You need to shut up. I know that bitch is out there, somewhere. I said, shut up! She doesn't know who she's fucking with."

Kathy's eyes began to well with tears. The emotional strain was breaking her down but she did not want to appear weak in front of John. As she blinked the tears away, she noticed John's focus drift to somewhere distant.

****

There were more footsteps. Terri stood there with her ear against the wall as she listened to the silence, waiting for what was next. Suddenly she heard the kitchen door swing open and closed; then someone was standing on the back porch.

****

She's gone, she's gone go, go, go! The voice in John's head took over.

A lizard caught John's attention as it simulated pushups one after the other in a rhythmic motion. Frogs croaked their chorus in the background. John felt the eye of the lizard staring at him.

"Stop looking at me," John commanded. The lizard did not respond as John took a step toward it. "What are you staring at? Are you laughing at me?" John spoke low and soft to the lizard as he took another step forward. The lizard continued his pushups. "I don't like to be watched." John began to hypnotize the lizard with his right hand. He cocked his head and the lizard stopped his pushups as if to acknowledge John. John's left hand came down and smashed the fleshy moving tail. The lizard struggled for his life, leaving his tail under John's fist.

John smiled as he grabbed the injured lizard with his other hand. "She doesn't know who she's fucking with, huh, little lizard."

Then John squeezed hard, extinguishing the life of the small creature in his hand. He threw its body out into the darkness. A warm tingling sensation raised the hairs on the back of John's neck and moved up to his forehead. He closed his eyes and enjoyed it, as if he was having a cerebral orgasm. His attention turned toward the house and when he heard the shower turn on, he knew he had ten minutes of peace. He practically started running down the wooden steps.

******

Terri turned and stumbled on her own foot. Too afraid to turn the flashlight on, she used the cold concrete wall of the cistern to guide her back to her corner. Reaching the corner of the cistern she ducked around it as she heard the door to her hideout swing open. Frozen in her tracks, she didn't know if John spotted or sensed her presence. The door remained opened for what seemed was too long. She resisted peeking around the corner.

The water pump came to life with a loud clank. It caught Terri's nerves off guard as she gasped out loud. Kathy must be in the shower. It clicked off as quickly as it came on, silence again. She heard John opening the ice chest, talking to himself in a sing song voice. "She's gone, she's gone, go, go, go. She's gone, she's gone…. Look at me, look at me!" His voice began to rise.

Terri shut her eyes as the blood rushed behind her ears with each beat. *Is he talking to me? He saw me!* Terri kept her eyes shut as she waited for his footsteps to come toward her.

"I'm going to poke your heart out, bitch. Ouch, shit. You like that don't you?"

Who is he talking to? Slowly she opened one eye, then the other. She didn't dare move any other muscles. She strained her ears,

221

VOLUME ONE: RAPTIS TRILOGY

****

trying to make out what he was doing. There were noises she couldn't place. The water pump suddenly came on again with a loud stutter. Terri peeked around the corner at John as the pump sprang to life, hoping the pump would mask any noise she might make.

John appeared to be poking at his tattoo with his needle. "Maybe I'll just carve your face off, and then you'll remember me." John was flexing his forearm. He talked to his tattooed hula girl as she sprang to life with a few movements of his wrist.

Terri watched with fascination as he seemed to be repeatedly stabbing himself in the forearm.

He stopped, and with a quick cock of his head, as if he'd just had a new idea, he turned around to the plywood wall behind him. He studied the wall for a moment, then picked up a pencil and began writing.

John, you're sicker than anyone knows. How have you hidden this? Terri couldn't stop watching as he continued to speak in broken phrases and write. *What is he writing?*

****

There were footsteps above, but John continued writing. Either he didn't hear, or he didn't care. The kitchen door to the outside swung open.

"John? John! Where are you?"

Terri heard John stand up, frozen, waiting for his intruder to go away. Terri heard the footsteps coming down the stairs, and realized it was Kathy.

"John! Where did you go?"

He scrambled to put everything away and walked toward the door of the hideaway as it swung open.

DIVE TOUR

****

"John? Are you in here?"

The faint, distant sound of croaking frogs somehow brought Terri relief. "What are you doing down here?" Kathy was in the doorway.

"It's this cistern, the pump is screwy, I've tried to tell you that before." John walked up to her so fast she was forced to back out of the doorway. He followed her out and stood in between her and the door.

"What do you mean it's screwy, I just took a shower and it worked fine."

"Well yeah, after I was down here helping it."

"What's wrong with it? A loose wire or something? Let me look at it."

John stepped forward and motioned her back as he shut the door behind him. "I said I fixed it."

"You said it was screwy. Maybe I can help."

Terri leaned forward trying to keep up with their conversation; her flashlight smacked the concrete wall.

The conversation stopped.

"What was that?" Kathy wondered.

"It's nothing, nothing in there, must be a rat or something."

"I thought you had left. John, I'm sorry. I don't want to fight again tonight. I just wish you would get help."

"I'm not going anywhere, Kathy. I didn't mean to snap like that."

"You never mean to snap like that, but you do! You've lost all this weight, you're not sleeping at night—and this drinking, I

VOLUME ONE: RAPTIS TRILOGY

****

don't understand! I think you're still doing drugs." Kathy's voice was flat, deadpan as if she had been saying the same line over and over. "I'm exhausted and going to bed. My God! What did you do to your arm?" The tone of her voice quickly changed to concern as she reached for his tattooed arm.

John looked down as he jerked away, afraid of Kathy looking too closely.

The head of his hula girl had grown into an exaggeratedly large lump. Now her face was swollen and disfigured. A drop of blood smeared across her head as if a flame was shooting upward. He had missed his vein and pumped his cocaine concoction into his muscle. The anesthesia of the cocaine kept the intensity of the pain at a pulsing throb. "A spider must have bit me."

"Wow, I guess so." Kathy's instinct was to take care of John as she always had, but now he wouldn't even let her touch him. She examined it from where she was standing.

Inside, Terri looked around the corner to see if John left anything out on his makeshift desk. It was dark except for the light coming through the open door. Taking a step forward to catch her balance, she disturbed the ground again and sent some pebbles rolling. She quietly lifted her foot upward and stepped back behind the cistern, afraid they might have heard the noise and investigate. John heard the footstep; he felt someone there in his dark secret place. He ignored the sound, not wanting to draw Kathy's attention to it.

"You had better take an antihistamine; you might need to see a doctor for that."

He covered the hot lump with his other hand.

"Look at your other hand John, where did that come from?" Kathy took a step backward and held on to the rail. The outdoor light was casting an eerie yellow shadow across John as he stood there, holding his lump.

"I smashed him."

"Smashed what?"

"I smashed the spider."

"Come on John, let's go upstairs, you wash that off. I'm going to bed." She stood there waiting for him. John wanted to investigate his visitor. Suspicious, Kathy didn't want to go upstairs without him.

Loneliness and subservience steered Kathy through her existence. She didn't want to be alone. The only thing she could do was suppress her real feelings and thoughts of despair. No one knew, had a clue, an inkling, just how alone she really felt.

The intruder in the cistern room had been unconsciously holding her breath, and now inhaled with a slight gasp for air. John's attention and eyes turned quickly back to his hole. *Someone's in there.*

"I know," John responded to himself out loud, confusing Kathy. Realizing she still stood there, John's attention snapped toward Kathy. She cocked her head and looked at him.

"I'm going inside before these mosquitos eat me alive." She was done. She couldn't stand being in his presence but she was also afraid to not be with him. He was like cement around her feet, taking her down with him. She exhaled a long sigh as she opened the screen door and walked through as she had a thousand times before. One foot in front of the other, she had no strength left. She didn't want to argue, or mother, or care. She wanted her own mommy.

John's adrenaline level evened off. He didn't say anything as he followed a silent Kathy indoors. He paused to glance back over his shoulder at the cistern door, another rush of excitement rushing up his spine. He wasn't sure what he had captured but was damn sure it could not get out. He would sneak down later, after Kathy was asleep.

VOLUME ONE: RAPTIS TRILOGY

****

****

As soon as Terri heard the door shut upstairs and the floor creak above, she stood up and stretched. Laborious in each movement, she ever so slowly tiptoed over to where John had been. "This guy is a bigger freak than I imagined," Terri whispered to herself as she looked over John's "tools" which he had shoved back on a little shelf. Terri was fascinated but didn't want to touch anything.

"Needles, yuk and yikes, who does that to himself?" Loud steps above drew her attention away, voices were once again escalating. Holding her breath she did her best to decipher the conversation. Kathy was once again clearly upset. She wanted to drive John to the hospital ... John definitely did not want to go....

Slowly Terri took both hands and pushed forward on the cistern door, not wanting the hinges to creak or the door to fly open in un unexpected breeze. She was met with resistance. She pushed again. Harder. Again, with force. Nothing, it wouldn't budge.

That bastard! He's locked me in! She pushed against the door, trying not to panic, applying the full weight of her body again and again, hoping to loosen weathered hinges or screws. In the moment feeling trapped, she kicked at the door in defeat.

****

John's head spun toward the sharp noise. He once again had Kathy perplexed as he began to grin in extreme pleasure.

Kathy took two steps back, wondering what had caused such a response in John. Clearly, she hadn't.

****

"Yep, he's locked me in! Damn it! Damn it!" Terri's whisper was strained, she didn't want to be heard but she wanted to scream and kick out of frustration. She didn't even have a real

226

DIVE TOUR

****

plan for how to escape. She asked herself, *How did this happen? How did I get myself into this situation with no way out?* She glanced over her shoulder into the darkness. Now the darkness seemed pitch black, and she was sure she heard something scramble across the dirt floor.

I hate the dark! Again, she pushed on the door hoping that somehow God would hear her plea and release her from hell, if she would only admit she was sitting in hell. But the door didn't budge.

Terri couldn't hold her frustration in any more. It started with one tear leaking down her cheek as she tried her best to keep from screaming out to the world. Squatting down, she tucked her head into her arms to stifle the sobs.

******

Again, voices from above her broke into Terri's thoughts and reality took over. Kathy was pleading with John to at least take a shower. On cue, Terri tucked her nose into her armpit and sniffed, dramatically throwing her head back reeling from a whiff of her own scent. John relented.

"OK, OK, I was going to shower later. I'll shower now. First I'll go jiggle the cistern pump handle."

"Enough of the God-damned cistern!" Kathy shot back. "You spend half your days and evenings down there dealing with the cistern. I'm going down to the cistern, you go take a shower." Kathy meant business as dynamics flipped once again: she felt like the mother lecturing the child.

John's emotions bristled. "No!" John puffed up and screamed back. *"I* will deal with the cistern!" He pointed to himself as he spoke.

Kathy took a step back as once again she could see Mr. Hyde rising further to the surface. She quickly changed her tone and wording. "OK ... how about if we go together and you show me what it is you need to do?"

VOLUME ONE: RAPTIS TRILOGY

****

It's a trap. She's setting a trap for you! John heard the voice in his head warn him. "I said *no!*" There was desperation in his voice, his hands were shaking.

Kathy could see John's physicality becoming increasingly agitated. She stood still, afraid to make eye contact as she contemplated her next words to try and calm him down.
"I—I'm sorry," she quietly spoke out. "I just wanted to—"

"I'll take a cold shower. Forget about the cistern." John wiped the sweat off his dripping brow with the back of his hand and wiped it on his pants. Sweat ran down his face, neck, and chest. Normally the sight of John's chest would excite Kathy, but now she was repulsed. This was clearly a different man.

As Kathy stood there in silence, John accepted his triumph over her, turned around and walked into the bathroom. He left the bathroom door open when he stepped into the shower stall.

DIVE TOUR

****

<u>32</u>

As soon as Terri heard the water come on she scrambled toward the front and began to examine the lattice for a way out. Afraid to turn the flashlight on and draw attention to herself, she gently pushed forward with her hands, looking for a loose piece to pry off. The vines were so intertwined that the wood slats were sewn together.

Working her way down she found an area where two sections of lattice butted together. When she pushed, they bowed out, only to be held together with a few vines. Terri began digging in her bag for her trusted kitchen knife—but the water abruptly turned off. She sat waiting, hoping John would turn the water back on.

Voices. Damn, he's out of the shower…. So in slow motion, she placed the edge of her knife against a vine and moved back and forth, holding on to the vine with the other hand, careful not to make a sound. One by one and with no concept of time, her ears listening for the slightest movement, she slowly, methodically worked her way from the top to the bottom, slicing through the vines.

The conversation and footsteps above stopped. Terri sat down and stared out the escape route. With a gentle push forward, the lattice would open just enough for her to turn sideways and slip through. The vines and lattice would make noise, though, so she had to plan her escape carefully.

Where am I gonna go? Crap, how am I even going to get there? Looking down at the still glowing hands of her watch, only forty-five minutes had passed, but it was beginning to feel like eternity.

******

John lay in bed, wide awake. He had his arms at his sides as Kathy curled away from him, asleep. Controlling his breathing to a rhythm, he lay still, waiting to make his next move. Every tick of the clock caused a twitch in his body he couldn't control, an involuntary muscle movement. He needed to get out of bed. He needed to pace, walk, run downstairs to find out just what he had down there.

****

Two hours into the silence, Terri convinced herself it was time, she wanted to get out of there, she *needed* to get out of there. She was afraid of John and of what he was thinking, afraid of being caught, afraid of the dark she sat in. Her heart was racing as she began to push forward on the lattice, wedging it outward. The vines stretched and shook with the pressure.

****

John heard vines rattle outside. He slowly sat up.

Kathy, who'd appeared to be asleep, now rolled over. "Wha... what's wrong now, John?" she murmured with her eyes still shut. She was unwittingly making things much more difficult.

She's still awake! Anger shot through John: his wife was not cooperating with his plans! He couldn't risk her knowing he was going downstairs one more time tonight. He hissed quietly, "Nothing, go back to sleep!" He looked down at Kathy, and saw that her eyes were still closed. Exhaling softly, he laid back down, his own eyes wide open, alert, unblinking. He could hear rustling down below; frantic movements, like an animal trapped in a cage, waiting for death to come.

But what if his prey was trying to escape? He had to stop it from getting away. John clenched his hands together in a fist on his chest, his fingers intertwined, his knuckles more white and bloodless with each sound he heard. All the while, he was waiting for Kathy to fall asleep.

"Go to sleep." John couldn't help but command her one more time in a low tone as if to hypnotize her.

Kathy didn't respond, she was now drifting off to sleep and chose to ignore any more of John's paranoia. This was becoming the most treasured time of her day, when she slipped off into dreamland to live in a happier world.

****

Terri looked down at the glow of her watch. Once again it felt like an eternity had passed since she had last heard John's voice. It was now twelve thirty.

She pushed it slowly through the opening of the lattice. The vines shook and rattled as the boards opened and contracted, the bag landing with a thump on the other side. She held her breath, listening for any signs from the house above.

****

John was trying his hardest not to fidget. Kathy was in a dream state, moving gently in her sleep, each time putting John's nerves on high alert. He heard the vines rattle outside and stop. He had to make his move. He listened again for movement outside, it was silent. Locking his eyes on Kathy, he slowly made his way to the side of the bed, being careful not to upset the balance of the mattress.

****

Terri convinced herself it was time to make a move. She spread the lattice open, slowly pushing outward with her hands. The vines began to rattle. Terri pushed the front half of her body through; her right hand landed on the ground in front of her, holding her up. A design flaw she had not thought of: once she let go of the lattice, it squeezed shut on her waist. She was half in and half out and on her hands and knees in two places. If she tried to move forward the lattice squeezed tight against her, jabbing into her ribs.

"Oh boy…." She lowered her head down onto her pack while she listened for movement upstairs. She heard the floor creaking. It was going across the house. "Shit. Shit…." She pulled with her arms. Her legs in their awkward position provided no base to spring from. She felt wedged in, stuck. The vines rattled louder as she struggled to free herself.

John could hear the rattle as he crept barefoot through the house as quickly as he dared to without waking Kathy. The rattle continued as he reached and turned the doorknob of the back kitchen door.

****

As Terri heard the door open she felt panic begin to well in her stomach. He was coming. She pulled at the lattice with her hands and started twisting her body through, wincing as the edges tore at her skin. She could hear John's footsteps stop at the cistern door and unlock the latch. The door was pulling open, John was coming in.

"OK, let's just see what we have here—or who."

She could hear John talking in a low voice behind her. Forgetting about making any noise, as now was *the* time, she pulled and pushed with all her might as the lattice tore down her side.

Hushed and right behind her: "Oh, you thought you'd get away?"

Terri's adrenaline rushed as John grabbed on to one of her ankles. She used the weight of her upper body and all her might to kick off John and pull herself all the way through the vertical opening. Catching John by surprise, his arm went through the lattice with her. Terri could feel his grip tighten as if she were a fish about to swim away. "You bastard! Let *go!*" She tried to disguise her voice as she kicked back with her free leg.

John's grasp released and the lattice snapped back, trapping his body inside, tightening more against his arm the more he tried to retrieve it. He pushed back the opening; he was too large to fit through. Watching through the crack, he could see someone running toward the road. He was sure it was Terri. How far could she go at this hour? The croaking of the frogs irritated him as he listened for movement upstairs.

Barefoot and barely dressed, John ran to the front of the house, looking back up at the windows for any signs of Kathy. Satisfied she was asleep, he snuck down the gravel entrance to the paved road.

****

Terri ran across the paved road and down through the brush to hide. With adrenaline and fear pulsing through her body, she didn't even notice the large cobwebs of five-inch spiders claiming their kingdom. At the moment, her fear of John transcended every other possible emotion.

She could see the beam from his flashlight pan across the road. She crouched down as low as possible and shut her eyes. She listened to John talk to himself as he walked one way a short distance, then turned and walked back.

"Come here, Terri." He called out to her as if he were calling out for a lost pet.

****

Kathy rolled over. John was gone. She listened a moment for the comfort of hearing him in the bathroom. When she didn't hear any movement, she decided to get out of bed and investigate. Walking through the front room she could see the beam of John's flashlight out in the road. She opened up the front door and called to him.

John and Terri heard her at the same time.

VOLUME ONE: RAPTIS TRILOGY

****

John turned his flashlight off and started to run back up toward the house. Terri stayed crouched down with her eyes shut, straining to hear any conversation.

Kathy could make out John in his underwear, panting as he walked up the short gravel driveway. "What are you doing?" she called out from the porch.

"There's someone out there!" John was reluctant to tell her who. "Wait, listen, I think whoever it is is gone. I'm coming back to bed." John stood below, looking up, hoping she would go back to bed.

Kathy rolled her eyes back. She didn't know what else to think at this hour. He was delusional. "You're supposed to meet the Captain and go diving in a few hours. And you're out here looking for someone?" Beyond tired and disgusted, Kathy couldn't keep the sarcastic undertone out of her voice.

Tell her what to do! "Go to bed! I'll be there in a few minutes."

John's tone had started to change and Kathy quickly clued in. Her life was being reduced to a walk across egg shells, never knowing which crunch was going to set John off. At present, her submissive side prevailed, so she just walked away from the turmoil, back into the house without a word. She switched the front room light off as she headed to bed, as if she knew or didn't care that John wasn't coming right in.

John stood there, silently watching her disappear.

****

"All right, I know you're out here…." John was back on the paved road. "Terri, I'm not going to hurt you, what do you think I'm going to do?"

Terri could hear John walking away in the opposite direction. "Terri! What are you hiding? People are worried about you." John stopped and turned back, getting more frustrated, peering into the bushes.

DIVE TOUR

****

Terri remained as still as possible, keeping her eyes shut for fear the flash light would shine off her eyeballs. He walked closer toward where she hid, his anger rising each time he called out her name.

It didn't take long for John's mind to drift. After fifteen minutes of frustration, he heard a voice in his head tell him: *Go on, Terri's not going anywhere, where could she go? Kathy's asleep.*

John turned off his flashlight and walked back up the driveway, stopping to look for any sign of Kathy, continuing around to the back of the house. Looking down at his arm, he became conscious of the warm painful throbbing which pounded with each heartbeat. His hula girl's beautiful face enflamed, oozing, distorted beyond recognition. He stroked her with his hand as if to assure her it was all going to be OK.

The voice was back: *They will never understand you, John, never....* He grabbed at the hula girl's face and squeezed as the voice became louder in his head. He was hoping the intense pain would stop the volume of that voice. He didn't understand, his mind was quickly slipping, he knew only one way to relax the beast inside. Like a thief, he slunk under the house to the cistern, careful not to draw attention or wake anyone.

******

Terri opened one eye carefully, open just to a slit, trying to make out the direction John was headed. Realizing he had walked back toward the house, she crawled out of the bush in slow motion, as if each leaf would chime out and reveal her. Reaching a curve in the road where she could no longer see the glow of the porch light, she stood up and listened. Satisfied no one was out there, Terri took a deep breath and sat down. She was tired, so tired she wanted to sleep, not stand.

Turning the flashlight on, she checked her watch, two forty-five in the morning. She had less than four hours to make her way to Coconut Beach and get herself situated. There was not a car in sight. But even if a car did pass by, in the glaring lights she would have no way of knowing whether it was John or someone else. Terri let out a long exhale as she prepared a plan.

She remembered what was in her pocket. She reached in and snagged the folded paper bundle with her fingers. Balancing the flashlight in her arm, she unfolded it. But her excitement quickly turned to disappointment as the results of her efforts were unveiled. Her body heat and moisture had proven to be too much for the fine powder. It was all but gone, and only a very small sticky white mass stared back at her. It had all melted around the lone kernel of white rice she left in the packet.

Taking it all in stride, she stood up and crammed the bundle in her mouth and began sucking. *There might be some value to that,* she thought to herself. Soon her mouth was numb and drool edged out the side. She attempted a smile as she began to walk with a passion. She finally spit out the wet paper wad and swallowed. Her mouth and throat were numb and for a moment she questioned her judgment about putting the whole thing in her mouth at once.

"Fucking addicts." She was wondering if her whole head was going to go numb as she stepped up her pace.

****

John sat in his chair and looked out from the porch. He never went to bed that night. He was listening, catching every croak and every chirp in the dark, hoping that if he listened hard enough, the voice in his head would stay away for the night.

At some point, Kathy would be up. He would have to function, converse, see Captain Jerry.... His heart began to pump harder as a vision of the man's face filled his mind. He could see his nostrils shooting out steam like a cartoonish bull about to charge. John turned his head sharply, closing his eyes and then opening them again, trying to look past the Captain's scorning face.

<u>33</u>

After an hour of walking, Terri's luck changed. Parked under a street lamp was a rental car with three drunken tourists. Lost on their way home from a night of dancing on the other side of the island, they had stopped on the side of the curvy, narrow, unnamed road to argue about which way to take. They were happier to see Terri than she was to see them.

Soon she was behind the wheel, driving her new friends to their condominium. They weren't too far off from their destination, and they were conveniently close to where Terri wanted to be.

"Come onnn, we're nice... Aren't we? Guys?" The young man sitting next to Terri was slurring as he tried to convince her to come back to the condo. They swore their girlfriends were there and that the girls were going to be all mad at them for being out so late without them. No way would those girls believe they'd been so lost.

"OK, look. It's late and I'm not stupid." She put on the best business voice she could manage under the circumstances, and put a snide tone into it, trying to scare them. "I deliver you to your condo, and I'm going to park in front of security. Then I must move on to my place, OK?"

Terri put the blinker on and turned right into the private entrance of the Royal Holiday Resort and Condominiums. Lava rock and native cacti dominated the landscape of the two-way road. The predawn hours made it look more like a moonscape than a tropical landscape. Turning a corner, spotlights on coconut trees surrounded by beds of lush foliage lined the road to the grand entrance, reassuring everyone that it was indeed the tropics.

VOLUME ONE: RAPTIS TRILOGY

****

"How about—" One of the men in the back leaned forward wrapping his arm around Terri in the driver's seat.

"Don't make me mad! I told you! I'm not stupid!" All three men sat back in surprise as they saw their new friend's attitude turn on a dime. Terri looked for a place to park and saw a golf cart driving toward her. This was a safe chance to ditch her new friends. She pulled into the first available parking space and came to an abrupt stop.

"OK guys, thank you, this is it, where I depart your company." She opened the driver's door.

One of the men said, "Oh no, damn, now this is going to be a problem!"

The three men looked at each other in disbelief.

"Hey now, I said don't get weird, I have no problem screaming you know." Terri warned them again.

"No, look!"

Terri turned and looked in the direction the men pointed. Marching toward them were three women and they didn't look happy. Each one had her hands perched on her hips. These women looked as if they were birds in predatory mode, puffing larger to scare and take down their prey. Terri stood there in the dark, trying to focus on what was happening. She didn't know who the prey was, herself or these men.

None of this looked good.

Each of the drunk men scrambled to his own girlfriend as she stood there waiting for an explanation from him. Each man then turned, looking toward Terri as if she was going to explain how they all ended up together.

"Thank you, Terri...." each one sputtered.

"We were lost—I mean, really lost...." They began to plead their case to the ladies.

"I never thought we would make it back it was so dark ... no road signs."

"Terri ... she was an angel."

"An angel from God," another agreed.

One thing was perfectly clear to their women. Their men were drunk. Clearly, very drunk.

"Well, she really doesn't look like your type, Chuck!" Chuck's girlfriend ran her garishly painted fingernails down the back of his shirt. She was coming purposefully close to making him wince with the pressure she applied, as if to make a point. He looked his girl in the eye, then returned the playful gesture by slapping her butt with a hard snap.

"I didn't want to say anything, we were so grateful for her help." As if on cue they all turned and looked at Terri. All three burst out laughing, knowing the punchline before anyone else. "When we were driving in the car, she smelled like she had been out in a jungle all day or something."

The girls began to laugh with their men as Terri grew more self-conscious by the second. Suddenly she felt the urge to explain. "Um, I was. Hey, sorry I didn't believe you, about your girlfriends and all." She turned to the girls. "Believe every word they say, they were perfectly drunken gentlemen. It's not too cool to be out hitchhiking this late at night. I was lucky to happen upon these lost boys." Terri started laughing along with them, feeling a warm moment of camaraderie.

Then Terri added, "Do you guys mind if I use your head real quick? It's a long story, I'm after someone." Looking at their faces, Terri could see that this was probably not the best way to describe her situation. "Don't worry—I'm not a freak, *he's* the freak."

The six looked at each other, trying to determine which one was the freak. "Hey! You said we were perfect gentlemen! A little drunk, but gentlemen."

"No, no, no—Not you guys, the freak I'm after."

Dead silence took over as they all began to look closer at their new friend, examining her.

Terri grew increasingly uncomfortable as her truly bizarre appearance grew more apparent. She saw the looks on their faces as they sized her up, trying to decide how to respond to her request to enter their world, *and just to use the head*....

Grass stains and dirt were ground into the knees of her wrinkled pants. A slight scent of urine wafted from her crotch area. The bandana she had set out with wrapped around her neck was now wrapped around her forehead to keep the stinging salty sweat from dripping into her eyes. Her hands were filthy, her short fingernails outlined in grime as if she hadn't washed in days. She brushed at her pants with her hands as they stood there silently looking at her.

"I—I spent the night last night—crap, this does look bad, I know...." Terri was fumbling to excuse her appearance, knowing that if her pants looked as bad as they did, she could only imagine what the rest of her must look like.

"I don't suppose it would hurt." One of the ladies offered as she reached her hand out to Terri. "Come on, this way."

****

Terri emerged from the bathroom refreshed and somewhat cleaner, a step closer to feeling like a human. She was shaking off extreme exhaustion and the mental notion that her body craved more of that white powder to keep functioning.

"Thank you very much." She had stepped out to an audience of all six of her new friends. The women were spread out across the huge king-sized mattress with its brightly colored floral bedspread. The men were reclining in various uncomfortable positions in the wicker chairs.

"I have to be at Coconut Beach in one hour, so it's time for me to move on. You all are my new best friends." Terri started for the door.

"Well, even I can get to Coconut Beach and back from here." One of the men stood up, looking for the car key.

"No, thank you, it's not far from here and you shouldn't be driving anyway."

"Here." The young lady who had offered her the bathroom now had the car keys. "I'll take you there, Terri."

"I'll go with you, too." The other women either didn't want to be left behind or let their friend go alone with this very nice but completely disheveled person, whose stability was still debatable.

Terri was indeed very tired, dirty, and her scent ... well, still detectable, to say the least.

So all the ladies jammed into the car, leaving their boyfriends behind as quickly as they had found them. Within five minutes, they were pulling into the vacant parking lot of Coconut Beach. The ladies were grilling Terri about life on the island, and telling her their dreams about what it would be like to live there. The first minute was fun for Terri, as she had all the answers down pat, having answered them all every day of her working life with tourists. The last four minutes became increasing long, however, as all Terri wanted to think about was how small her island had become.

VOLUME ONE: RAPTIS TRILOGY

****

DIVE TOUR

****

34

The predawn hours on the water were always the most special time for Terri. The water was at its calmest, and there was the quietness that came with the changing of the guard at the ocean's edge. Nocturnal birds and fish quietly found a place to spend the daylight hours hiding and sleeping. A few day birds began to wake and call out. Sea birds would begin to gather, their airborne habits suggesting the weather forecast. Those fish who had been feeding all night were now swimming and crawling into their crevices, their camouflaged resting spots for the day.

"Thank you once again for all your help." Terri was ready for this party to end, and she wanted her new friends to go quickly. Paranoia was beginning to seep in. Quickly looking over both shoulders for any other signs of life, she noted only one larger vessel, anchored off in the distance. All the interior lights were off, and it looked harmless, probably a charter out exploring new territory.

"Good luck, Terri! Don't let them get you!" All three girls giggled as the car shifted into reverse and then forward.

Yeah, don't let them get me. Shit, they have no idea. Terri was finally alone, all by herself on a beach. This alone place in her head was becoming more and more her favorite place to be. *People, so fucking exhausting.* A short laugh erupted as her head swirled in thought.

****

A man leaned against the galley opening, observing with binoculars from the yacht, and went undetected by the party on the shore. He was watching as Terri exited the car and walked around in a circle, waving goodbye.

DIVE TOUR

****

35

Terri walked down to the surf and looked to the left up the rocky shoreline. In her head she could map out every diveable square foot of this water. This was *her* office. "What in the hell are those two doing out there?" she asked herself out loud as she gazed back the other way, to the right where she'd seen Jerry and John dive before.

She'd explored out that way on several occasions. There was really nothing there other than a sloping, sandy bottom. But with a wicked current when the tides changed, it became more like a channel. She continued walking around the entrance to Underwater World.

The man with the binoculars lost sight of her when she walked away from the beach.

The aquarium was completely empty at this hour in the morning. There wasn't even the sound of a janitor wheeling around. With a layout open to the parking lot, it was possible to walk all around the locked buildings.

Terri had never paid any attention to this area before. Why would she have? Slinking around now, she made her way to the rocks that lead down to the water on the other side of the park. From there, she looked out into the sea. It was beginning to swirl with the first signs of the waking tide, gently slapping against the rocks of the jetty.

Terri knew that from this perch she would be able to track the bubbles of John and the Captain, to see their path under water. She found a rock and watched as the yacht in the distance had pulled up anchor and was gently moving past her view. Its wake was slowly reaching the jetty she was sitting on, causing

VOLUME ONE: RAPTIS TRILOGY

****

a gentle lapping sound on the rocks below. Terri wanted to close her eyes.

The darkness of the sky was just starting to yield in the gentle colors of dawn. Terri was bored. An hour had passed and she was obsessing more with each minute that went by. She was wondering and wondering where they were. Did Jerry know where she was? What did John say? Or would John say anything at all about last night? Did John even make it down to the docked ship to pick up the Captain, as he usually did?

Flaw after flaw in her plan was becoming more and more apparent in her head. It was now after six and a tear ran down Terri's cheek. She was starting to unravel.

Just how stupid are you, Terri? Really? Next she was obsessing about her disheveled appearance. *Look at you, look!* Next she was wondering what she could do after all this. "Now what are you going to do? What are you going to say and just how are you going to say it?" She asked herself aloud, demanding answers she didn't have.

****

Headlights turned onto the entrance road and headed for the beach. Her heart started pounding as she climbed down a little to watch it drive up to the parking lot. It was a car, but not John's truck. It idled in the parking lot. Her hands were shaking, and she had to admit she was a little scared.

Leaning forward, she looked again. It was just one man sitting in the car, looking out. It might have been a rental car, no frills. *Hopefully just another lost tourist ending a night at a shore or a bar or someone's hotel room.*

Nervous, she decided to sneak back to her post on the rocks and wait for John and the Captain to pull into the parking lot.

She heard the car go into gear, then sluggishly move toward Underwater World's parking lot, then come to a stop. She scrambled further away from the lot and crept up toward the

DIVE TOUR

****

buildings. She was very nervous now. She made a dash through the darkness between the buildings. But then, to her surprise and horror, she was blinded by the beam of an unknown light.

"Excuse me!" The man called out.

Terri realized this was a flashlight hitting her eyes. "Hey! Your flashlight, in my eyes!" Terri instinctively pulled her arm up across her face to keep the beam of light from penetrating further into her hurting pupils, looking both ways for an exit to run away.

"I'm lost and I can't find myself on this map. It's like the whole island is shut down, no one else is awake." The man kept talking as he stepped closer to Terri and dropped the blinding lights out of her eyes. He had some kind of accent, Latin.

She could make out his face as her pupils adjusted. Her quick character study: *Handsome face, nicely dressed—pressed slacks at this hour? Wow, those shoes, an unfolded map in his hands.* He appeared harmless.

"Mmm, I don't live here, I don't know." She wasn't planning for this diversion. *What if John drives up?*

"This will just take a second, do you mind?"

Just as Terri was thinking, *mind what,* he drew closer. Terri could smell his crisp minty breath on her face. The map dropped as he squeezed her shoulder. She felt something sharp and painful poke into her butt. A needle. He never said another word.

Terri tried to scream, but the man, already two steps ahead, had already reached up and cupped his hand around her mouth. Only muffled gargles and noises came out at she struggled, trying to open her mouth and bite his fingers. A sensation of wooziness first hit her head, then a wave of euphoria washed away any strength she had left in her body.

VOLUME ONE: RAPTIS TRILOGY

****

With all her remaining strength she struggled, managed to get loose momentarily, and half attempted a swing at her assailant. He stepped back and watched her body follow her fist like a rag doll as she spun around in a twisted circle and fell to the ground, her head hitting the asphalt with a thud.

Moving quite rapidly, he dragged Terri over to his car and mindlessly heaved her into the back seat, being careful not to get any dirt on or any wrinkle in his clothing. Satisfied, he closed the door on his prey and drove away into the dawn.

PART FOUR

SURVIVAL

DIVE TOUR

****

36

She opened her eyes slowly. The pain in her head throbbed with each beat of her heart. Light hit the pupils of her eyes. The slightest amount blinded her for a while, until she could focus.

Trying to raise her right hand to investigate the source of her pain, both hands moved clumsily, tied together in front of her. "Ouch! What the—"

She sat up and blinked in an effort to see. She was in a room, a small room. She was on the floor with her hands tied in front of her. The room swayed and her stomach swayed with it. Her stomach revolted and waves of saliva ran to her mouth as she began heaving.

Sweat ran off her forehead into her eyes as she tried to lean forward for some relief. Her feet were shackled with handcuffs. She closed her eyes, trying to envision a horizon so she could focus on her breathing. The smell of engine fuel filled her nostrils and she heaved again.

Slowly she wriggled herself onto the small bunk she was leaning against. She could make out the sound of an outboard motor; a distinct, two-stroked, high-pitched sound as the throttle turned and faded into the distance. The room swayed once more from the small wake left behind. *Anchored out. God knows where, not even a window. I'm feeling sick again....*

Using her forearm to wipe her brow, she saw her hand covered with blood. "Hey!" She shouted and then listened for any movement. "Hey! I need some help here!" She couldn't hear anything, any voices, music, boats in the background. Suddenly the boat moved under a heavy quick momentum, and she heard footsteps.

The boat bobbed with the movement along with her stomach, all in one symphony.

Why didn't they just shoot me? I hate being seasick.

Without a horizon to focus on, she was at the mercy of her middle ears. They predisposed her to intense sea sickness. She shut her eyes and tried to meditate herself into some kind of trance to block out the boat's motion.

The door swung inward. She didn't recognize the man in the doorway. "You are quite a fighter, chica," the man said in broken English as he walked in. Grabbing Terri by her bound hands, he yanked her up off the bed.

"Do you feel tough now, chica?" he snickered at her.

"Who are you? How did you get me here?" Terri tried not to act scared. Inside she was petrified.

"You were too easy. Did you really think you were hiding all this time?" He started to laugh out loud. As he pressed his face up to hers, a piece of his spittle landed on her cheek. She tried to reach up with her shoulder and wipe it off, but couldn't reach.

Terri never could tolerate anyone laughing at anyone, especially at her. Indignant and pissed off, she butted his chest with her head. "You bastard!"

As she screamed, he laughed louder. She tried to move toward him with her feet bound. With each inch she moved, he moved back six inches, each time laughing harder. Her toe twisted and she crumbled to the ground.

"You are helpless, chica. I have something for you." Again he jerked her up by her bound hands, up into his face eye to eye. She complied with his movements. His tone was quiet, nurturing, different now. Terri stopped and looked him in the eye, confused, as if he were offering to let her go. Feeling submissive like a little girl wanting a reward for being good, her face softened as she looked back at him.

"You are making this too much fun."

Terri had a confused look on her face as he turned her and shoved her down face first. Her head slammed against the wall. Stunned, she couldn't kick or scream, and she wanted to pass out. He yanked her pants down and plunged a syringe into her butt, releasing the fluid.

Terri was grateful. She could pass out now.

****

"OK big shot, time to wake up." It was four o'clock in the afternoon. Terri had been out for hours. Her head was heavy and groggy. It throbbed so much, she didn't want to open her eyes. There was a gag around her mouth. Her body was like lead, not one part of it could move.

One of the men sat her up on the bed and she slumped over. Another man came in and together they picked up her dead weight and began moving her. Hoisting her into an inflatable dingy, she looked back at the vessel they just removed her from. Trying to take a quick inventory: *No noticeable markings, just a large yacht, maybe forty-five feet? Name? Can't see name. Registry? What color is the trim?*

A blanket over her head quickly ended her view. She struggled for a breath with the gag in her mouth and the blanket over her. The heat of the day was beginning to bear down as her body sweat out what fluids it had left. Helpless. She was helpless.

She shut her eyes and prayed. She felt the tug of the cord on the outboard engine and it sprang to life. A swell splashed over the bow of the small inflatable as they took off, drenching the blanket with sea water. She welcomed the relief.

VOLUME ONE: RAPTIS TRILOGY

****

<u>37</u>

A nondescript white rental car pulled into the side parking lot of the dive shop, where no one lifted a head to take notice. Everyone was focused on cleaning up after the end of the day, getting ready for tomorrow. Another big day: six cruise ships, so many new tourists all seeking a new adventure of a lifetime.

But John was waiting out in front, five o'clock straight up, just as he'd been told. Staring down at the ground, he kicked at a small hole in the asphalt as if to open the wound in the road bigger. His arms were crossed down in front to hide the blistering wound on his forearm. A gentleman got out of the car and walked up to John with an outreached hand.

"Hi, are you John?" He kept his arm stretched, waiting for John to respond.

John looked up, half annoyed because this man was interrupting, and half scared because he did not know him. With the stark contrast in appearance and confidence between the two, John's eyes cast down in shame. Somewhat reluctantly, he extended his hand and slowly looked up.

The neatly dressed gentleman locked his eyes on John's as if he were reading John's mind, taking in every thought in John's head. He shook the hand with one firm, short stroke. "Hey John, so good to see you, been a while and can't wait to catch up. Let's go diving!"

"Um, uh, sure...." John played along. He looked over each of his shoulders to see who exactly was taking notice. He had been instructed to stand out front of the dive shop with his own diving equipment and a complete rental setup. He was supposed to meet a mutual old friend of theirs, the Captain had said, a friend from Aruba.

VOLUME ONE: RAPTIS TRILOGY

****

"Let's take my car," the gentleman insisted as he popped the trunk.

"I've got to use the bathroom first," John insisted.

"Nonsense." The man looked at John as he began to hoist the equipment up and into the trunk. "Get in the passenger seat."

****

An emptied surf truck pulled up to the front of the shop for a final cleaning, and for an inspection for any remaining saltwater or sand. Its driver inadvertently blocked the white sedan from backing out.

"Hey! You're blocking my car! Didn't you notice when you were parking that thing?" The gentleman was clearly irritated.

Hearing an irritated raised voice commanding him, Hook shook his head. No time in his life for people in such a hurry. Making a loud sucking noise with his tongue through his front teeth, for a moment he seemed as if he were actually contemplating moving. But he looked away and continued to sweep out his truck.

The man behind the wheel responded with a honk of the horn. Hook slowly shook his head. Again another honk.

"Look, mesonnnnnn, you plenty room, stop bot'erin me. I not moving me ol' woman, she tired you know."

"Just move your damn truck, OK? So I can get out of here!"

Hook walked over to the front of his truck, slowly examining the situation as the gentleman grew steadily impatient.

John looked down and shut his eyes, hoping Hook wouldn't notice him.

DIVE TOUR

****

"OK mon, pull da wheel left mon, das it!" Hook was motioning with his arms to pull forward, back up, pull forward, back up in three inch increments.

The man complied with Hook's orders. He realized his quick temper might have drawn too much attention.

******

Terri was lying like a sack of potatoes on the floor of the back seat. Several beach towels were draped over her, hiding her from view. She could hear Hook's voice in the background giving orders, but felt paralyzed with her own weight from the last injection. Her hand was crammed up to her face. She used all her focus and might to pull at the edge of the towel to reveal her face. It was as if each finger had a ten pound weight attached. So hard.

The quick, jerky movements of the car worked in her favor and she could see light! Hook's voice was still in the background. As she struggled to catch a glimpse of him, she couldn't make out where he was. She hoped someone would spot her.

There he was—Hook! Hook! Look at me! she shouted in her head. She wanted to talk but her mouth wouldn't cooperate, making only inaudible low sounds as she tried to scream.

"Ngaugh," was all that came out, and that in a hoarse whisper at best.

It was so weak she wondered whether Hook could hear her over the car engine. Then, there were his eyes! Hook's head cocked to the side with a questioning look. *Does he see me? Does he see me?* For a moment Terri felt sure she had locked eyes with Hook. But it was a long shot that Hook would even recognize those eyes as her own.

Suddenly the car lurched forward and shot out into the road, leaving the dive shop behind.

Oh please God, Terri prayed. *God, I'll call my mom every month if you just help me, somehow.*

"Who are you?" John finally spoke, breaking his silence. He looked back behind his seat and saw Terri's eyes glaring back at him. If looks could kill, he would've been dead on the spot. "Is that Terri you have in the back?"

Again the man did not answer. Soon he was slowing down and pulled off the road into a private driveway. The gravel popped loudly under the wheels, and each pop set one more shattered nerve pulsing in John's head. He was craving his drug. He compulsively asked again as the car slowly pulled down the single lane road: "What are we doing here? Where is the Captain? I don't even know you!" John was backing himself into the door panel as his paranoia and agitation grew, and Terri could hear a quiver in his voice.

"What are you? Some kind of moron?" The man reached under his seat and pulled out a gun.

John slowly inched deeper down in his seat.

"Wow, you act suspicious, you look suspicious, and where in the hell did they find you?" The man lit a cigarette and sat back.

John looked back at Terri. She froze. But she was oddly enjoying this, seeing that someone else finally agreed with her opinion of John.

Another car pulled in behind and Terri could see a small cloud of dust filter past the windows. She could hear the Captain's voice.

"Well, John. How are you?" Jerry's voice had a snide, cynical tone. "And how is our guest?"

Terri looked up and could see the Captain upside down in her vision, staring back at her. She did her best to scream at him. "Ngaaugh" was again all that came out.

DIVE TOUR

****

The men shared a laugh.

"Oh, you are funny, Terri," he said dryly.

The driver's side door opened and she could feel the car lift as the driver got out. Terri listened. She heard footsteps but no conversation, and she couldn't see anything. Someone sat back down in driver's seat. There was the click of John's door opening.

Maybe that bastard will panic all over them, Terri thought.

"You stay there, cowboy." It was the Captain's voice.

******

The air conditioner had long since turned off and Terri was beginning to overheat. The windows in the back were rolled up tight.

"Damn it's hot in here." John was pulling at his clothes. He was feeling so uncomfortable that he didn't want to sit any longer. He needed a fix. The heat made it feel like his head was going to explode and the ache in his arm seemed to grow more intense with each heartbeat.

"Ooohnnn." Terri tried to say John's name. He was so jittery his body jumped at the sound. She heard the driver's door open.

"Is our guest giving you a hard time, John?" It was Jerry. She felt the car lower down as he sat in the driver's seat. "I'll be taking over from here." The car backed up and made a u-turn. It followed the lane back out to the main road.

John's body felt some relief from the air conditioner—but not his head. He looked down at his hula girl's swollen, disfigured face sticking out like half of a golf ball. He squeezed his fist and released, watching her hips swing.

"Christ! What in the hell did you do to your arm?" The Captain was looking straight at it.

John snapped awake to attention and covered her with his other hand.

"Spider bite ... big God-damned spider bite. Where we going, Jerry?" John tried to divert the attention away from his arm.

"We're going on a dive, John. All three of us."

"I thought you had to be on the ship. Isn't it sailing right now?"

"I've got exactly one-and-a-half hours before anyone begins to look for me. Just enough time to complete our task."

John transfixed on his hula girl, squeezing his fist and letting go, wincing in pain with each clench. He was thinking of where he was to poke her next to help smooth the distortion. Glancing at the Captain through the corner of his eye, he reached down and rubbed the contents in his pocket. "I thought you said we were just going on a dive?"

The Captain's temper rose with John's questions: "You're just another sick junkie, aren't you?" The tone was harsh and disgusted.

The Captain's just now figuring that out? Who's the bigger moron? Terri wanted to talk so badly.

When John didn't respond, Jerry demanded an answer. "Aren't you!" He reached over with his right hand and pulled John arms away, revealing his tattoo.

The Captain was being aggressive and forceful, so John reverted to his childlike look and didn't resist. "It's a spider bite."

A curve in the road brought the Captain's attention back to his driving. It took two hands to drive there. "Where did you tell

Kathy you were going? Did you tell her you were going diving this evening?"

John hesitated as he thought his answer out in his head, making sure he had done everything exactly as he'd been told. "Yes. Yes I did. … I told her I was taking out a private tour, a friend of yours. Just like you said, Jerry." His body was rigid still, and his teeth clenched as he craved a fix more and more. The air conditioner wasn't enough to keep the sweat from dripping into his eyes. The salty sting was another pain to focus on beside the crave in his body. "Um, I'm gonna have to piss soon. Before we get wet."

"Yeah right," Jerry made a noise with his mouth suggesting his disgust. "You can piss in the water."

John closed his eyes upon hearing this news. He clenched his fingers into his fists even tighter, daring the tips of the fingernails to pierce the palms of his hands. "How is Terri going to dive? She can't even walk."

"When we get her into the water she won't have to move. She should be able to hold the regulator in her mouth. That is, if she *wants* to breathe. That shot won't wear off her body for another hour, so she can't fight back." The Captain chuckled.

John wasn't seeing the big picture yet.

"The only unfortunate part is, Terri will most likely run out of air and drown before the fun part. The blades turning on."

"Blades? Turning on…?" John said it slowly. Then his mind put two and two together. He knew exactly where the minute body parts must have come from a couple weeks ago. The visual of Terri being chopped up into tiny pieces caused the corners of his mouth to extend upward in a smile. He imagined the look on Terri's face as the blades rushed on and she was sucked forward into them.

"You like that, John? See if she's still alive back there, will you?"

John turned around and looked down at Terri. She was still there, glaring back with those eyes. She had heard everything and was wondering when that muscle relaxer would wear off. Her arms and legs still felt like dumbbells, but she was finding more range in her fingers. Fortunately, she couldn't feel the bumps of the road. The car turned into the entrance to Coconut Beach.

She moved her jaw and tried to speak again. Her attempt met with laughter from both men, and then with John mimicking her, acting like a little boy himself. This really pissed her off. She decided to shut up and keep any found strength to herself. It would have to be a surprise attack. It would. If she pulled this off, it would surprise her as well.

Her only hope now was Hook. Back at the shop, from deep inside the car there, she had been convinced that she and Hook and had locked eyes for a moment as she lay helpless on the car floor. *Did anyone think I was missing? Am I missing? Does anyone care? Melvin thinks I'm on vacation. He's not at the dive shop at this hour anyway. He's on a ship or something ... he's picking up Mitch.* She tried to look for some hope. Thinking of Mitch, she said his name over and over in her head, as if he would pick up on the telepathic message.

DIVE TOUR

****

38

Hook was just finishing the rinse on his truck when Mitch slowed down and pulled over. He was hoping Terri might be hanging out in front, but she wasn't. Jackie had called Mitch earlier at his office and invited him over to the ship. She felt terrible, she said, and wanted to make sure Terri was OK.

But Mitch still hadn't seen her. He'd disembarked at the ship's next port and flown to Aruba hoping to find her. After no luck there, he returned to St. Todos. No one had heard a word from her, and he was considering calling her parents to see if she had flown home. But he didn't want to alarm them.

Jackie was out front waving at Mitch as he drove up and got out. It all somehow seemed different without Terri's contagious banter and giggling about what could happen next.

"Wow, nice car!" Jackie gave Mitch a peck on the cheek. For this, he bent down and she stood on her tippy toes.

"Thank you. It gets me there." Mitch blushed with modesty.

****

Surf buses were pulling up, returning loads of passengers to the *Captive Sea* at the end of their day.

Hook pulled into the lot. Seeing Mitch with a pretty woman, he strolled over. He never missed an opportunity to introduce himself to a woman, especially one in a ship's uniform.

"Now, Mitch, I see why Terri's gone hiding from you, mon. Dis lovely lady, she som' competition." Hook smiled widely as he took Jackie's hand, gave her a slight bow, and her hand a light peck. Hook considered himself quite the ladies' man.

"I don't think Terri's hiding from me."

"Well den, she hidin' from someone."

"What do you mean she's hiding from someone?"

"Oh, you know dat Terri, dat John went diving, I tink, wit' dis—" Hook had to stop himself from saying anything derogatory in front of his new lady friend. "Dis rental car. Wat, White. Anyways, I look down and t'ers Terri, back floor de car, unda stuf, behind dem."

"What? You saw Terri?" Mitch stood at attention.

"Ya mon, hiding in back seat of dis big white rental car, with dat John. I know dat her."

"That was today?"

"Yea mon, bout fifteen minutes ago. Dey drove off. Coconut Beach, diving I tink."

"Why would Terri be in the back seat? Covered up, you say? Big white rental car?"

Jackie was confused.

"I donno, mon. Terri, she get crazy ya know. She was just ... lyin there. Covered. Maybe she hide from dem?"

"Well, I do know Terri, and that doesn't sound like her, to just lie there. I'm going to go find her. She might be in trouble. Who was with John?"

"Not from here, he had accent, maybe."

"Wait, how far away is Coconut Beach?" Jackie was tugging at Mitch's arm as he looked at his watch. The sun had dipped behind the ocean and soon the light would be gone.

DIVE TOUR

****

"Ten, maybe fifteen minutes."

"Oh, I know this is crazy, but I'm coming with you!" Earlier that afternoon, Jackie had felt an inexplicable, intuitive shiver as she noticed the Captain getting into a white rental car on the dock. At the time, she thought it was odd that he didn't hire a taxi as usual, and that she didn't recognize the man in the driver's seat. She hadn't seen him since, and it was less than an hour and a half before ship would be readying to sail.

"What about your ship?" Mitch asked. "I don't know what I'm going to find."

Hook chimed in. "I will meet you at da' beach, I'm der in less dan' twenty minutes. If Terri in trouble, we find her."

VOLUME ONE: RAPTIS TRILOGY

****

<u>39</u>

Mitch was in the front seat of his car already. He didn't want to waste a minute more. He looked at Jackie, still in her crisp white uniform, and wondered: *If there's going to be trouble, what good will she be?*

Mitch quickly shrugged and said, "Come on, get in." He motioned Jackie over; she got in and buckled her seat belt. Then Mitch said, "Hook, if you would, maybe you can meet us there."

"No problem, mon." Even in a hurry, Hook sauntered to his open surf bus, not wanting to break his cool.

******

Meanwhile, Kathy was walking down from the dock of another ship. She had stayed as long as she could, surrounding herself with the joy and happiness of those on board. It was time to return to the dive shop with the day's accounting.

Her head was down as she walked in deep thought. She felt like a pariah; no one wanted to be her friend because of John who no one wanted to connect with or like. Hell, she didn't even like him, but couldn't find courage to leave.

Hook saw her walking by his truck. "You OK, Kat'y?"

She looked up to see a friendly familiar face. "Hey, Hook. I'm just headed back to the shop."

"Ya mon, I'm goin' to da' beach, you know if John, he diving?" Hook liked Kathy. She was always really nice to him.

"I guess. John mentioned earlier today he had to go diving. I don't know anything about it." Nor did she care.

"I'm on my way to Coconut Beach now. Mitch an Jackie, dey already left."

"Why are they going out there? Why are you going out there?" Kathy was confused by Hook's line of questions.

"I saw Terri in da' back seat. Mitch, he worried about Terri you know."

"Terri? In the back seat?"

"Ya mon, on da' floor like she was hiding."

Kathy's head was swirling with details as she tried to make sense of all this. "And you're going out there right now?" she questioned Hook again.

"Yea mon!" Hook motioned for her to get in. "I'll drop you off at the dive shop." The engine was already purring.

Kathy didn't know what to think. Her nerves were shot. She was feeling extremely confused for some reason she couldn't quite explain to herself. A looming dread filled her mind and body. Something was screaming out to her, something wanted her to pay attention. Kathy was intensely unsettled by these feelings, whatever they meant. "No. Not the dive shop. I'm coming to the beach with you," Kathy said as she climbed into the front seat.

Hook manipulated the long gear shift handle into first and the truck rolled away carrying the two of them to Coconut Beach.

DIVE TOUR

****

<u>40</u>

The Captain pulled into the parking lot at Coconut Beach. Early dusk was setting in. There was still going to be light for a while, but he had to move quickly. No time to waste. The air was still, the water calm. Sand flies began their nightly tour for food, testing the air for the smell of warm blood.

John was ordered to get out of the car and get ready. He needed a fix so badly he fumbled his kit out of his pocket and onto the car floor in front, hoping Jerry would not detect his movements.

"Let's go John, we have to move fast."

John couldn't concentrate without a fix, that was all he could think about. As the trunk of the car swung open John quickly unraveled his kit. *Now, now! He's busy, go, go, go!* Shaking, John fumbled with the contents. Pouring white powder into a cap, a drop of sweat splashed into the white powder.

"John!" the Captain barked. He sounded pissed off.

John dropped what he was doing and scrambled to the back of the car next to the Captain, leaving the door ajar in hopes of finishing his task. Terri lay as still as she could, continually testing her ability to move her limbs without any success. She did have a sense that perhaps the stuff would wear off soon; she could wiggle her toes.

"Open that back door, we need to get Terri up."

The door swung open and Terri could see John's sweaty face above her. Pulling on her hands like a handle, he yanked her up to the back seat. She let her head fall back and made him handle dead weight in an effort to slow him down. His wild eyes looked into hers and she tried her best to show courage. John let go and scrambled to the front to continue with his fix. He removed a wet cotton ball from a baggie and squeezed it into the cap. The cap was a moving target as his hands were shaking uncontrollably.

"You just couldn't take it one more minute, could you." John swung around to see the Captain standing behind him. Half the contents of the cap spilled onto John's fingers; he eagerly stuck them into his mouth and sucked.

"Go ahead you fuckin' junkie, so you can function."

John didn't know whether it was a trick, but Jerry's voice was strained. "And then take this down to the water's edge." The Captain spoke in stern, short orders. When John was back from the water, the other man had his tank on already.

"Put your tank on." He then turned to Terri without offering John any assistance.

"We're going on that dive I promised you, Terri." He yanked at her arms and Terri slid out of the car. She rolled onto her side. At the very least, she was not going to make this easy. "Help me grab her."

The two men each grabbed an armpit and lifted her up. Her head dangled and her feet scraped on the ground as they dragged her down to the water. They entered the water to waist deep so Terri would float.

"No—no one is gonna believe Terri in a rental tank. When they find her...." John's voice sounded nervous. "Don't you think they're gonna try and pin this one on me?"

Jerry ignored him as he strapped Terri into her scuba tank's floatation device.

Terri's head flopped forward into the water as the Captain tightened the straps around her shoulders. The cloth gag let salt water leach into her mouth, causing her a gag response.

DIVE TOUR

****

John yanked her head out by her pony tail. Jerry untied the gag. She sucked in a large breath through her mouth, breathing so fast she almost hyperventilated.

"John, you idiot!" were the first words to leave her mouth. She gasped for another breath. "Can't you see he's playing you for the fool! You're totally being framed!"

She threw her head back and attempted to struggle as the Captain tried to shove the regulator mouthpiece between her teeth. "Shut up, you little wench! I've had it with you and your mouth. This is what happens to girls with big mouths." He crammed the mouthpiece until Terri had no choice but to accept it or have her teeth broken. "Don't let her spit this out."

Her body involuntarily convulsed as salt water slipped down her throat.

"And here's some insurance," the Captain continued as he removed two weight belts from around his waist and began to strap them around Terri. Twenty pounds of lead; she was going to sink like a stone.

"I think she's right, Jerry. Everyone knows I'm here, no one knows I'm with you." John looked over both shoulders to see if anyone was watching.

"No one's seen Terri. It's all planned."

"No one told me the plan." John was concerned in his own muddled way.

Jerry glared at him, exasperated and angry. "Look, you just shut up and do what you're told, and you're home free, OK? *That's* the plan."

Muffled sounds of anger came out of Terri. The Captain shoved her head underwater and removed any air from her buoyancy device.

Without another word, Jerry was under the surface. He routinely checked his pressure gauge one more time; twenty-two hundred psi. In six feet of water, Terri sat on the bottom with a thud. The extra twenty pounds of lead held her slender body down. She was helpless and without strength.

John dropped down next to them.

She could feel herself being yanked along as Jerry held her pressure gauge like a leash. Her butt and legs dragged through the sand. She scraped across what she thought was a low piece of coral. Without a mask on her face, she could squint and make out some shapes. The deeper they traveled, the heavier she became.

DIVE TOUR

****

<u>41</u>

"How much further?" Jackie was sitting forward in her seat, her right hand on the dash to keep steady and her eyes going back and forth between the road and the watch on her left hand. It wasn't the speed at which Mitch was driving, or the quick accelerations to pass slower cars, that made her sit so upright. It was that nagging feeling in the back of her mind. Trying to dismiss her feelings as mere guilt, she knew nevertheless that the Captain left early that afternoon in a strange white car, and that she hadn't seen him since. She'd had a strange feeling about this, but couldn't quite figure it out.

"We're almost there, two more minutes." These were the first words Mitch had spoken after putting the car in drive. His total focus was absorbed in driving as fast as he could to the beach. In the open air truck, Kathy and Hook were miles behind. In the truck, no matter how urgent or unimportant it was to get to Coconut Beach, it would always take twenty minutes.

****

Forty feet underwater now, the trio had passed the barren point and swum up to the open culvert guarded by the sentinel of large blades. Terri's legs were badly scraped and poked as the two men callously dragged her across the ocean floor. Sea urchins were stuck in her right shin.

She could see the opening as they pulled her up to it. *What is this?* Terri had never seen it before. There was a deteriorated metal barrier across the opening, obviously meant to keep fish out. Perhaps people, too. And there was a half-faded danger sign hanging. *As if that would make sense to anyone stumbling across all this.* But there was never a reason to swim this far around the corner, not with this sandy bottom, so few corals.

VOLUME ONE: RAPTIS TRILOGY

****

Here, there was nothing of interest at all—except a current that would rip around the corner during the full moon.

The rush of the bubbles streaming upward past her ears made things seem still more ominous. And Terri was still trying to figure out exactly where she was. She really had no idea.

******

Leaving the limp woman in John's hands, the Captain swam up and opened the metal grid, pushing it to the side. He looked inside. He was supposed to retrieve the two single tanks he and John had put in there. But both tanks were gone. Where they'd left them, there were only silt outlines. Jerry checked the watch on his wrist. He had to keep moving quickly and get back to the ship. Plans for the tanks must have changed. *Now for Terri.*

He snatched at Terri's straps, pulling her toward him while releasing the buckles holding the tank of air on her back. With the buoyant tank removed, she dropped like a boulder with all that lead strapped around her. Feeling some strength and sensation returning to her limbs, she let her body stay limp like a rag doll. Clenching tight to the regulator mouthpiece as the tank dangled above, she focused: *Control your breathing.*

The Captain shoved Terri's tank between the blades, dropping it inside. She clamped down hard on the mouthpiece as her head jerked up and followed the hose attached to the tank. Terri tried to swing her body sideways, while both men tried to maneuver her through the blades face first. John grabbed her feet and together they pushed her in, John pushing extra hard as his final farewell.

With the silt stirred up around her face, she squinted and lay still, trying to get her bearings. Was she up or down in here? She could make out the light at the opening and inched her body around to face it. She gave a hard yank on the regulator in her mouth, which pulled the floating tank up to land beside her. Her hands and ankles were still bound, and that extra twenty pounds of lead crushed her waist. She had to get out of there.

DIVE TOUR

****

******

Satisfied that Terri was taken care of, Jerry checked his dive watch again and reached around to the back of his tank. John was still looking down the tunnel to watch Terri struggle. He wanted to see her expire, slowly.

Terri could see the large blades spanning the diameter of the cylindrical entrance. Someone was still outside. Inching closer, she could just make out John holding his hand up. He was giving her the finger. She held her bound hands as high as she could and managed to extend both of her middle fingers. Her strength was returning. *I hate that guy, I hate that guy,* she chanted in her brain.

The Captain reached over and gripped John by the right shoulder strap. He yanked the surprised man around suddenly and faced him, eye to eye.

For John, there was a moment of complete confusion before the bang stick loaded with a single twenty-gauge shotgun shell exploded into his chest wall. His torso blew open in a large mass of green fluid and internal organs.

The mask on John's face filled with blood that streamed from his nose. Blood flowed until it half covered his wide eyes, an expression of complete disbelief frozen on his face. Jerry continued to hold on to the shoulder strap, looking into John's eyes and watching the glow quickly extinguish.

Terri bolted upward with attention when she heard the explosion, the shock waves putting pressure on the slits of her eyes. As much as she wanted to investigate, she kept her eyes shut until the vibrations died down.

When she opened her eyes, she could make out a silhouette falling away as Jerry released all the air out of John's buoyancy compensator and pushed him away.

Terri put her head down and shut her eyes for fear the Captain would return for her.

The dead man landed on his back on the sandy slope below. His entrails rose out of his open gut, small fish feasting on the soft flesh. A cloud of green haze surrounded him as his blood drained into the ocean. Swimming down to John with powerful, fast strokes, Jerry was now in a race for time. He had to place the bang stick on John and get back to the cruise ship. He had forty minutes left. Not a second to waste.

Terri maneuvered herself to the entrance to watch Jerry swim away. Bigger fish were coming in to examine the feeding frenzy below. She had just witnessed cold blooded murder. Her brain was spinning. She could feel her breath becoming labored.

The deep blue color of the ocean turned darker in front of her eyes: the sun had dipped now, and it was dusk. She needed a way out. The next breath was harder to pull. She reached down to her waist searching for the buckle to the weight belt. Couldn't find it. The next breath ... it was still harder. She reached out to the fan blades. *How do I get out of here?* The next full breath was not there.

She had run out of air.

DIVE TOUR

****

<u>42</u>

Mitch's car raced to the bottom of the Coconut Beach parking lot. He drove up and parked next to the white rental, the only other car parked at the beach. It was getting dark, so Mitch turned his car off but left the headlights on and shining out to sea. There was nothing to see, just a mild surface current and a larger yacht motoring off in the distance.

Mitch examined the other car. There were blankets in the back and what looked like a syringe coming out from under the passenger side seat. Mitch's automatic headlights suddenly went off, causing Jackie to jump. She had recognized the white car from earlier.

"I don't know, I can't see too much out there." Mitch had stepped back from the white car, turned his own car lights back on, and grabbed a flashlight. He started walking toward the water, scanning out to the left and the right with his flashlight, looking for anything—a dive light, bubbles, something.

****

Jerry swam quickly with long stiff strokes of his legs, time closing in on him. He was around the point, closer to the beach, into shallow water. He reached for the hose of his buoyancy compensator and gave the bladder a shot of air, raising him to surface before his exit onto the beach. He needed to make sure he was still alone. The top of his head slowly broke the water like a periscope, his mask looking forward toward shore. He held his breath and his heart skipped a beat as he saw a car parked next to his. Two people with flashlights were on the beach heading over toward the shore, scanning the water with the narrow beams of light.

****

VOLUME ONE: RAPTIS TRILOGY

****

"Hey! I think I see something out there! Over by the rocks, inside the point!" Mitch had caught a reflection off the metal on Jerry's mask as his beam of light glanced over it. The Captain quickly ducked underwater. Mitch could see the air bubbles rising from below, expanding and popping together as they hit the surface.

"Where? I can't see!" Jackie was straining and waving her flashlight toward Mitch's target.

"John! Is that you?!" Mitch yelled out.

"John!" Jackie cupped her hands to magnify her voice and yelled as loud as she could.

Jerry was now swimming back to the point to figure out his next move. Submerged, the sound of Hook's truck driving into the beach parking lot confused him—and was that Jackie's voice? He had to take the chance to see if it was. From behind the rocks, he slowly looked around the point back to the beach again.

Kathy opened the passenger door and jumped out of Hook's truck before it rolled to a stop. She was running toward Mitch by the time Hook could turn the engine off.

Retreating back behind the point, out of possible view, Jerry heard the sound of a larger engine a distance behind him. He watched as lights motored closer, in his direction. The directions he'd been given included a back-up plan; a boat would be out there if support was necessary. De Gerlick had assured him of this. The Captain flipped on his back and began kicking out toward the oncoming boat as it approached and slowed.

******

"What's going on out there?" Kathy was panting when she caught up to Mitch and Jackie.

****

"I don't know, I think I see someone out there. Right now it looks as if whoever it is is swimming toward that boat." Mitch was shining his light out toward the boat but the beam was not strong enough to make out any details, just watery shadows.

"John!" Kathy screamed out.

******

Jerry kicked up closer to the boat as it shifted into neutral. He could make out someone in the back stern motioning for him to swim over.

The muffled sound of a shot ricocheted off the peace of the evening hour; it hit the Captain's head with a deadening thud. With his buoyancy compensator still inflated, his head was snapped back. His mask was shattered into slivers and splattered with oozing blood, a rubber strap clinging to what was left of his head.

The boat sprung into motion and sped off into the black of the night.

******

"John! John! Oh my God—did someone just shoot John?" Kathy was screaming at the edge of the water as Mitch threw his shoes and pants off and quickly swam out to sea toward the floating victim. Hook was on the CB radio in the cab of his truck, summoning help.

DIVE TOUR

****

43

Terri tried not to panic as she squinted, her eyes burning with hope, searching for her next source of air. *Air. Air. Please air.* She did not allow herself to feel desperate; she couldn't let herself go right now. *Stay focused,* she urged herself. She very rapidly scanned everything around her in the cylinder. As she did, she realized she was seeing a large metal chest with several heavy duty chains bound by huge locks, almost invisible, there at the end of the cylinder. *What?!* She so much wanted to go to that chest and find a way to get it open. *What the hell is in there? What? What kind of secret could someone want to lock up so well and hide down here of all places?* But she could not let herself wonder right now. She had to get air. Had to or die. *This is it!!!*

Looking up to the top of the cylinder, she could make out what she thought was the reflection of trapped air glistening above her. *Yes! Yes! Yes!* Her only hope for a breath was up. *Yes!!!* she told herself. Immediately she spit out the rubber mouthpiece, the lifeline she had been clenching onto for dear life, and rolled forward on her knees. The extra twenty pounds of weight felt like a hundred.

With one thrust, pushing with all her might, she lifted her face up to the top of the cylinder until her nose crackled and crunched against the metal wall. *It was air!* Lifting her lips up like a straw, she slowly opened them, her tongue pushed up against the back of her teeth to prevent an onslaught of water rushing in. She opened her eyes and took a chance as she tried to inhale slowly, fighting the urge to gulp. Her neck was crunched all the way up and hurt. She slowly savored another long inhale before dropping back down to her knees.

The air tasted bad. Her mind was racing, and each heartbeat sent a throb of pain to her head. She needed to get the weight belt off fast. *Rule number one: When in trouble, drop your weight belt.* She had practiced this maneuver over and over with her students. Now with her hands tied in front of her she reached down and felt the weight belt. She followed the lead pieces with her fingers to the left until she couldn't reach further: no buckle. Moving her hands the opposite direction, feeling her way around the belt; lead, lead, lead, twisting as far right as her body allowed, and still no buckle. The Captain had clasped the belt so tight around her it wouldn't budge, and the quick-release buckle was at the small of her back.

With the CO_2 in her body beyond comfortable limits, her lungs wanted to inhale, urgently. She stood up again, jamming her nose back up into the cylinder. She controlled her body to reach her lips up like a straw and inhale slowly. *Think.*

The surface was twenty-five feet above. John's lifeless body, swarms of fish pecking at his entrails, was fifteen feet below. She had twenty pounds of lead strapped around her, and she was out of air. She shut her eyes and let her mind race to an ending.

It was inevitable now. She thought she was going to drown. They probably wouldn't find her for a few days at least. *That is, if anyone would even bother to look.* Terri was beginning to resign herself to a not good outcome. That would be it: John's body would drift away, and no one would look for Terri.

She had two choices, both risky, one better than death. The first choice was to do nothing, which made little sense. The second choice was to swim for the surface twenty-five feet above, with twenty pounds of lead strapped around her waist and no fins to propel her or to keep her afloat when she surfaced. Holding her breath as long as she could, she concentrated. *Now: A slow, controlled exhale.* There wasn't much oxygen in the residual air she was breathing, and she was becoming increasingly light headed.

She had to make her move.

DIVE TOUR

****

<u>44</u>

The Captain's lifeless body was bobbing in the yacht's wake when Mitch swam up to it, not knowing who he was going to find.

"Oh my God!" Mitch stopped short of the body, frozen in shock when he realized he was only looking at half a head. The mask down around the neck line was filled with blood. An involuntary gag response overtook Mitch and he couldn't keep from heaving at the horrific sight. He didn't know who it was and didn't want to look closer. Grabbing the regulator mouthpiece floating near him, Mitch turned toward shore and started swimming, towing the carnage behind.

Kathy was in the water up to her knees, sobbing loudly. Jackie paced between Kathy and Hook as he was speaking through the CB mouthpiece to the police chief, already on his way.

Mitch made his way to the shoreline, panting. Kathy made her way over, stopping short and letting out a scream when she saw the head.

"Sorry, Kathy." Mitch was panting from the long, hard swim. "Couldn't—couldn't catch my breath to tell you in time." Mitch was holding on tight to the regulator hose like a leash, but he didn't want to look at the body as it bobbed toward them in the surf.

Hook and Jackie were hurrying down to the shoreline. "That's Jerry! That's the Captain!" Jackie was the first to notice it wasn't John. All four looked down at the gory sight of the slumped headless body in confusion. Each one of them was thinking something different.

VOLUME ONE: RAPTIS TRILOGY

****

"Then where is John?" Kathy had stopped crying and was scanning out to sea with her flashlight, hoping to see John swimming toward shore.

"Where the hell is Terri?!!!" Mitch shouted at the Captain's half head with its mouth frozen open.

Hook quickly walked back up to the truck to reposition headlamps for a better view. They were looking for any signs of life. Bubbles, gear, anything.

DIVE TOUR

****

45

Sucking in as much of the foul air as she could hold, Terri dropped down to her knees in the culvert and crawled under the shaft to the opening. She looked through a space between two of the blades. The ocean was slowly transforming to a shade darker as the sun was setting further.

Terri could barely see John's body right below. Praying hard, she quickly worked her body through the blades. Once the weight belt went over the edge, she quickly sank to the sandy bottom. Landing with a thud then a brief skid, silt stirred everywhere. She squinted through the floating dustbowl, looking for John.

Two feet to her left was John's head. She grabbed it with her two hands tied together, finding his hair, and working her fingers down his facial features until she found the round regulator mouthpiece still clenched between his teeth. Precious air bubbled out of the circular second stage as she pressed on the purge button, tugging it out of John's clenched jaw. She pulled herself over and shoved the mouthpiece into her mouth, simultaneously pressing on the purge button to blow out any salt water while gasping for the precious air.

She calmed herself with slow deep breaths, fighting back the fear that was quickly overtaking her thoughts. *Breathe, breathe, breathe.* She focused on the sound the bubbles made as they rushed by her ears. She groped down to John's face for his mask. Grabbing it with her right hand, she pulled it off and lifted it up to her eyes. It was two breaths before she looked up and exhaled through her nose, clearing the water out of the mask.

With even deep breaths, she slowly looked at the landscape around her. Looking down, she was almost on top of John, face to face. The regulator hose was stretched as far as it would go. She slid over to the other side of the body to have the full length of the hose.

John's eyes were a blank stare, wide open. She was transfixed, staring at his lifeless expression. She'd never seen a dead body so close.

Maneuvering with her bound hands, they caught on something. Her wrists had snagged in a dangling intestine. She pulled hard. Fish darted closer for the new feast of particles coming out. With a clear look down at John's gaping stomach cavity breaming with activity, Terri shut her eyes and looked away.

Already having to swallow back her deep fear of the dark, not to mention her terror of sharks, Terri also never wanted to look at John's stomach cavity ever again. She was beginning to shiver as her body temperature dropped. Slowly the sea was sucking at her in another way now, sapping her strength, holding on to her as she fought against it. It was as if the darkness below had bigger plans for Terri. Her hands shook uncontrollably as she reached over for John's buoyancy compensator hose.

Terri tried to remain calm, to control her breathing to preserve the air in the tank. Pressing down on the fill button of the buoyancy compensator, she could see the air expanding in John's buoyancy bladder. And his upper half began to rise, taking Terri with it.

DIVE TOUR

****

46

On the beach, Mitch, Kathy, and Hook were scouring the water's surface for any signs of life. Jackie was now on the CB with the ship's radio, informing them of her whereabouts and of the Captain's as well, agreeing with them that the second in command was in charge for now.

"John!"

"Terri!"

"John!"

"Terri!"

It sounded like a shouting match as they walked up the beach, shouting and looking out to sea, looking for a light, for bubbles, for anything out of the ordinary. Sirens wailed in the background as a police car and an ambulance pulled in to the parking lot. Two more semi-official cars pulled in and parked next to the police car.

Clift stepped out as Mitch was rushing up to him.

"I think Terri's out there, Clift. Maybe with John, I don't know."

Clift looked out to sea while Mitch reached down for his knees. A wave of nausea was climbing up his throat.

"So dey out for a nite dive?" Clift motioned to the other cars. The men got out, opened the trunks, and began pulling out diving equipment. The men in the ambulance began preparing a stretcher.

"I don't know. The Captain of the *Captive Sea* has been shot dead, over there."

They walked across the sand to the body.

Mitch's breathing started to labor as he neared and saw Jerry's head again. That close up vision of gore was now forever emblazoned into Mitch's memory. "Out there. I swam out to him. I thought it was John." Mitch focused on Clift's eyes as he spoke.

Jackie walked over and rested her hand on Mitch's shoulder.

"I saw Terri in da' back of dat car." Hook pointed to the white rental car. "Sh' was hiding me' son. I tink John, he got her."

"Did you bring more flashlights, Clift?" Jackie needed her own, she was hating being dependent on someone else's beam.

The trunk of the police car popped open and everyone reached in for a searching tool. Mitch grabbed the electronic megaphone and turned it on, walking down to the shore. He called out John and Terri's name at the highest crackling volume the megaphone would turn up to.

The main lights of Underwater World were off. No one was around to question them as they began to expand the search to other places.

"Hey mon! Hey mon!" One of the officers was shouting from the opposite side of the aquarium. His light shined out toward the channel. "I tink I see sometin out dere!"

Mitch was running across the pavement in his bare wet feet, racing toward that policeman with everyone else close behind. Skimming his flashlight out into the channel, he could see the orange color of John's buoyancy compensator's expanded bladder. It was floating on the surface.

"Oh my God." Kathy started to cry again, seeing whoever it was face down and lifeless.

DIVE TOUR

****

Clift used his megaphone. "Terri! John!" reverberated across the channel.

Hook walked back to the other beach to get the search divers who were entering the water from the other side of the peninsula.

"I'm going in. Shine your lights on it, don't let it out of the beam of your light or your sight," Mitch shouted to them as he climbed down the rocks to the water.

"Mitch, be careful!" Jackie pressed her index finger up to her teeth and bit down as she held a light beam on his path. The others kept a diligent eye on the orange bladder.

VOLUME ONE: RAPTIS TRILOGY

****

DIVE TOUR

****

47

Terri was getting weaker. Her body was extremely dehydrated and hypothermia had set in. Now her body shivered uncontrollably as her teeth clenched the mouthpiece. She had wedged her forearm between John and his weight belt to keep her attached. With the weight of the lead pulling her down, she tried to relax and focus on her breathing. She could feel John's body slowly drifting with a slight current. Looking out around her, that current was now the darkest shade of blue. There was black darkness below.

Small fish began appearing around Terri as the scent of John's dead body indicated a leftover trail of food. New and bigger fish were coming in to investigate the activity. Terri shut her eyes and tried to think good thoughts, but she was exhausted. Unable to curb her fears, sharks started swimming in her mind's eye. *Don't think about it, don't think about what's swimming up next.* It was all she could do not to see herself as a dangling piece of bait in the darkness.

Her thoughts were scrambling. She almost wished to be back in the womb, in the security of the womb, or even in that tomb, that cylinder where she had been trapped just a while ago. She began to cry through her regulator as her fears took over.

I'm trying, I'm trying, was all she could say to herself, almost talking through her sobs as she held on. The thought of her parents being told she had drowned flashed through her mind. She couldn't let that happen. The lead was bearing down on her hip bones, it felt like two hundred pounds now. She was so weak she couldn't even sob any more, couldn't move. She exhaled and lay still, too tired to take another breath so soon.

In the silence she heard a muffled sound above. She listened again. She couldn't make it out—wait, someone was there! A

VOLUME ONE: RAPTIS TRILOGY

****

burst of adrenaline shot through her as she found a glimmer of hope!

She used all her strength and yanked up and down on John's regulator hose, trying to pull him up and down like a fish on a line, hoping to attract someone's attention.

DIVE TOUR

****

<u>48</u>

Mitch had started to swim out, keeping his head above water and the orange vest in view. The vest suddenly pulled down below the water then bobbed back up. Mitch stopped swimming and watched. Again the vest jerked underwater, then bobbed back up. Mitch turned and looked toward shore to see if anyone else was seeing the same thing.

"Shark!" Clift called out on his megaphone, waving his arm, watching the orange vest bob up and then go back down.

"Shit!" Mitch screamed out loud toward the floating vest.

VOLUME ONE: RAPTIS TRILOGY

****

DIVE TOUR

****

<u>49</u>

Bright stars started to fill up the back of Terri's vision. She had stopped pulling and fighting for life. A calmness began to take her body over. Shutting her eyes, letting the stars behind her eyes take over the darkness, felt good. Her breathing slowed.

"Terri... Terri... Terri..." She could hear her mother's voice calling her name in the distance, and didn't want it to stop.

"I'm sorry mom, I'm sorry mom," her body felt unattached now. She could no longer feel the piercing pain of the lead against her hips. She kept her eyes shut, waiting to fall away into a deep sleep.

******

"It stopped moving, mon!" Clift shouted through the megaphone to Mitch.

Mitch was twenty feet away treading water, watching. He didn't want to swim into a shark's feeding frenzy. A crowd of bystanders had gathered on the beach to watch the events unfold. Some had their flashlights on the orange vest, others had a light on Mitch. Together they all watched one man have the courage to swim out.

Mitch swam closer. He saw bubbles rise to the surface. Bubbles again, a pattern! He swam full speed ahead toward the body without a thought of a shark in his mind. Someone was alive.

Mitch swam up to the bladder and grabbed it, turning the body over on its back.

******

Terri was under John, drifting into a state of unconsciousness, letting go, listening for her mom's voice to guide her. Suddenly there was a jerk and her face was following the regulator hose up as John's body turned over. With her wrist still attached to John's waist belt, she moved with John's body. Terri's weight caused John to flop back over face down. She could sense the movement above but didn't have any strength. She was watching herself from afar now.

Mitch looked under the water to see what was pulling on John. Terri was there, dangling lifeless, three feet under the surface, her wrist wedged in John's belt, her eyes shut and her teeth clenched around the regulator. He reached down to pull her up. So heavy!

Reaching around to the front of John, Mitch pulled on the buckle of John's weight belt and released the excess weight. It dropped down into the darkness. Terri's wrist released, and she began to sink down holding the regulator, her clenched jaw still locked.

On shore, they watched as Mitch struggled.

Looking underwater, he could see Terri had an over-weighted belt on. He dove down to look for the buckle.

Terri felt an angel, an angel coming to lift her away. She relaxed her mouth as her unconscious mind wanted to see the angel, to open her eyes. Relaxing her mouth, the regulator slipped out from between her teeth and she began to sink.

Mitch had his hand on Terri's belt. He did his best to hold her up as he searched for the buckle.

Released.

The weight dropped away and Terri's descent stopped. Grabbing her arm, Mitch swam for the surface. He could hear the whine of a two-stroke outboard engine heading toward them. He raised one arm and started waving. He held Terri's head back and above water with the other. She wasn't breathing. Pulling her head back, he clamped her nose shut, and with one quick kick upward his body rose up out of the water above Terri and he blew with force into her mouth. Her chest expanded. Water gurgled out of her mouth as she exhaled. He pulled her head back and blew again.

A small fishing boat pulled up alongside the two and shifted into neutral as Mitch held his arm out, holding the boat steady. Two men reached down and pulled Terri aboard. Mitch climbed in and attended to Terri as the unknown heroes shifted into gear and headed back to shore. They left John and the orange vest unattended.

Everyone was on the shore waiting, including the paramedics.

They pulled Terri out of the boat and onto the stretcher. One paramedic swiftly attached an IV while the other took over resuscitation. Mitch stepped back and watched, holding on to her hand.

DIVE TOUR

****

<u>50</u>

Jackie walked up and put her arms around Mitch. They held each other as they watched their friend.

Terri began to regurgitate. The paramedics quickly moved her head to the side and cleared her airway. She took another breath. They put an oxygen mask up to her mouth and she opened her eyes.

She was alive.

"Terri!" Mitch was at her side.

Her eyes blinked and she took another breath.

Mitch and Jackie walked alongside the stretcher as the paramedics took Terri to the waiting ambulance.

"I thought I was dead," Terri managed to whisper as they pushed the stretcher into the opened back doors.

Mitch climbed in with her, still holding her hand. "I thought you were, too."

Terri went on whispering, struggling to speak, "You need ... to go ... after the Captain. ... Mitch ... he tried to kill me. ... He killed John, ... I saw it." Tears began to well up in her eyes and stream down her cheeks.

"We got the Captain, honey," Mitch said.

Terri could see Jackie standing at the back of the ambulance. "Where is he, where's the Captain, Mitch?"

"He's right behind me." Mitch motioned to the yellow plastic behind him.

"... He's dead?"

"Very dead."

Terri put her head back and shut her eyes. Her body let go. She smiled and drifted off on the combination of drugs and sheer exhaustion.

"You go with her, Mitch. I can take your car and meet you at the hospital. I think Kathy is going to need someone."

Mitch handed his keys to Jackie.

The men in the boat went back and retrieved John's body. They could hear Kathy in the background sobbing. Hook had his arm around her. He guided her away when he saw the condition of the body....

DIVE TOUR

****

<u>51</u>

"Mitch? Can you please bring me another beer? Are we all out of chips?"

Terri was milking Mitch's guilt for all it was worth, which was plenty. They were sitting out on his porch watching the clouds change colors in the sunset.

It's easy to be spoiled up at Mitch's house, Terri thought to herself.

"Here you go." Mitch walked out holding a drink tray in one hand and clenching a bag of chips in the other. He put the tray down and handed Terri a bottle of beer.

"Ahhh. Thanks, Mitch." Terri was smiling as she handed him her empty and grabbed the full one. "I've just got to say it again, Mitch...."

"Go ahead. I'm actually getting used to it—"

"I told you so!"

The two of them laughed together.

"Can you believe that guy? Nothing but a coke junkie. He just had to have a fix. I saw it! Did you see that tattoo on his arm? Did I tell you about the tattoo on his arm?" Terri's breathing escalated as she thought about John. She was starting to get herself all worked up again.

"It sounds like you saw a lot of things, Terri." Mitch tried to calm her down with a soothing voice.

Terri caught herself and quieted her breathing, just saying, "Anyway, I never saw what was in those tanks the Captain and John had."

"Maybe Jackie will find out something this week."

"Right, like she'd tell us." Terri looked down and kicked at the ground with her foot." She thought I was a kook, or something like that."

Terri wondered what else Jackie might know. *Probably very little,* Terri said to herself, *and probably she has no idea about that big, chained-up metal chest hidden down there in the cylinder. Gee, maybe no one alive has any idea it's out there, maybe no one but me.*

"You know Mitch, I—" Terri stopped herself right there, deciding not to tell even Mitch about that strange metal chest down there in that underwater hell hole tube, not to tell anyone at all for now.

Mitch looked at her. Was she OK with all these memories? Was she still in shock? "What, Terri. What were you saying?"

"I, uh, I was just saying, well, Jackie, yes Jackie was starting to act like she thought I was crazy or something. You know this."

"Now, Terri. You were acting … a bit … like a kook." Mitch finally had to say it.

"Hey now. After all I've been through!" Terri sat up and looked at Mitch, just a little hurt. But this moment of hurt was good, because with this, she shifted out of possibly hinting about that locked-up chest. This was hers and hers alone to know, so far as she knew. She didn't want to draw any attention to her secret, not yet anyway. It could wait for a later time, a much later time. *If ever.*

Mitch looked back and said, "Well who's the kook now?" The two of them started laughing together again.

Terri stopped laughing and switched to a serious tone. "I really feel sorry for Kathy, Mitch. That guy John sure had her coming and going. He had me too, wow, I sure felt like I was tap dancing at the edge of insanity there with John. Mitch, you have *no idea*. Dealing with his craziness was making me feel like I was losing it. And everyone seemed to be protecting him. You have no idea what all went on between John and me, both above and below the surface...."

Terri knew she could never explain in full detail the madness of the whole ordeal from the very beginning to the very end. *No one would be able to know what it was really like, the hell I went through, the edge I was on, no one*, she told herself. She figured she would have to deal with all this on her own. And also, she figured she could never find a way to tell Mitch how hugely grateful she was that he had saved her life—that is, after she had already saved it herself, of course. *But really, Mitch is the reason I'm still here. I love you always, Mitch*, Terri thought to herself. *How do I tell you this? Will I ever find a way?*

"I think I have some idea what you went through, some anyway, Terri," Mitch said. But Mitch had no idea what all Terri was thinking. He knew he could never really know all that she had been through, not in totality. He could not know what that life and death struggle was like, the sheer extreme she had been through there on the edge, under the water. He only knew a little about it, the little he imagined, the little Terri had been able to talk about so far. It could be years, if ever, before Terri could relive and then share all the details of that terror, and that triumph over that terror. She would be forever marked by this experience, that Mitch knew.

"No, really, it was so frustrating knowing I was right about John and that Captain when everyone else thought I was the problem! Sorry if you got hit in the emotional massacre. Sorry Mitch, sorry...." Terri suddenly found herself gasping for no clear reason. She realized she was feeling queasy. "Oh gee Mitch, I just want to relax now. Let's relax."

"Let's do that. Relax, yes," Mitch nodded as he saw Terri wipe a tear from her cheek. One tear, but definitely a real one. Mitch knew it would be a long time before she would be able to talk much about being down there. And her finding John like that, and having to breathe John's air and be tied to John's dead body to do it? That must have been even worse than his own horror finding half of Jerry bobbing on the surface.

Mitch decided to shift the subject some. "Yep, poor Kathy. She's a mess. And Melvin tried everything to get her to stay on, because she was really good."

Terri agreed. "She's so freaked out, she still can't stop crying. I don't blame her for wanting to go home. Back to the States."

"Melvin thought it might be a good idea for you to go home, too—"

"What?" Terri shot Mitch a dirty look as if he were once again part of the conspiracy.

"For a *vacation*! Relax! He knows he can't run the shop without you!" Mitch ended with a low chuckle to help keep her ego in check.

"Yeah. He needs me, doesn't he, Mitch?" Terri took a sip of her beer, watching the clouds move with the breeze and change color in the fading light.

"We all need you, Terri. Me too." *Terri, you have no idea how much I need you, how much you mean to me.* Mitch fanaticized he was actually telling Terri this. *Maybe someday you will know.*

Mitch's voice sounded too serious for Terri right then. But she was so deeply touched.

"Everyone needs a little excitement now and then," Terri grinned. "Including me." Terri giggled, knowing only she had any idea how much excitement might be still to come. The chest down in that cylinder kept calling her. *But mum's the word,* she told herself silently. It might be a very long time before she could get herself to go back there.

DIVE TOUR

****

Terri's infectious giggle set Mitch off, and the two started laughing from the bottom of their hearts. They looked at each other fondly, dearly, wisely.

Terri held her beer bottle up to Mitch.

"A toast!" Mitch held his bottle up. "Toast to another day in paradise!"

They clinked their bottles and drank to each other, to the sea and the sun, and to life.

THE END

VOLUME ONE: RAPTIS TRILOGY

****

Basic Scuba Diver Gear Diagram

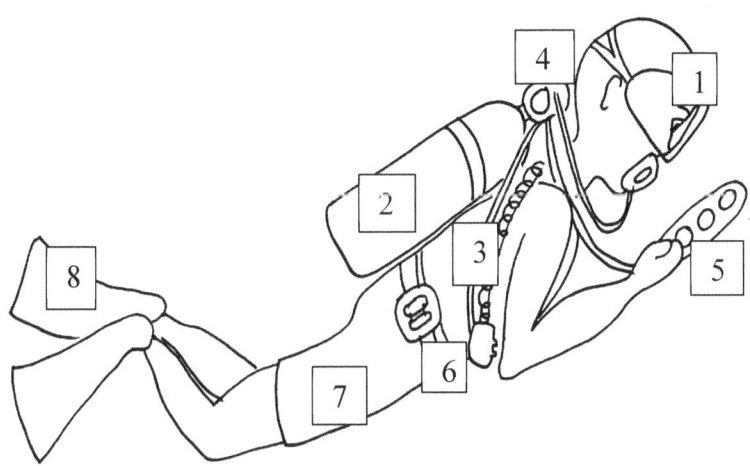

DIVERS:

(1) Our **DIVE MASK** provides a space of air to see through.

(2) Our **TANK** of air is attached to our backs.

(3) Our **BOUYANCY COMPENSATOR** is worn like a vest. It fills with air from our tank.

(4) The **REGULATOR** comes in two STAGES. The 1st STAGE attaches to the tank's valve and breaks down the immediate pressure from the tank. You also attach all your gauges to the 1st STAGE as well. The 2nd STAGE goes in your mouth: you inhale and exhale through the 2nd STAGE.

(5) Our **PRESSURE GAUGE** is attached to the 1st STAGE of the regulator. It tells us in PSI, pounds per square inch, how much air we have.

(6) Our **WEIGHT BELT** offsets the buoyancy of our body fat and wetsuit.

(7) We lose body heat in even the warmest of oceans. The layer of water between us and our **WETSUIT** keeps us warm.

(8) Our **FINS** propel us through the water.

See the following pages for other
Diving and Boating Terms
used in this book...

VOLUME ONE: RAPTIS TRILOGY

****

Scuba Diving and Boating Terms
Used in This Book

ANCHOR LINE: The ANCHOR is attached to the bow of the boat with a long nautical rope, the ANCHOR LINE. Dropped down into the water, it sinks to the bottom and holds the boat in place.

BANG STICK: This is a long cylindrical "stick" with a handle on one end. The other end holds a bullet. When the stick is pushed into an object, the bullet is triggered and released into that object. Some divers use the bang stick for safety (for example, as a shark deterrent).

BOUY: This is a round bright marker floating on the ocean's surface, usually left to mark an area for certain use (such as an underwater fish or lobster trap, or a place a boat can tie up to).

BOUYANCY COMPENSATOR: This is a vest the diver wears, attaching it to the TANK. This COMPENSATOR VEST controls the diver's BUOYANCY on/above and below the water's surface. A hose is attached to the 1ˢᵗ STAGE of the REGULATOR to fill the vest with air from the tank or with air by mouth (when simply blowing the air in). As the diver descends deeper into the water, compressing and becoming heavier, adding air to the vest helps achieve a NEUTRAL BOUYANCY, a suspended floating.

BOW: The front of the boat.

CLEAT: This is attached to the top side of a boat, used to fashion rope around to hold it, or to attach different objects.

CONTROLLED BREATHING: Because the diver is breathing air that is compressed, and is further compressing when DESCENDing, the diver must be aware of breathing at all times. The diver CONTROLs breathing to conserve air. The diver also CONTROLs breathing when ASCENDing. While ASCENDing, the COMPRESSED AIR in the diver's lungs expands so the diver must consciously exhale slowly.

DINGIIY: A small boat used to maneuver to shallower areas larger vessels cannot reach.

HOOKAH RIG: Instead of wearing a TANK, the diver can have another air source, an AIR COMPRESSOR, floating on the surface. To this compressor, long hoses are attached and on the other end is the diver's mouth. A single AIR COMPRESSOR on the surface can serve more than one diver at a time.

PORT: Looking forward toward the BOW, the PORT side of the vessel is to the LEFT.

309

PRESSURE GAUGE: This gauge is attached to the 1ˢᵗ STAGE of the REGULATOR. This gauge informs the diver of the amount of air in the tank, by PSI.

PSI: POUNDS per SQUARE INCH is the pressure of the air the diver puts into the tank. Tanks are designed to hold between 2250 PSI to 3000 PSI of air.

REGULATOR: The 1ˢᵗ STAGE of the REGULATOR attaches to the tank's VALVE and controls the air pressure in the tank. The 2ⁿᵈ STAGE of the REGULATOR is attached with a low pressure hose to the 1ˢᵗ STAGE. The diver puts the 2ⁿᵈ STAGE in the mouth to inhale air.

SAFE BOTTOM TIME: Because the diver is breathing compressed air, there is only so much time the diver can stay underwater without having a NITROGEN build up in the diver's body. The NAVY SUBMARINERS developed tables for divers that tell them the safe time limits for remaining down at certain depths. Too much NITROGEN will make the diver sick.

SCUBA: This is the general acronym for SELF-CONTAINED UNDERWATER BREATHING APPARATUS.

STARBORD: Looking forward toward the BOW, the STARBOARD side of the vessel is to the RIGHT.

TANK: The diver brings air down underwater compressed into a tank which is worn on the back. On top of the tank is a VALVE with a handle. When the diver attaches the REGULATOR, then the VALVE can be turned on to release the air to the 1ˢᵗ STAGE of the REGULATOR.

TRANSOM: This is the rear outside of the boat. A platform with a ladder can be attached to the TRANSOM for divers to use to climb up onto the boat.

VISIBILITY: This is how far the diver can see underwater. Mud, silt, and sand in the currents all effect visibility. In ZERO VISIBILITY, the diver sees only 6 inches in front of the mask.

WEIGHT BELT: The diver wears a belt with lead in it to help offset the POSITIVE BUOYANCY of the body fat and of the wetsuit if wearing one. This belt has a quick release to ditch the lead in an emergency.

WETSUIT: Even the warmest ocean waters are below the diver's body temperature and eventually the diver gets cold. The diver uses different thicknesses of neoprene, worn as different WETSUITS. It is the layer of water there between the suit and the body that helps keep the diver warm.

RAPTIS TRILOGY
Volume One: DIVE TOUR • Volume Two: TREASURE HUNT • Volume Three: REDEMPTION

Raptis Trilogy
Afterword

This keen, sharp, edgy sense, this suspended from real life sensation, this journey into a terribly thrilling, frightening, disturbing, even evil situation, this is the thriller reader's experience. A great thriller writer is an artist. And we turn to this art to not only distract us from life, but to let us live out our worst fears in the world of fiction, to allow our imaginations to do this in fiction and then when done, simply close the book. We love the suspense, we even crave it. We may hate the fear, but we can't turn away. Instead we turn the page for more.

So what is a thriller? Well, if you've been on the edge of your seat, or at least feeling on edge while reading these books by Tracee Raptis, you know the thriller reader experience. And indeed, Tracee Raptis knows how to bring out in we readers a strange suspended curiosity, a sort of must-know what next, almost a temporary addiction or at least compulsion to read on and on, to want to know what the bad guys are doing, to want to know whether and how our heroines and heroes survive, to want someone to survive.

Suspense, fear, hate, love, perseverance, twisted brilliance, the odd, the strange, the evil, the good, the hero and anti-hero, are all involved. (Of course here in these Raptis Trilogy tales, our greatest hero is a heroine named Terri who may, we hope, survive all three of these Raptis Trilogy tales.) Author Tracee Raptis knows these emotions, she knows how to bring these out in readers, even in her characters. Her wisdom screams into our minds that this story is, or at least could be, real real real, really real and this is all the more unnerving. Fasten your seat belts, readers. Something's lurking in the shadows....

Dr. Angela Browne-Miller
Editor-in-Chief, Metaterra® Publications
www.Metaterra.com

TRACEE RAPTIS

THRILLERS

I'd like to thank my editor, Dr. Angela Browne-Miller, for believing in me and showing me the way. And a special thank you to my family and friends for their encouragement and support.

Tracee Raptis

About the Author
Tracee Raptis

Adventurer, painter, sculptor, diver, author Tracee Raptis was born and raised in the Coachella Valley, in Indio, California. She fell in love with the ocean as a child and spent as much time as possible with her family in the Corona Del Mar coastal area, in Orange County, California. Tracee became a certified scuba diver at the age of fifteen. At the age of nineteen, she followed her dreams, left her life in the U.S., and headed off to the Caribbean islands where she taught scuba diving and led scuba tours for many years. There her life was filled with adventure, romance, and a great love of the underwater world. One of Tracee's most exciting adventures in the Caribbean was working with an underwater archeological expedition company, discovering how much mysterious and intriguing history is down there under water, and searching for treasures lost in time. "There is a whole wild and mysterious world down there, one that reveals its beauty, secrets, and dangers as it wishes to. You have to really live in it, be with that world for a long time, to start to see what it is all about," Tracee says. Tracee now lives in California where she is writing several books and book series.

About the sequels …

YOU HAVE JUST COMPLETED

**Raptis Trilogy, Volume One:
DIVE TOUR**

NOW YOU CAN READ THE
SEQUELS TO
DIVE TOUR:

**Raptis Trilogy, Volume Two:
TREASURE HUNT**

AND

**Raptis Trilogy, Volume Three:
REDEMPTION**

***

**Brought to you by
Metaterra® Publications**

*Stay tuned for more from
Author Tracee Raptis….*

**Find these and other books by
Tracee Raptis
on
Amazon.com**

Watch for announcements on…

TraceeRaptis.com
and
Metaterra

www.ingramcontent.com/pod-product-compliance
Lightning Source LLC
Chambersburg PA
CBHW070217260626
47160CB00002B/581